Someday

Jae Henderson

Someday

RiverHouse Publishing, LLC is registered in the United States Patent and Trademark Office.

All **RiverHouse, LLC** Titles, Imprints and Distributed Lines are available at special quantity discounts for bulk purchases for sales promotions, premiums, fund-raising and educational or institutional use.

Imprint: *RiverHouse Publishing, LLC*

ISBN: 978-0-9832186-2-3

Printed in the United States

This book is printed on acid-free paper.

This book is dedicated to my family. It's because of you that I am the woman I am. For your love and guidance, I am extremely grateful.

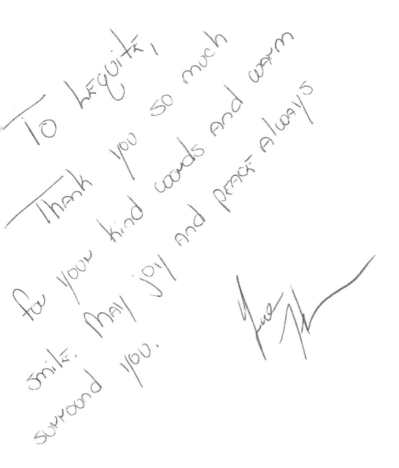

Acknowledgments

This is my first book and as much as I would like to thank everyone who has ever had a positive influence on my life, I can't. So, if I didn't mention you please charge it to my head and not to my heart. I give special thanks to:

My heavenly Father from whom all blessings flow. I am grateful that you chose me to deliver the messages contained within this book. I am more grateful for your love, grace, favor and mercy. You are better to me than I could ever be to myself. You get all the glory, all the honor, and all the praise!

My parents, Lillie and Gean. I probably don't say it enough, I love you. I am so proud to be your child. Thank you for loving me.

My siblings, Reggie, Van, and Andrea. You are truly a blessing.

My grandparents, Mae and Alfred. You have gone on to glory but the love of Jesus you helped to infuse in me shall travel with me all the days of my life.

My uncles and aunts. Thank you for lending a hand in raising me. I always tell people that I am everybody's baby.

My nieces and nephews. Auntie loves you and I hope you are proud of me. May you find wisdom in these pages to help you as you mature.

The rest of my family. I am so blessed to have wonderful people such as you in my life. You are irreplaceable.

My Olivet Fellowship Baptist Church family. Your encouragement and support means more to me than you will ever know. I am so happy to be a part of "The Place of the Outpouring".

My Riverside Missionary Baptist Church J 1:22 crew. The moments we shared and the lessons that were taught helped me get through one of the most pivotal points in my life. We had the best Bible study group on the planet!

My publisher, RiverHouse Publishing, LLC. Latrivia Nelson, you are not only my friend and my publisher but an inspiration to women everywhere. You truly are a super woman. I couldn't have done this without you. Greater things we shall do!

My editor, Janice Williams Miller. Your hard work and suggestions were instrumental in the completion of this book.

Be blessed!

Chapter 1

I'm A Good Woman
Tee

I allow my body to melt slowly on top of the man lying beneath me. My muscles relax, and I lay my weary head against his chiseled chest. I don't care that I just got my hair done and this will certainly flatten it on one side. I don't care that I'm wearing linen and should we decide to go out I will be a wrinkled mess. I listen to the even beat of his heart. It seems almost like music to me. Thump, thump. Thump, thump. Thump, thump. This is the heart that keeps this wonderful specimen of manhood alive to make me feel beautiful. Having him in my life gives me the ability to give love and receive it in return. He brings me happiness, most of the time. I feel the sleeves of his starched shirt brush against my warm skin as his arms enclose me in an embrace. I breathe in his essence. I'm not sure what he's wearing today, but intermingled with his natural scent it's almost intoxicating. I take a deep breath allowing the scent to further inebriate me. Our time together makes me wonder if this is a small fraction of what heaven is like. Life seems so easy and problem-free when I'm with him. Well, there is one problem. I press my head further into him, continuing to listen to the strong beat of his heart, and I imagine that it's telling me to be strong. This one is truly going to be "the one," and if I'm patient, the love I've been waiting for is just around the bend. *Please don't let him make a move on me*, I pray silently. In one sweeping gesture designed to demonstrate power and desire, I find myself no longer on top of my man, but on my back beneath him. I knew it was a bad idea to watch TV in his bedroom. He never even cut it on. I search his bright brown eyes for an explanation.

"What are you doing?"

"Wait and see. You'll like it. Close your eyes."

I uneasily do as I'm told, and begin to feel soft lips on my lips and familiar hands on my hips. The lips stay in place while the hands migrate inward and begin to unbutton my dress.

"No, please. I can't," I say with his lips still on mine. "We discussed this. I can't."

"Yes, you can. You mean you won't."

Choosing between God and man should seem like such an easy decision, but when that man is MacKenzie Elbert Patton, III, known as Mac to all his friends, there's no way it could be. He has a body that I'm sure the Creator took great time and care to mold because of the intricate definition and attractive details throughout his physique. It's so perfect! I watch in awe every time he enters the room, and take great pride in knowing that it all belongs to my man. The curve of his jawline, that curly hair, pecs, biceps, and triceps. Oh my!

Now Mac is on top of me, asking me to make that choice AGAIN. At this moment I'm torn between the love my heart wants, the attention my body desires, and my dedication to the God I have vowed to serve with celibacy until marriage. He tries to continue to undo my buttons. I clasp his hands in mine. God wins again. Mac begrudgingly stops unbuttoning my dress and breathes a heavy sigh of exasperation.

"I can't do this anymore, Tee. I have a beautiful, sexy, woman in my life, but I still go to bed horny every night. For the last three months, I have done everything in my power to show you how much I care for you and that I'm not going anywhere. Baby, I need you—all of you, but I'm not going to beg. I want to make love to my woman tonight! After everything we've shared, are you really going to lie here and tell me no again? Why isn't the fact that we're in a committed relationship not enough to put your mind at ease and your body in my possession?"

"Mac, I told you when I met you I was celibate and had no intentions of having sex again until I was married. Why are you asking me to do what I told you I wouldn't? You said you understood and respected my decision."

"Because I can't take this. I have to be honest with myself and be honest with you. I NEED SEX."

"Baby, you don't need sex. You need Jesus. Let's pray."

Mac's usually calm demeanor seems to travel from frustration to rage in an instant. His butterscotch-hued skin is now red, and the veins in his neck are bulging. I have never seen him like this. Mac is usually so laid back and reserved. He looks like he is about to explode.

"I'm telling you I want to physically express my emotions, and you want to pray. Girl, that crucifix around your neck must be too tight, because it's cutting off the oxygen supply to your brain and causing you to spew ignorance in my direction. You say you want a future with me. Then prove it! Do you know who I am? I'm one of the most successful attorneys in Memphis. I can have any woman I want, and I choose you. You should be honored I took the time to reach down in the gutter and pick up a ghetto girl like you. You try to act all refined, but I know who you are and where you come from, Ms. High Society Event Planner. I'm trying to give you more than you'll ever be able to obtain on your own, and instead of being grateful, you behave as if you're sooooo holy. You're enjoying this aren't you? You want a man to go through hell and high water just to get your goodies. Well, I won't do it because I don't have to. It's not worth it; you're not worth it. Tina Long, you don't have to go home, but you have to get the hell out of my house!"

I try to sit quietly through his rant in hopes he will feel better after he got it out of his system, but there is only so much I can take.

"Mac, what are you saying? You would really end our relationship over sex?"

"I'm not ending it. You are with this archaic desire to wait until marriage. No one does that anymore, Tee. We try on our shoes and walk around in them until they are slightly worn and very comfortable before saying *I do* these days. You and I have different beliefs about what constitutes a relationship, and I cannot conform to yours just to suit you. I am only going to tell you civilly one more time. Tee, I need you to leave."

"I'm not going anywhere. We are going to sit here and discuss this like adults. We've only been together three months. Why rush things? You're thinking with the head in between your legs right now instead of the one on your shoulders. You told me you would wait. You can't change the deal now because you're horny. Mac, what we have is special. It doesn't come along every day. We can work this out if you just calm down," I say in an attempt to appeal to his rational side. He's a lawyer. He knows what good can come from two people engaging in dialogue.

"Tee, I've been trying. I do think you're special, but not special enough for me to torture myself. This celibacy thing isn't for me. I am going to have sex tonight with or without you. I can't remember the last time I went this long without sex, and I don't plan to continue. I feel like I'm about to implode, and you are both the cause and the cure. But since you refuse to administer the medicine for what ails my mind, body, and soul, I know someone I can call who will."

Mac is now sitting upright on the side of his king size sleigh bed with his feet planted on the floor. He moves away from me as if I have some disease and walks over to the mahogany dresser to retrieve his cell phone. He dials a number, and I distinctly hear the voice of a woman answer with, "Hey, baby!"

"Hello, Leslie. How are you? Are you busy? Good. I was thinking about you. You and I haven't enjoyed each other's company in a while, and I miss you, sweetheart. Why don't you come over so we can make up for lost time?"

This can't be happening. This man is actually making a booty call in my presence. Well, I'm not having it! I walk over to him and attempt to snatch the phone, but Mac holds it out of my reach with one hand and pushes me down on the small almond-colored ottoman beside the dresser with the other. Before I can stand he places his hand on my shoulder and pins me in place. I struggle to jump up and get the phone, but he has me firmly confined to the ottoman. The best I can manage is a small bounce aided slightly by the cushions. He brings the phone back to his ear and resumes his conversation. Physically, I am no match for him. Even with one hand occupied, he easily limits my movements. I continue to struggle in vain.

This can't be happening. Not only is he disrespecting me, but he has his hands on me. Mac's grip on my shoulder becomes more forceful as he digs his fingers into my skin to hold me in place.

"Let me go! You're hurting me," I scream.

Mac completely ignores me and continues his conversation.

"I'm looking forward to it, baby. Wear that little red thing I like ... Oh that noise? It's just the television. See you soon."

He hangs up the phone and looks down at me, smiling as if he's won some glorious battle.

"You see how easy it is, Tee? Did you think you were irreplaceable? In this city pretty women come a dime a dozen, and I'm Mr. Moneybags. I got a whole pocket full of change and a lucrative bank account if I require more. Exit my domicile, woman."

Mac has never spoken to me like this before. I always knew he had a pit bull inside, but I had only seen it unleashed in the courtroom, never with me. I will myself not to cry. I cannot let this insensitive, selfish, jerk see me cry. He's right. I should leave. He takes his hand off me, and I leave the ottoman to put on my shoes and locate my purse. I don't want to lose him, but there is no way I'm going to let a man, no matter how fine, refined, or rich he is, treat me like this.

"Or," he says licking his thick, luscious lips, "I can call her back and tell her I changed my mind. All you have to do is give in to all these desires you've been suppressing for years and let my please you unmercifully. Stop acting so sanctified and spread those legs. I bet you're good, too. The biggest freaks I know go to church every Sunday."

When standing close to Mac you cannot help but become fully aware of his size and height. At seven feet, two inches he towers above me. I'm not a big woman. Some may even describe me as a little on the thin side. But I never let my lack of width deter me from engaging in a verbal or physical confrontation with anyone who challenges me.

"Who do you think you're talking to? I'm a good Christian woman. Not some whore walking down Third Street. There's no way I'm going to have sex with you just so you won't have sex with someone else. Ultimatums may work with other women, but not me. For all I know, you've been sleeping with that woman the entire time we've been together. I'll leave, but believe me when I walk out that door there will be no turning back. Do you know who I am? I'm the woman who put up with your pompous, spoiled, arrogant behind in hopes that you could see that real love is based on a deeper connection than sex. So don't get it twisted, Mr. Moneybags. You're the lucky one. Not me. All the money in the world wouldn't make me sleep with you now."

This man is all wrong. What was I thinking when I let him into my life? He's right about one thing, though. I am from the hood. And the same girl who would beat a brother down for calling her names still resides within me and does not appreciate being disrespected in any form or fashion. Now that I'm a Christian, I try really hard to quell her wrath, but some days she won't be shut down. I can feel her just itching to get out.

"Don't do me any favors, mademoiselle," he hisses in a low growl. "Would you like me to walk you to the door?"

I don't move.

"It's now or never, Tee. I've spent way too many nights just kissing and holding you. I need more. Make a decision. I've made mine. You're just a poor girl from the hood who got a lucky break throwing rich folks' parties. I'm offering you a golden opportunity to truly belong to the social circles you cater to instead of receiving a visitor's pass. Think carefully. You may not get this chance again because my girlfriend for tonight will be here in about 30 minutes."

"Maybe I didn't grow up with money, but your Armani suits don't make you better than anybody else. You are going to regret this. Good women like me don't come along every day. So if I have to make a decision, I'll say NEVER! And by the way, don't you ever put your hands on me again!"

I grab Mac by the lapels of his shirt. As his body jerks toward me, I issued a strategically placed knee to his groin. He buckles over in pain and falls on the ottoman in the exact place he had previously pinned me. His hands are now clutching his genitals. It is obvious that he is in excruciating pain.

I retrieve my purse from the lavender chase in the corner of the room, and proceed to the door. Before making my exit, I bend over my former boyfriend, being careful to stay out of his reach. "Goodbye, love. And tell Leslie I said hello. You're all hers. I hope you can still perform tonight."

He yells some gibberish peppered with several expletives and buries his contorted face deep into the cushions of his furniture.

The only sound I hear is the hollow clack of my stilettos as I walk down the hardwood hallway floor to the front door. I turn its golden handle, open it, and slam it tightly behind me to make sure Mac knows that I have gone, not only from his expensive home in the exclusive South Bluffs community, but from his life.

It is summer time in Memphis. The temperature is 90 degrees at night, but the rise in mercury is nothing compared to the temperature of the blood boiling within me. The nerve of that man! He's so used to talking to people any kind of way because he has money that he forgot to mind his manners when in the presence of a lady. I was raised that no one, regardless of their status or finances is better than me. That should teach him!

As I descend the front porch steps and walk down Mac's well-lit, well-landscaped street, the thought of taking my keys and carving my initials into his customized red Mercedes SLK enters my mind. He's lucky I'm allergic to jail. Plus, assault and vandalism in one night would be a bit much for a law abiding citizen such as me. Lord, forgive me for my actions, but he deserved it. Besides, I'm not quite sure vengeance would lessen the hurt, embarrassment, and anger I'm feeling right now.

I walk through the artsy South Main District of downtown Memphis, passing some of my favorite art galleries, eateries, and retail shops, but barely even notice they are there. After walking for nearly 40 minutes, I realize that I am nearing the famous Peabody Hotel. I feel like diving into the fountain where they keep their famous ducks to cool off.

I don't want to call any of my friends or family to pick me up because I will have to explain what happened, and I'm not ready to talk about it yet. I hop into the backseat of one of the cabs parked outside the entrance. It smells like stale popcorn. The driver doesn't seem too pleased that I interrupted his nap. If he doesn't want to work, he shouldn't be sitting in the area that is designated for working cabbies. A grumpy driver is the least of my concerns. I give him my address and relieve my feet of the brand new, red crocodile shoes that I purchased earlier today. Bad "A" shoes aren't made for walking long distances, and these are sho'nuff some bad "A" shoes. I just happened to catch them on sale at Macy's. As I rub my French manicured baby toe, I sink down in the well-worn seat and start praying for strength to get through this trial.

The journey to my house is a long, quiet ride. As we move along I-40, I keep thinking, why me? I gave him everything I had to offer except sex. I cooked. I cleaned. I ran his errands. I listened attentively when he talked about a big case. That man broke all kinds of attorney client privileges with me, and in return for his trust I never told anyone but my journal what he said to me. I even gave him my signature Tee's Baby Massages, lovingly rubbing his neck, shoulders, back, and feet after a long, stressful day at the office. Those massages are exclusively reserved for the man who is lucky enough to wear the title of Tee's Baby. Afterward, I would hold him in my arms and sing to him softly until he drifted off to la la land. He really was my big baby.

I'm a good woman, looking for a good man. Unfortunately, I keep coming up short. This one is fine and wears $1,000 tailored suits with diamond cuff links and

Italian shoes. He is prince charming if I ever met him, or so I thought. Maybe I should have given him some. Hundreds of women would love to be in my place. He isn't all bad.

MacKenzie Elbert Patton, III was born into a politically powerful family in Richmond, Virginia. He is extremely attractive and rich. Every time I think about him, I almost have to repent for having lustful thoughts: smooth, creamy skin; the physique of a tall, toned basketball player; a gorgeous smile with the whitest of pearly whites; and eyes that beckoned you to "come hither" all times of the day and night. I'm almost certain those teeth are veneers, although he would never admit it. But what I love most about him is his intellect. His parents made sure he became well-rounded by travelling the world. Mac has been to 19 different countries and can speak four languages, including French, Japanese and Spanish. He graduated from Harvard Law School at the top of his class. At the age of 30, he used his family's money to start a law firm, which in the last five years has grown to one of the more successful small firms in Memphis, TN. Like most rich people I've encountered, he's used to getting what he wants. I guess after three months of wining and dining me without being allowed to partake of my forbidden fruit, his fragile ego couldn't take any more. I told him when I met him that I am not having sex again until I get married. I guess the challenge my celibacy presented was one he couldn't resist.

Unfortunately, Mac is the latest casualty in a long list of failed relationships. Why didn't I see what a jerk Mac was before?

Chapter 2

Kissing Frogs
Tee

My sister's restaurant, Mae Lillie's, is abuzz with activity. The lunch crowd is heavy and although Sandy is sitting with me as I relay the drama of another failed relationship, she is also observing her wait staff to make sure they are attending to her patrons' needs. Today is Catfish Tuesday, and the smell of the favorite southern dish is heavy in the air. All the guests seem to be enjoying their meals of deliciously fried, baked or blackened catfish, and completely oblivious to the saddened soul that sits among them. My sister is trying to console me as best she can, but I know she needs to get back to running her business.

"I don't understand," I say in utter disgust. "I tell a man from the beginning that I'm celibate so he won't be surprised when I turn down his sexual advances, but when he tries and I tell him NO, he still gets offended. This one had the nerve to tell me I was a waste of his time. I didn't ask him to send four dozen roses to my job. I didn't ask him to take me to expensive plays and restaurants. And there my dumb behind was, thinking that he really liked me and wanted me to experience the finer things in life, when all he was doing was trying to get my defenses down so he could get in my pants. I'm not for sale, Sandy!!"

"I know," she soothes. "Be patient, Tee. There is a man out there that's on the same path as you are. You just haven't met him yet."

"Why do men say they want a good Christian woman, and then, when they realize the work that comes with one, they run? I'm getting so good at saying good bye to men that I'm thinking of putting it on my resume!" Tears start streaming down my face, and I quickly dab them with one of my sister's pristine, white cotton napkins. I find a tissue in my purse and blow my nose.

"Why can't I find a man who loves the fact that I love God more than I love my flesh? I'm so tired of the relationship revolving door. Maybe I should give up on love, because Cupid seems to have his foot permanently lodged in my behind."

Sandy attempts to lovingly bandage my emotional wounds, like always.

"Tina Desiree Long, don't talk like that. God has not forgotten you. You are not the problem. Their lack of spiritual maturity and dedication is. Be patient, baby sis."

"That's easy for you to say. You're married!"

I dab the new tears that seek to escape my brown eyes. "Sandy, do you think all men are dogs?"

"No, darling, I don't. However, I can honestly say that quite a few are, and some of them occasionally migrate to canine tendencies. But there are some really good men left out there. If you think about it, you've actually dated a few. Unfortunately, it wasn't meant for you to be with them. Remember Dontae? He adored you. What happened with you two?"

"Yeah, he was a really sweet guy, but, unfortunately, when the puppy love phase wore off, we realized that we didn't have very much in common."

"There you go. That's one good one. And what about the keyboard player, Myles?" Sandy says as she rolls through her mental rolodex of Tee's adventures in dating.

"Sandy, did you forget he stalked me for almost a month after I refused his proposal? I had to get a restraining order against him! Myles seemed nice at first, but he was crazy. That man wanted to marry me a month after we met. He was so sure God had sent him his wife. It was scary. I wasn't ready for that type of commitment. After I broke up with him, he would show up at my house or my job all times of the day and night, crying about how he couldn't live without me. Funny how life turns out. Now, I would almost give a kidney to have a man begging me to be his lawfully wedded wife--even if he had been hiding in my bushes for two hours waiting for me to come home."

"Well, you're older and more mature now. Why don't you look him up?"

"You can't be serious! Even if I did want him, he's happily married with three kids and a Pomeranian. His sister does my hair, and she gives me an update every now and then. They're building a love nest in Collierville, TN right now."

"Oh," says Sandy, scrambling to find something else to say to make me feel better. "Well trust me. There are some good ones out there. I assure you. When the time is right, God will reveal a saved, successful, fine brother, without codependency issues, that he has set aside especially for you."

"But you're forgetting one thing, Sandy. I was getting my freak on back then. I screwed both of them regularly. And although they were nice to me, our relationships were lustful. I don't understand. The woman I've become is three times better than the one I used to be, but I can't keep a man longer than six months. What am I doing wrong?"

"Have you heard from Jarvis?" she asks.

"Are you trying to make me feel better or worse?" I laugh. "That man dropped me like I tried to steal his wallet, and he hasn't looked back since."

"I was just asking. It's hard to believe that he worked so hard to get you and then did you like that. I was hoping maybe he had come to his senses."

"Well he did, and he hasn't. Please don't bring his name up again. It still hurts."

"I'm sorry," Sandy says.

I am no longer laughing. Even though people are all around us talking, eating, and clinging cutlery and dinnerware, an awkward silence engulfs the table. I love Sandy, but her efforts to cheer me up aren't working this time.

Sandy, formally known as Cassandra, is my amazing big sister and my best friend. Five years my senior, she is wiser and always there when I need her. We have the same mother but different fathers, and we don't look a thing alike. I'm tall and slender with skin the color of cinnamon. I keep my hair natural, often in an afro. Sandy is 5'4" and robust with big momma boobs. Her light skin reminds me of the golden sun as it sets. Her relaxed hair is long and silky. Whenever she throws it over her shoulder, she looks like one of those women you see in the shampoo commercials. It has so much shine and body. Our mother told us that her father was Creole, but we never met him. He left Momma while she was pregnant. Momma said he wasn't the type to be tied down. It's his loss, though, because I couldn't have wished for a more wonderful sibling. My daddy treated us both like we were his until the day he died. He even legally adopted Sandy and gave her his last name.

Unfortunately, her husband, Patrick, doesn't know what a jewel he's got. Well, yes he does, but sometimes he develops temporary amnesia. I assume Sandy was referring to Patrick with her remark about canine tendencies. He had an affair with the receptionist at his office a little over a year ago. He felt so guilty about it that he told Sandy soon after it happened. She started to leave him, but, being the rational individual she is, she weighed her options. After making him grovel and beg her for weeks not to leave him, she told him she wouldn't. She said she wasn't going to walk away from all they had built together because some gold digger thought she could take her spot by sleeping with her husband. With two kids, a successful restaurant, an equally successful dental practice, a 5,000 square foot house, and a ton of debt, I had to see the logic behind her reasoning. She looked above and beyond her pain to preserve the security of herself, my adorable, seven-year-old niece, Nicole, and handsome nine-year-old nephew, Donovin. I fully commend her for being strong enough and level-headed enough to do so. Sandy also had to admit that even though he had messed up royally, she still loved her husband dearly. She told Patrick that he had to fire his receptionist and get an HIV test. And if it ever happened again, she would divorce his behind and attempt to take everything they owned. The two of them have been going to counseling for months now and seem to be doing just fine. I really do like my brother-in law. For the most part he has been a good husband and he's an excellent father. Little does my sister know, I am helping Patrick plan a surprise birthday party for her this Friday at the restaurant.

From where I'm standing Sandy still got the long end of the stick, at least she made it to the altar—even if her hubby did defile the sanctity of their vows. I'm still outside the church waiting for an invitation to approach the altar.

Their restaurant, Mae Lillie's, is named after two of the most amazing women to walk the earth: our grand-mother Mae, who passed three years ago, and our mother Lillie. Mae Lillie's is a fine dining experience that can best be described as upscale soul food. The tables are set with white linen table clothes and napkins. The crystal chande-liers hanging above are absolutely exquisite, but it's the beautifully adorned walls that set the ambience. Colorful African American art is displayed throughout. My favorite is an oil on canvas piece called "Soul Mate" by a young lady named Morrisette. It depicts a woman with long brown hair massaging the shoulders of her attractive ebony prince. I guess I adore it so much because that's what I'm looking for—my soul mate. The real draw of any restaurant is the food, and Mae Lillie's is no excep-tion. When you enter, you are transported to Grandma Mae's kitchen: fried chicken, smothered chicken, ox tails, catfish, chit'lins, spaghetti, mac and cheese, ribs, mixed greens, squash, cabbage, cornbread, pecan pie, sweet potato pie, her special molasses cake ... well you get the picture. The restaurant is located in a suburb of Memphis called Cordova, and the folks out here keep the place packed. Mae Lillie's is proof that good cooking is color-blind, and my big sister can throw down with the best of them. I've seen blacks, whites, Hispanics, and there's a

Chinese family who comes here to eat at least twice a month.

The restaurant has been open for six years and rarely has a slow night. Sometimes it seems like every woman who didn't feel like cooking decided to feed her brood at my sister's place. It's not uncommon for people to wait for over an hour to get a table. Before, Mae Lillie's folks would have to go into the Memphis city limits to find good soul food, but Sandy, being the savvy business woman she is, saw a void in the area and sought to fill it. It has worked in her favor.

I normally help out on Sundays after church when it's really packed. I also come as often as I can during the week for a free lunch. However, today I am seeking emotional nourishment because I fell for a man who was everything I wanted, but hardly anything I needed. *Lord help!*

Chapter 3

The Magnificent Michael Stokes
Michael

As we make our way through the airport to board the plane to Memphis, I get this eerie feeling that someone is following me. It started in the lobby of my hotel, and it seems to get stronger and stronger with every step. I can't go on like this. This is crazy. No SHE is crazy, and she is ruining my trip.

Today was the last day of the celebrity charity golf tournament at Bobby Jones Golf Course in Sarasota, Florida. I normally love these all-expense paid, guest appearance trips. Heck, I love traveling, period. I use it as my escape. For a few days, I can leave my problems behind and focus on entertaining others. But my problems seem to have followed me here. When I checked out of the hotel, there is a note waiting for me at the front desk. It read,

If your stroke on the green was half as good as your stroke in bed, you would have won. Get some rest. You look DEAD tired.

This is the second note this week. She left the first one at the front desk of my hotel in Atlanta. My agent and manager, Peter, was so rattled he tried to get me to cancel all my engagements. How does she keep finding me? I know she is enjoying making me squirm. I refuse to go into hiding. I am a grown man. More importantly, I've got God on my side and the body guard that my manager made me hire when I'm traveling. Isaac looks like he's the one who should have played football instead of me. But I don't think he knows how big he is, or he would buy his clothes in a larger size. His bulging arms and legs always look stuffed into his shirts and pants. I have to introduce him to my tailor when I get back home. Every man should look good in his clothes, and he looks downright uncomfortable. I noticed a couple of teenagers laughing and snickering at the big man in the tight outfit as we passed through security. I wonder if he recently gained weight and that's why nothing fits. He's not very friendly, and he doesn't say much. But Peter says he's tops at private security.

It's an early evening flight, and I am rather tired. I can't wait to board the plane so I can take a nap. I approach my assigned gate and hear the flight attendant call for passengers in my section. Normally, I fly first class but when I changed my flight, first class was already at capacity. I would have to take a seat in the rear of the plane or take another flight. Another flight wasn't an option because tomorrow, Wednesday, I'm scheduled to speak to some boys and girls at a children's hospital and Thursday I'm the keynote speaker at a charity event to raise money for HIV/AIDS research. I need to get to my hotel room and get some rest while I can.

God has truly blessed me. I went from retired professional athlete to motivational speaker in one very challenging year. I questioned so many times why I had to injure myself and be ejected from the one thing I loved more than anything, but that was the problem. I loved football more than God. Almost everything I did centered around football. He needed to get my attention, and he got it in a very big way.

Isaac and I make our way to our seats. I realize that we are only five rows away from the rear of the aircraft. I'm missing first class already. Isaac takes the seat in front of me. I throw my carry-on bag in the overhead bin and settle into my aisle seat. I buckle myself in and see a blonde white woman boarding the plane. I thought she was afraid to fly. I quickly unbuckle my seat belt and get ready to defend myself. I tap Isaac on the shoulder and give him a head nod, the gesture we previously designated to signal possible danger. As the woman approaches, I see that it's not Becca. Not only that, but this woman has two small children with her; the girl is on her hip drinking from a bottle; the other, a boy in overalls carrying a security blanket, is toddling slowly in front of her. Yeah, she looks real threatening. I laugh at myself. Except for the blonde hair, she bears no resemblance to the woman who is trying to kill me. What is she going to do? Beat me with her diaper bag? Besides, she has her hands full. I have to stop trippin'. This can't be healthy. Despite the fact that I have armed security accompanying me every-where I go, I haven't slept in days. I close my eyes and try to relax, but how do you relax when you know someone wants you dead? I feel someone tap me on my shoulder. I'm too tired to even be startled.

I slowly open my heavy eyelids. There is a woman, who looks to be in her 50's, standing in front of me, "Excuse me, sir. I believe I'm sitting in the seat next to you." I stand up to let her pass. The woman reminds me of my mother, short but regal with salt and pepper hair. She's wearing horn-rimmed glasses with a gold chain fastened to each end that kind of gives her a professorish demeanor. After we both sit down, she introduces herself.

"Hello, young man. My name is Dr. Ida Foster. How do you do?"

"I'm fine, ma'am. My name is Michael Stokes."

"Honey, I know exactly who you are. My grandson Steven is absolutely crazy about you. Wait until I tell him I sat next to you on the plane. I'll be the coolest granny on the block." She lets out a hearty chuckle. "He's only 17 and he plays free safety on his high school team. He might possibly be your biggest fan. Steven was devastated when you got injured. How are you holding up?"

"I'm actually doing really well, Dr. Foster. My knee is pretty much healed, and therapy has helped me regain strength in it. I'm happy to hear I've still got fans. I have some autographed pictures in my bag. I'll give you one for your grandson before we land."

"Thank you so much! Steven will love that. Well, don't mind me. I saw you had your eyes closed. I won't talk to you death. You can go right back to your nap."

Wrong choice of words, lady. I think about death often these days.

I close my eyes. It doesn't take long before my body gives into fatigue, and I am fast asleep. I begin to dream about my days in the NFL, except instead of some arena, I'm in my high school stadium in Akron, Ohio. The stands are full, and people are shouting my name. "Michael! Michael! Michael!" Evidently, my team is winning. I turn toward the crowd to acknowledge their cheers, and I am tackled to the ground. Next thing I know, I'm lying flat on my back with a woman enveloped in black standing over me. I can't see her face, but what I can see is a large steel butcher knife coming right at me. As the knife is about to connect with my face, I wake up to Dr. Foster wiping my brow with an airline napkin.

"Son, it's okay. You're safe," she says.

Isaac's muscular body is positioned above me. Waking up to a huge man in a tight shirt is not exactly how a grown man wants to end his nap.

"Mr. Stokes, are you okay?" I am a little disoriented and unsure of my surroundings.

"What? What happened?"

"We probably should be asking you that, seeing that you were screaming in your sleep. I assume you had a bad dream," says Dr. Foster. "Young man, you can go back to your seat. He's fine. I've got him."

I echo her sentiments. "I'm fine, Isaac. You can sit back down," Isaac nods and retreats to his seat. What exactly does a man say to another man to comfort him after he's had a nightmare?

"Here. Drink some water," offers Dr. Foster. "The stewardess gave it to me, and I haven't taken a sip."

I slowly drink the water and allow its wet, refreshing sensation to coat my mouth and throat. I am hot and sweating profusely. The cotton t-shirt under my bright yellow Polo shirt is moist, and it is clinging to my skin. I have to cool myself or this will be a miserable trip. I reach up and turn the small personal air unit in my direction, allowing it to blow the air directly on my face. That feels better. I look at my watch and realize that we have been on the plane for at least 30 minutes and we are still on the runway.

"Why are we still sitting here? There's nothing wrong with the plane, is there?" She wouldn't try to kill me by sabotaging the plane, would she?

"It seems there's a severe storm in our path, and we haven't been cleared for take-off yet. The Captain said it might be another hour before we can leave, so I hope you don't have to be anywhere soon," responds Dr. Foster.

"I've got a few hours to spare."

"Good. I don't mean to pry, but I'm a licensed therapist. If you want to talk about those demons in your dreams, I'd be more than happy to listen since it looks like we'll be here for a while. I promise to treat you like one of my patients and give you strict confidentiality."

Dr. Foster seems very sincere. Maybe it's the fact that she reminds me of my mother that makes me want to open up to her. Or maybe it's that I haven't shared the entire story with anyone. I can't tell my parents because I don't want them to know about my past indiscretions, and there are very few people I trust with my personal business. I can't tell my manager, Peter, because he is so judgmental. He always has to criticize and tell me how I'm too this or too that. A talk with Dr. Foster may be just what I need.

"Well, it's a long story. And if you don't mind, I'd like to start at the very beginning."

"I don't mind at all. Don't leave out a single, solitary detail."

"Yes ma'am. Well, here it goes."

I allow myself to go back in time, remembering each detail and almost every conversation word for word. It feels like I'm in an extended version of the flashback scenes you see in movies.

Chapter 4

You Know A Tree By The Fruit It Bears
Tee

My sister excuses herself from our table and goes to check on the kitchen. I finish my lunch of catfish, carrot soufflé, broccoli with cheese sauce, and a lemonade ice tea mixture we call Sweet Thang. Then, I gather my plate, utensils, and glass and take them back to the kitchen, carefully placing them in the sink. I wave hello to the staff. The waitresses, bus boys, and cooks are busy doing their assigned duties. I spot my sister talking to the head chef, Mr. Norris. His white uniform is covered in spices, sauces, and what appears to be blood from some type of meat. I have never understood why chefs wear white uniforms. Each one I've seen is always absolutely nasty after being splattered with the day's orders. I politely interrupt them so I can give my sister a hug and thank her for listening to me before I leave. She hugs me back and speaks softly into my ear.

"I'm always here for you, Tee, but let me give you something to think about. Maybe the reason you keep getting hurt is because of the kind of men you allow to come into your life. How do you expect to have a saved relationship with unsaved men? You have to be equally yoked."

"They all say they're saved," I respond just as softly.

"That may be true, but you know a tree by the fruit it bears. Pay closer attention to their actions before you go getting all attached. That's what will tell you if they are really saved. Think about it. Mac didn't even like to go to church."

I know she's right. I give Sandy another hug and a weak smile and walk out Mae Lillie's heavy steel back door to my white Yukon Danali. As an event planner, I need a nice truck to haul things. I always have guests or clients, decorations, gifts, and other odds and ends I need to take somewhere.

I drive to my downtown office at Innovations Marketing and Events and listen to my favorite gospel radio station, Hallelujah FM. They play the best gospel, and it helps me keep my mind stayed on Jesus. I need that like the river needs rain. It's so easy to lay down your religion and cuss someone out, especially in my business. But I won't do it. I have got to stay saved!

I turn into the entrance to the parking garage and greet our guard Herman. Herman is the sweetest old man on the planet, and he has looked out for me the entire five years I've been with Innovations. He is in his usual dark brown security uniform that he didn't bother to iron. I wish he would stop doing that. If he doesn't want to iron it, the least he could do is take it immediately out of the dryer and hang it up. He always looks like he slept in it. I also wish he would get some dentures. Herman gives me his one-of-a-kind gummy grin with several teeth missing in the front. He's attractive for an old man, but you almost forget that as soon as you see those gaping holes in his mouth. I asked him once why he didn't get some new teeth, and he told me that would be one more thing he had to keep up with. He said he had enough trouble remembering where he put his gun every morning. Maybe it wouldn't be so bad if his lack of teeth didn't cause his speech to be somewhat impaired. He is always spitting! When you talk to Herman, you better make sure you've got at least two feet between you, or you'll be taking a shower, whether you need one or not.

"Good afternoon, Mth. Thong. You thookin mightly fine this day," he spatters as I drive through the gate. I flash him a smile and respond with a polite thank you. He is sweet, though. When my Grandma Mae died, he sent me a sympathy card and a dozen red roses. He said it was to give me a reason to smile when I felt like I didn't have one.

But old men with missing teeth aren't my type. I've had the same criteria since I was in college. I want a man who is God-fearing, intelligent, hardworking, goal-oriented, articulate, attractive, physically fit, sincere, romantic, thoughtful, honest, and trustworthy. Now, don't misunderstand me when I say attractive. I don't mean drop-dead-gorgeous attractive. He just has to be attractive to me. As long as I think my man looks good, I don't care what anybody else thinks. He must also have a gorgeous smile and a great sense of humor, and he has to love his momma. If a man mistreats his momma, you better believe he won't think twice about mistreating his woman. Did you notice I left out rich? I learned a long time ago that a man who's intelligent, hard-working, and goal-oriented at some point is going to start bringing in the dough, and I have no problem with helping him work his way from the bottom to the top. I've got my man's back. I'll date a grave digger if he's smart enough to put forth a plan that will have him owning a funeral home one day!

Mr. Righteous seems to be paddling in a canoe to get to me when I need him to be on a Learjet, because at 30 years old I'm not getting any younger. I want some babies. I know it could be worse. I do pretty well by myself, so I try not to complain. But Lord knows single life can be downright depressing at times.

I find a spot in the parking garage and make my way to the elevator. I press the button for the 10th floor and after a brief ride, I exit facing the entrance to the Innovations office suite. The first person I see is my co-worker and confidant Edgar. He became the company accountant around the same time I was hired. Every woman needs at least one good male friend, and Edgar is mine. He's from Mexico, but moved to the U.S. as an infant and is fully Americanized. He's also a major metro sexual and gives every woman in this office a run for her money in the style department. Today he is wearing dark green slacks with a mint green shirt and a Ralph Lauren pink and dark green tie. Edgar doesn't agree with my decision to be celibate, because he believes I would be married by now if I was giving up the goods. He loves me just the same, though, and hates to see me hurt. I already gave him an update on last night's events, and I'm sure he has been anxiously waiting to give me his two cents in person. He doesn't even say hello first.

"Girl, you are too hard on a brother. What do you expect? You are the total package: brains, beauty, and booty, and you ain't giving it up. That's like telling a man he can own his dream car, but he can't drive it. Do you really expect a man to make payments on a car he can't drive? These men aren't going to keep wining and dining you if they're not getting any. A man likes to feel appreciated."

"Well, good afternoon to you, too, and shut up, Edgar. I'm not a piece of depreciating machinery. And tell me something. When did sex become the universal sign for thank you? But, if you want to make such an absurd analogy, then you must understand that when a man is dating a woman, he hasn't bought his dream car. He has merely found it on the lot. By engaging in premarital sex, he is asking to take it for an extended test drive or, at best, lease it for weeks, months, and possibly even years before deciding if he wants to purchase it. What if he decides not to purchase it? Then, where does that leave me? I'll tell you where. With no ring, a few extra miles, and a few more emotional dings than I had before. I am only available for purchase. I don't see why I even confide in you, because all you do is criticize," I continue in my nastiest "don't go there" tone. I quicken my stride to my office.

"You confide in me because I'm male and you always want a male opinion. Well, here it is. Until you start letting a brother sample your sweet chocolate, he is not going to buy your candy, Godiva. The goodies-stay-in-the-jar routine is old now."

"I disagree, Nookie Monster," I say playfully in an attempt to lighten up the mood. "I serve a God who rewards the faithful, and I have been ever so faithful. I truly believe this is just a trial to get me ready for my one true love."

"Baby girl, I love you like a sister, but it appears to me that getting you ready for prince charming is killing you. The heart can only take so much pain before it puts up a wall and refuses to let anybody else in. I just don't want to see you turn into a BBW."

"What are you talking about, Edgar?"

"A Bitter Black Woman, baby. The kind of woman no man wants and all will run from like she's wielding a chain saw," he explains.

"I'm still the same kind, loving woman I've always been."

Edgar stops and pulls me gently by my arm, spinning me towards him. Once I am facing him, he uses both hands to grab me firmly by my shoulders, and looks me squarely in the face. I wince. My shoulder is still a little sore in the spot where Mac dug his fingers.

"No you're not, Tee. Over the years I've watched you become more and more feisty and defensive. And I must say it doesn't look good on you, mama. It doesn't look good at all," he says, shaking his head from left to right to emphasize his disapproval. "These tears you've been crying over men who just want a little lovin' have been washing away the sweetness you used to possess. You've changed, pretty lady, but the change has been so gradual you don't see it."

I break away from his grip and walk around his dumpy body in an attempt to escape to my office. I don't like the direction this conversation is going. Edgar refuses to let me get away so easily, and follows. As we near the entrance of my office, I spin around quickly causing him to almost run straight into me. There's no way Edgar is bringing such negativity into my personal space. This is my private domain, and I like it as peaceful as possible at all times.

"Maybe I have changed, but it hasn't had anything to do with men. It has to do with trying to make it in this industry. I got tired of people taking my niceness for weakness. I got tired of other people getting the large events and the huge checks when the events I plan are twice a fabulous as theirs. I got tired of people thinking I wasn't aggressive enough to get the big jobs done. So yeah, I became a little hard, maybe a little to serious at times, but look at me. I'm 30 and I'm one of the best darn event planners in the city, and you know it! I've got more creativity in my little finger than most of my colleagues have in their whole body. I work harder than anyone else, because I have to. As a black woman I'm constantly being asked to prove why I should get the job, even though my track record clearly states why. You act like it's a bad thing that I haven't let every Tom, Dick, and Harry run up in me with no commitment and then run and tell their boys about it! Why should a man buy the cow if I'm giving away the milk for free?"

"Even with a commitment they still couldn't get it. We men like to see if the milk is spoiled before we spend money on an expensive ring. Calm down, girl. Your problem is you ain't getting any, and it's got your emotions on red alert. You're wound tighter than a spool of thread. It's not healthy for a vibrant young woman not to release the tensions of this rat race called life with a little pelvic cha, cha, cha. You need some sex," Edgar says.

I shouldn't have to come to work and defend my religious beliefs with my friends. Has he been talking to Mac or something? I look at Edgar and speak as calmly and as slowly as possible so the other people in the office don't realize we are having a heated conversation.

"You're just mad because I would never break you off. And truth be told, your situation is three times worse than mine. I'm single and celibate by choice. You've been married two years, and you're always horny, because your ungrateful wife won't give you any. You pay all the bills so Marva's trifling behind doesn't have to work. And what does she do? She rations the lovin' like you're in the army, your platoon only has enough supplies for three day, and the rescue chopper won't be there for at least a week. I guarantee you, when I do get married, that will be the least of my husband's complaints. I'll make sure he goes to work every morning with a smile on his face, some pep in his step, and a brand new bulge in his pants every time he thinks about me. His daily motivation will be to hurry up and get home so he can make love to his wife again."

"That's cold, Tee, and that's exactly what I'm talking about. You're turning into an ice princess. No wonder you can't keep a man."

"You keep pushing my buttons, Edgar, so what do you expect? And for the sake of our friendship, I'm going to act like you never made that last statement. Leave this alone. Go to your office and do some to work."

I shut the door in his face before he can respond. I try to remain classy and professional but no one knows how to get your blood pressure up like your friends and family.

That's enough of this nonsense. I've got a gala benefitting HIV/AIDS research in two days, and I need to put the finishing touches on my plans. First, let me throw out all these roses Mac sent yesterday morning. He was only trying to butter me up for sex. Suddenly, they smell real stank!

Ten minutes later, Edgar returns to my office to apologize. I accept his apology and his offer to take me to lunch next week. I never could stay mad at him.

Chapter 5

Once Upon A Time
Michael

"Dr. Foster, someone is trying to kill me. It's my ex-girlfriend Rebecca DeFoy, to be exact. I dated her about five years ago. I met her at the grocery store one evening in the produce section. Those green eyes were what got me. Becca was beautifully biracial. Long honey-blonde hair, bewitching emerald green eyes, slim nose, with Angelina Jolie-like plump pouty lips. Below the neck she was absolutely delicious. Baby had back, hips, thighs and double D breasts, and she knew exactly what to do with them. We had some amazing nights.

"Her appetite for me sometimes seemed insatiable, and her energy level was higher than any woman I've ever known. After our all night love fests, I would barely be able to make it out of bed to get to practice. Becca, on the other hand, would have gotten up, worked out in my home gym, and cooked me breakfast by 7:00 a.m. She also loved sports and drank beer. She was too good to be true.

"Becca moved in with me a couple of months after we met. She was spending almost every night at my house anyway. I enjoyed having her around but something told me to do some investigating. It was too perfect. She told me she had relocated to Miami from Dallas, and that she had dated NFL players before. So, I called up one of my old Cowboys teammates, Roscoe Floyd. Floyd told me she was a platinum groupie and had been with half the team. He figured she only moved because she had exhausted all her options. According to him, it was clear she wanted to be a player's wife. Of course, no one on the team would take her seriously, because she had been with so many of them.

'Steer clear of that one, homie, or just use her for what's she's good for—a good time. And make sure you always wear a condom. There's no telling what she's got. It's probably something they don't even have a name for,' Floyd told me.

'You know what her nickname is, homie? It's The Silencer.'

'The Silencer? Why that?'

'That girl is a super freak, and we called her the Silencer because when she's done, it's lights out. When she's finished with you, you're worn out and all you want to do is be silent and go to sleep.' He laughed, 'I'm sure you know what I mean.'

"Yeah, that was Becca alright. There was no denying that. I was upset, but not surprised. Like I said, she just seemed too good to be true. I thanked Floyd for the info and got off the phone. Then, I called my manager and told him to find out some local info on her. I needed to know if she was messing with anybody in Miami. Peter is like a PI when there's something he wants to know.

'No need,' he said. 'I know her. I've been with her, and I know a couple of other people who have been with her, too. I told you when you meet someone to bring her around so we can check her out, but you're so afraid somebody's going to steal her from you like they did Alicia. I didn't know you were messing with her, Mike, or I would have warned you. When are you going to learn that lots of women are scheming to land a guy like you?

And they will make themselves seem like everything you've been looking for. You can be so naive sometimes.'

"I was pissed. Even my married manager had been with my girl! I felt so stupid. I hate when he mentions Alicia. She was my girl in college and the first woman to make me feel like a fool. We started dating my freshman year. She had my nose wide open. I was in love and didn't care who knew. Once, I even had my barber cut her name enclosed in a heart in the back of my fade. She was also the first woman I had sex with. Alicia was beautiful and smart. She was two years ahead of me when we met at the University of Miami; her major was molecular biology. I was so proud of her. I bragged on her all the time, and introduced her to everyone I knew. I guess I showed her off too much, because one of the other players noticed how great she was, too.

"His name was Terrence Duckett. He was the star quarterback and there was no doubt he was going to go pro. Agents were already trying to woo him by giving him gifts on the low. He had a convertible and his own apartment, and I was just a lowly freshman driving my mom's old Toyota Corolla and living in the athletic dorm. Long story short, Alicia broke up with me and started dating him. I was depressed for a month after she left me. I couldn't eat. I couldn't sleep. I barely attended class, and I wasn't performing well on the field. I almost lost my scholarship because of her! But when coach called me into his office, briefly offered me his sympathy, and then cussed me out and told me to stop being whipped or he was going to put me off his team, I came to my senses. Only a fool would let a woman take away everything he had worked for. I let my pain motivate me on the field, in the gym, and in the classroom. I put on 30 extra pounds and it was all muscle. Every time I walked across campus in my wife beater, all eyes were on me. I got a tutor, made up the work I missed, and by the end of the season I was starting. And I was only a freshman! I also had a 3.8 grade point average.

"Alicia and Duckett stayed together for a while, but in the end they both got theirs. Duckett dropped out of school and entered the draft. He was picked up by the Pittsburgh Steelers during the first round. After he got a taste of the good life and groupie love, he broke up with Alicia. Near the end of his first season with the Steelers, he shattered his ankle during a freak accident. His career was over before it even got started good. At least I got a decade out of the game before I had to be benched for life.

"Alicia tried to come back to me, but I wasn't interested. I was one of the star players, and had women coming at me from all angles. I was like a kid in a candy store, and I was satisfying my sweet tooth like crazy. What did I need Alicia for?

"After I graduated and joined the NFL, I dated a few women. Nothing serious. They didn't have the qualities I wanted in a girlfriend. You have to be more than attractive to get with me. They were bedroom buddies at best. But then I met Becca. When I found out that she had been spreading herself around, it no longer mattered how I felt about her. I confronted Becca and at first she tried to lie. She said they must have her confused her with someone else. When she saw I wasn't buying it, she confessed. You know what she told me?

'Don't push me away, baby. I've made some mistakes in the past, but you and I could have the real deal together. You know I make you happy. Please don't do this.

That was my past and you're my future. Michael, I love you. I really, really love you.'

"I had no intentions of trying to turn a whore into a housewife, no matter how fine she was. Your woman is supposed to feel like a prize, like you won a million dollars in the lottery. Sure you know that other people have won the lottery before, but everybody hasn't won it. That's part of what makes it so special, not to mention the fact that you've gained someone who is willing to work with you to elevate your life. The Bible calls your wife a help meet. I didn't see how an overused, drug addicted, sex fiend could help me. Yeah, she had a drug habit, but it was minor by my standards. I never used, but when you're in entertainment, there are drugs everywhere. You get used to seeing it. She never did it in front of me, so I let it ride.

"I told her to get her stuff and get out. The happiness she had given me couldn't compete with the stupidity I felt at being duped. I was glad I found out who she really was before I married her. I even thought I loved her, but I later realized it was lust. No woman had ever made me feel like that before. Looking back, all we really did was have great sex.

"After Becca, I went on a women binge. I was bedding anything that moved. At one point, I was so out there that I was dating triplets, and they didn't mind sharing me! I was mean, too. It was nothing for me to do a woman and then ask her to leave or get up and leave myself. The only reason I slowed down was because I messed up and slept with my old tee ball coach's daughter. I didn't realize who she was. The only thing she told me was that she had, had a crush on me for years. When I put her out my hotel room she threw a fit. The next day,

she called my momma and told her what I did! My
parents went off on me! After that happened, I knew I
had to make a change. I felt horrible. I had become a
cold-hearted monster. All because a woman hurt me. Pain
can make you do some crazy things."

Chapter 6

When It Rains It Pours
Tee

I drag myself out of the office around 7:00 p.m. The Give Life Gala is in two days and everything has to be perfect. Event planning isn't an easy business. In a lot of ways my job is to cater to the client's every whim, no matter how ridiculous they may seem. I spent most of my afternoon taking last minute requests from the marketing manager of the I Will Live Foundation and trying to make them happen. The drive home is a quiet one. Sometimes, I prefer not to listen to anything but the engine of my Denali as I zoom along I-240. I pull into my driveway and exit the truck. My cell phone rings. It's my old flame Jarvis. I haven't heard from him since he cheated on me with some woman he met at a club. My first mind tells me to let it roll over to voice mail, but I decide to answer. Maybe my sister was on to something earlier. Maybe he had realized the error of his ways. I could use an ego boost right now.

"Hello," I answer trying to sound perky, even though every part of my body could use a long hot bubble bath and some rest between 800 thread count, soft as silk sheets.

"Hey, Tee. This is Jarvis. How ya doing?"

"I'm good, Jarvis. How about yourself?"

"Fantastic. I've never been one to beat around the bush, so I'm going to skip through the pleasantries and get straight to the point. I called to tell you something. I didn't want you to hear it through the grapevine."

"Okay. What is it?" I ask.

"I asked Terry, the woman you saw at my house that day, to marry me. She said yes and we're getting married next year."

"But you've only been dating her six months!"

"Yeah, that's true, but I know she's the one. I've never known anyone who understands me the way she does."

"Congratulations, Jarvis, but I don't understand why you felt the need to call and share this with me. We haven't spoken since I caught you cheating," I say sarcastically.

"I wanted to say thank you. I had never been in a real relationship before you. You taught me so much. I know what I did was horrible, but celibacy is your thing, not mine. And I should have told you that. But, Tee, you have to believe me when I tell you, you were the first woman I ever loved. You were just about all my firsts. You were the first woman I took to a fancy restaurant, the first woman I introduced to my entire family, the first woman I bought an expensive present for. I gained a new respect for women because of you. I'm sorry I hurt you. I just needed someone who didn't have a problem with me hanging in the streets. And I needed a little lovin' on the regular. Terry was patient with me and waited for me to slow down. Now, I have, and I'm going to marry her."

I can't believe what I'm hearing. Is he serious? This man is marrying the woman who slept with him the same night she met him and calling to tell me thank you! I grip the phone tightly, wishing it was his neck. The whole world is full of horny, stupid men who are thinking with the wrong head.

"So basically, you're thanking me for being the training ground for another woman!" I yell.

"Well, don't think of it that way. I'm thanking you for making me a better man," Jarvis says.

"For another woman!"

"I guess that means you don't want an invitation to the wedding? I was hoping you and I could be friends. I still care about you, Tee. I've been wanting to call you ever since we broke up. I just couldn't work up the ne---,"

"You know what, Jarvis?" I say cutting him off. "I always questioned the level of your intelligence when we were together. I knew something was wrong when you kept saying that the wine during Communion tasted like grape juice, after I told you it was grape juice. You have now confirmed it for me. You are indeed an idiot."

I hang up the phone and look down at the small two-carat diamond and white gold ring on my right ring finger. Jarvis gave it to me last Christmas. He called it a commitment ring, and said it was a symbol that he was serious. That was also the day he told me he loved me for the first time. It's so beautiful. Even though we're no longer together, I continue to wear it. We were only together four months, but I can honestly say I had fallen for that man.

We did have our issues. He is five years younger than I am and always wanted to hang out with his boys and play on his xBox 360 or go to the club when I felt he should be spending time with me. I knew we weren't a perfect match, but there was something about him that drew me to him. He was handsome in a b-boy, hip hop kind of way. When he wasn't in his delivery uniform, his attire was usually jeans, a t-shirt, and tennis shoes or Timberlands. He was also extremely sexy.

My house is on his delivery route. At first, I wouldn't give him the time of day but my resistance just made him try even harder. He left notes in my mailbox until I agreed to meet him for coffee. He asked me to give him a chance to show me that he could make me happy. I did and he did make me happy…in the beginning.

He was a little rough around the edges. He had a lot to learn about women but he was so eager to learn that I didn't mind teaching him. I told him I was celibate, and he said that sex wasn't the reason he wanted to be with me. Although he was used to getting some, he was willing to try it for me. Midway through the third month, he wasn't trying any more. He would go two or three days without calling. If I called him, he may or may not return the call. Previously, he would call me right back. After about two weeks of that mess, I stopped by Jarvis' apartment one morning to talk. He answered the door in his boxers and a t-shirt with lipstick on the collar. He looked surprised and ashamed at the same time. I immediately knew what was up. I walked past him and headed straight for the bedroom. There was Miss Thang, topless and fast asleep in his bed. Before I could give her a rude awakening, Jarvis pulled me out of the room. I didn't even try to fight him. All I could do was cry.

He said, "I'm sorry. I never meant to hurt you. I tried, Tee. I really tried, but a man like me has needs. If it makes you feel any better, this is the first time I've cheated on you. It wasn't like this was something that was going on all along. Actually, I just met her last night at the club. I love you, Tee. I just can't do what you're asking me to do. Don't blame her. Blame me. She doesn't even know you exist."

I told him to lose my number and stomped out of his apartment. I haven't spoken to him since that day, and when I do, he tells me he's getting married. If he had broken up with me first, I would have at least had some respect for him. He didn't have to cheat on me. If he had come to me and told me the truth, I would have understood.

Celibacy isn't always easy. It can be a struggle. Especially the days when your loins feel like they are on fire. You're hoping a man doesn't so much as bump into you, because your panties may fall down all of a sudden. And since you're half way naked, your body may somehow convince your brain that you might as well give him some to quench the fire.

"Loser!" I yell, yanking the ring off my finger and throwing it into the middle of the street. I listen to the clinking sound of the metal as it hits the pavement and bounces twice. Here I am trying to be a Godly woman and set some standards. For what? To get told time and time again that I'm not the one. Life isn't fair. Why should she reap the benefits of my hard work? I know I'm better off without him, but that doesn't stop this feeling of nausea rumbling in my stomach. It doesn't stop the tears that begin to stream down my face for the second time today. It also doesn't stop this escalating fear that I'm going to grow old alone. During my final days, I'll be in a nursing home being spoon fed green Jello by some woman with bad acne who's only doing it because she's being paid to do so.

I open my door, walk in my house and head to my bedroom. I don't even stop to pet my cocker spaniel, Chesnutt, who is jumping up and down to greet me. At least someone is happy to see me. I am exhausted. I throw myself face first into one of the jumbo size pillows on my bed and wait for the Sandman to come and relieve me temporarily of my present agony. Sandman is my nickname for sleep. I know I should wash off my makeup and get out of my Donna Karen suit, but doing so won't make a bit of difference in my personal life. Once again, I'm like the ugly guy at a Sadie Hawkins dance who didn't get picked to two-step. Cupid really does have his foot permanently lodged in my behind, and it feels like he's got on cleats.

I kick off my shoes and lie there waiting for sleep to overcome me. I was raised in the church. My mother taught me that my body was precious, and it wasn't meant to be shared with any man I found attractive. I didn't lose my virginity until I was 22 because I was waiting for someone special who appreciated me. My first love didn't last, but I continued to be selective when it came to the men that I let in my life and in my bed. But this new age custom of sleeping with every man you enter into a relationship with didn't sit well with me. I knew that something wasn't right about the way I was doing things. I found out the hard way that some men will say and do the right things to make you feel comfortable enough to sleep with them. Even give you a commitment. Afterward, they'll reveal their true selves. I didn't always like what I saw. And after it ended, I often found myself feeling used.

Once, I attended a single and saved conference and learned that when women have an orgasm our bodies release a hormone called oxytocin. It creates a feeling of bonding. It's also released during birth and while breast-feeding. That explained why so many of us get attached to men we barely know and accept behavior from them we know is wrong. They put it on us, and we have that oxytocin in our systems!

I decided to stop doing things my way and do things God's way. I became celibate. Since I'm no longer having sex, I am not falling for the lies and the lines. If a man isn't willing to take his time to get to know me, as far as I'm concerned, he is not worth my time. The clarity I have with men is amazing. I can truly focus on the person and decipher whether or not his intentions are honorable---most of the time. But if they aren't, I didn't give him all of me so I don't feel so bad.

The peace that comes with knowing I am living within God's will is immeasurable. Not to mention the joy, that unspeakable, make-you-jump-up-and-down-and-dance-until-your-clothes-come-off-like-King-David kind of joy. I used to feel good about my decision to give up sex. But lately, it seems my decision is bringing more sorrow than joy. I'm no saint, and I'm far from perfect, but I try to be a good Christian. But I'm starting to get weary. All I want is a man who is capable of loving me and respecting my decision to remain celibate until marriage. Does he exist?

I try to go to sleep and forget tonight happened. After about 30 minutes, I am still wide awake. Men! Even the Sandman won't act right.

I decide to get up and do a little work to take my mind off things. I open my briefcase and look at my notes for the Gala. Retired NFL player Michael Stokes is going to be our keynote speaker. He's been called one of the best running backs of all time. His bio says he was a star player at his high school in Ohio. After high school, he accepted a full athletic scholarship to the University of Miami, where he still holds several school records for catches and touch downs. He was an All-Star Athlete and even won the Heisman Trophy! It goes on to say that he decided to finish college before entering the draft. After graduation, Michael was selected as a first-round draft pick by the Washington Redskins. During his 10 year career, he played in eight Pro Bowls and four championship games, winning two of them. He was voted MVP two times! He was later traded to the Dallas Cowboys and he rounded out the last three years of his career with the Miami Dolphins. Last year, he tore up his knee during the playoffs. Unfortunately, surgery was unable to repair the damage enough to allow him to continue to play.

Michael looks really good in the photos his booking agent sent. I wonder if he's this fine in person. I have a meeting with his manager in the morning, but I have no idea what he wants to talk about. He wouldn't tell me when I spoke to him earlier today. All he would say was that it was urgent.

Chapter 7

You, Me, and Baby Makes Three
Michael

Dr. Foster has been quietly listening to me tell my story for almost an hour. She doesn't interrupt to ask a question or make a comment. Occasionally, she nods her head or laughs as I give her the low down on my life. The Captain announces that the storm has subsided, and we have been cleared for take-off. I am happy to be on my way. While I'm not afraid to fly, it's not my favorite thing to do. I listen as the flight attendants give their routine safety and emergency spiel about seatbelts, exits, breathing and floatation devices. After the plane ascends to the sky and then levels, I resume my tale.

"About a month ago, I came home and found Becca standing outside my condo. I don't know how she got my address, because I had moved twice since we dated.

"I had returned to Miami that day after an extended stay at my parent's house. After I found out I wasn't going to be able to play ball any more, the only place I could go to find refuge was home in Akron, Ohio. I had been there almost three months eating Mom's cooking, fighting depression and trying to figure out what I was going to do with my life since the one I knew had been shattered. It was there that I returned to my home church, dedicated my life to Christ and turned over a new leaf. No more partying. No more sleeping with women I barely knew.

"The day Becca stopped by was warm but rainy. I thought the storm had ended, so I walked to a nearby store to pick up a few items. On the way back, it started sprinkling. She approached me while I was at the front of my place punching in my security code. I was extremely surprised to see her. Not happy or angry, just surprised. She didn't have an umbrella either, and I wasn't going to stand in the rain and talk to her. So, I told her to come in. Besides, I felt sorry for her. She didn't look good. I almost didn't recognize her. She looked like she had aged 20 years in five. Since finding Christ, I was full of forgiveness for everyone who had hurt me.

"I opened the door for her. Instead of entering the building, she ran over to an old, raggedy Oldsmobile parked out front. She returned with this adorable little girl who looked to be about three or four years old. I didn't say anything at first. I just opened the door a little wider so they could both come in. Becca informed me that she was her daughter. When I looked down, she said, 'Hello, I'm Michelle. What's your name?' And held out her hand. I stooped down to her level to shake it.

'That's a pretty name, Michelle. I'm Michael.'

'Nice to meet you, Michael. I'm hungry. Are you hungry?' asked Michelle.

'A little,' I chuckled. 'I'll see what I have to eat.'

'Good cause I'm staaaaaaaaaaaarving!'

'Oh really?' I chuckled again.

"She had her mom's honey-blonde hair, except hers was extremely curly, brown eyes and a dimple in her chin. Like I said, she was adorable, and it was obvious that her father, whoever was, was black. Becca's skin was light enough to pass for white but Michelle's skin was more of a tan color.

"I was in a good mood, and when I'm in a good mood I like to cook. So, Michelle was in luck. I made my way to the kitchen, Becca walked around looking at my place, and Michelle grabbed the remote, settled into my brown leather Laz-E-Boy, and cut on the TV. She was making herself right at home.

'This is a nice place you have here, Michael,' said Beccca.

'Thanks.'

'It's a lot smaller than the house where we used to …' Becca stopped and then looked at her daughter. 'Well you know.' She gave me a seductive wink. I wasn't enticed. I tried to ignore the last comment.

'Yeah, I realized I didn't need all that space. Plus, my little brother was living with me then. You remember Maxwell, don't you?'

'Yeah, I remember him. How's he doing?'

'He's great. He's a sophomore at UCLA majoring in biology with plans to be a doctor.' I am quite proud of my little brother. He is the brains of the family, and there is no denying it. He was the valedictorian of his high school, got a perfect score on his SAT, and a full scholarship to UCLA.

'What? I thought your brother was in college when I met him. He told me was.'

'That doesn't surprise me. He actually attended a charter high school that was located on a college campus.'

"Becca got this really distraught look on her face, but as fast as it came, it was gone.

'He was a lot younger than I thought, wasn't he?'

'Yeah, he was. He was always telling people he was in college, trying to date college girls. I came home more than a few times to a grown woman in my house. He used to beg me not to blow his game by telling them he was really in high school, but I couldn't let him get away with that. I always gave him an ultimatum: You tell her or I will. So, he had to tell. I was trying to teach him not to play with women like that. Trying to passing on some of the lessons I learned the hard way.'

'That was good of you. I'm sure he's a better man for it. Now, how's his big brother doing? I heard you hurt your knee and can't play football no more.'

'That's right.'

'What are you going to do now?' Her questions were starting to bother me.

'I'm going to do motivational speaking. I actually have a few jobs lined up already. People are willing to pay top dollar to have a future hall of famer come speak at their functions.'

'Sounds like a plan to me. You always were an excellent communicator. I used to love to sit and listen to you conduct business on the phone. You always sounded so confident and knowledgeable. So are you seeing anyone?'

'Becca, you said you had something important to talk about. What is it? I am not going to discuss my personal life with you. It's none of your business,' I said.

"Michelle stood up in the chair and said loudly, 'Michael, I'm staaaaaaaarving! You still gonna feed me, aren't cha?'

"I take a break from Becca, and go over to her.

'Alright, shorty! Be patient. I told you I was going to feed you, didn't I. Demanding aren't you?' I scooped her up with one arm, carried her to the kitchen, and I gently sat her on the counter.

'I was thinking of making my special spaghetti. Do you like spaghetti?'

'Yeah, I looooove spah-spetty!'

'Ok. I have to cook it. I may need some help.'

'I can help you. I loooooove to cook!' she yelled, clapping her hands with excitement.

'That's good to know. I would be honored to have you assist me.' I get my ingredients ready: tomato sauce, basil, garlic, salt, ground pepper, bell pepper, onion, ground beef, and spaghetti. I also get some crackers.

'You can take these crackers and munch on a few of them since you are staaaaarving. And when I get to the part where I need your help, I'll call you.' I set her on the floor and motioned for her to take her crackers and finish watching the cartoons she found on TV. Michelle didn't move.

'I wanna stay here with yooooou, Michael.' She took her little body and bear hugged my leg. I think my heart melted at that moment. I was smiling from ear to ear.

'That's fine with me cutie.'

'YEAAAAAAH!' she screamed, jumping up and down. Michelle was so easily excited. I loved it. She reminded me of some of the football fans. I turned my attention back to Becca.

'Do you want to tell me why you are here Becca?'

'Sorry, but it's not suitable for children. It will have to wait until Michelle isn't around.'

'Fair enough.' Why did she bring her kid if she couldn't talk around her, but I was too hungry to give it much thought. My spaghetti was my main concern at that moment. Becca had a seat on the bar stool while Michelle and I cooked. Her contribution was rolling the ground beef into meatballs.

'I used to love watching you in the kitchen, almost as much as I loved watching you on the field. You always looked like you belonged in both places, and you were equally talented at each,' Becca said.

'Thanks, but if memory serves me correctly, you made a delicious Belgium waffle.'

'And I still do. Maybe I can show you sometime.' She used her seductive tone again. I really wished she would stop bring up the past. I needed to nip that in the bud.

'Sorry, but I don't think that's possible. You two are my guests for this evening and only this evening.' Becca got the hint. She sat there a few more minutes, watching us in silence. Then, she turned around to watch television.

"When the spaghetti—complete with Michelle's gigantic meatballs—was done, we all ate hungrily and quietly. You can tell when people are hungry because there is little to no conversation. After dinner, we watched TV. Michelle fell fast asleep with her head pressed against the side of my arm.

"I knew she and her mom had stayed too long, but I was enjoying their company. Becca wasn't a bad person. She had just made some terrible decisions. Because of her past, we had no future.

"I picked Michelle up, carried her to my bedroom, and gently placed her in my bed. I headed back to the living room so Becca and I could talk. Afterward, these two had to go. I was not going to give Becca the opportunity to come back into my life. I don't care how cute her child was.

"Becca wasn't attractive to me anymore. She still had those great green eyes but she also had wrinkles popping out everywhere. Her figure looked more like a two liter than the Coke bottle it used to be. She was dressed in faded black jeans and her pink 'I love football' t-shirt had bleach stains in it. She had really let herself go. I suspected she was still doing drugs.

"I went to the kitchen and grabbed us some beers from the refrigerator. I rarely drink but I had a feeling I was going to need one, and Becca looked nervous. I was hoping a little liquor would help her relax so she could say whatever she had to say and then leave. It was my first night back in Miami, and I wanted to relax alone.

'So what's up, Becca?'

'I believe you are Michelle's father,' she said matter-of-factly.

"I wasn't even rattled by her statement. 'Oh really? From what I heard, plenty of people could be her father. So what makes you think it's me? We used condoms.'

'We used them most of the time, not all of the time. You know---'

'Didn't you start messing with some lawyer right after our relationship ended?' Actually, you did. And would you like to know how I knew that? He was my lawyer.'

'Time out! Put the gloves down, Binky.' She held her hands up in defense, and then put them in a T symbol. 'I didn't come here to get beat up by my past. I came here to try to find my child's father so he can be a part of her life. I had both parents in my life, and I want to give that to Michelle, if I can. She's a good kid. She deserves that, Binky.'

"I always hated when Becca called me Binky. It was the pet name she gave me when we were together. It sounds so unmasculine. She started scooting closer to me with that same unenticing, seductive look on her face.

'You look good, Michael. Real good. I bet I can make you feel as good as you look.'

"She started kissing on my neck. Even though I didn't find her attractive anymore, it felt good. It had been months since a woman who wasn't a doctor, nurse, physical therapist or my mother had touched me. Becca began to slowly unbutton my Kenneth Cole shirt, and as she undid each button, she kissed my chest. I laid my head back on the couch and began to imagine she was Halle Berry. Maybe a little attention wouldn't hurt.

'See, Michael? See how good we are together? What you're feeling right now is that connection we had that's still there after all these years. I still love you. You, me, and Michelle--we could be a family. I know how much you wanted a kid and now you have one.'

"I suddenly snapped back to reality. Same Becca. Still looking for a meal ticket. I removed her hands from my body and placed them at her sides.

'That's it, Becca. I admit there is a possibility Michelle could be mine. I am willing to take a DNA test, but you have got to leave NOW.'

"She burst into tears. 'Michael, don't say that,' she sobbed.

'I'm sorry, Becca, but I don't back track. I'll go get Michelle. You have to go.' I stood up and buttoned my shirt back up.

'Michael, I don't have any place to go! Michelle and I have been living in my car for a week. Why do you think she was so hungry? I don't have a job, and I don't have any money. We've been getting our meals at a local church. Michael we're homeless!' She stood up, wrapped her arms around my neck, and started sobbing relentlessly on my shirt. I hate to see a woman cry.

'Okay, you can stay here tonight. Just stop crying. I can't stand it. You and Michelle can sleep in my room. I'll take the guest room. But I'm locking my door, so don't even think about trying to come in there with me. Tomorrow, we are going to get a DNA test. If Michelle is mine, I will take care of her. Stop crying and get some rest.' I took her arms from around my neck and led her to my bedroom. I was proud of myself. I was stern, yet feeling. There was a time when I didn't care if a woman cried until her eyes were swollen. I wouldn't feel a bit of emotion.

"I showed her to the master bathroom so she could wash her face. While Becca was in the bathroom, I selected a few personal items to take into the guest room. I stood by my bed and looked at the sweet little girl lying there. What if she was mine? I didn't think it would be the worst thing in the world. She even looked a little like me. I bent down and said a prayer of protection over her. I wanted God to bless her.

There was a strong possibility I could have been Michelle's daddy, but I couldn't let myself get attached until I knew for sure."

Chapter 8

Child's Play
Tee

After reviewing my notes, I decide to take a shower. Hot steamy water may be exactly what I need to relieve the tension I'm feeling. My muscles are tight, and I can feel the beginnings of a headache. As the water and soap cascade over my skin, I try to release the anger and sadness that have invaded my psyche. Neither Mac nor Jarvis deserve my tears. I make a silent pact with myself not to shed another tear over either of them. My head knows I am better off without them, now I have to convince my heart.

I step out of the shower and wrap myself in a large terry cloth towel. I go to my dresser to get my lotion and notice that my cell phone is indicating that I have three missed calls. They are from my former business partner, Eric.

Eric and I used to promote concerts together when I was in my early 20's. They were mostly hard core hip hop, but after I got saved, my spirit would no longer let me promote artists whose lyrics were riddled with profanity, vulgarity, violence, sex, and drugs. I tried to get Eric to bring in more socially conscience rappers and even some holy hip hop artists, but he refused, saying that he couldn't make as much money off them. I told him I had to get out or, better yet, God was pushing me out. Eric wasn't happy because I was good at what I did, but we remained cool. He continued to promote shows, and I began to focus solely on event planning. He's evolved since then. This year alone he brought Jay Z, Kanye West, Mary J. Blige, Usher, and Rihanna to Memphis. I know Eric well enough to know that if he is calling this many times back to back, it must be important. I dial his number, and the phone only rings once before he answers.

"Tee, I'm so glad you called me back. I need you to handle a situation for me."

"What's up, babe?"

"Tasha is having our baby, and I have a show going on at the Mid-South Coliseum tonight. It's this kid called Icy Blak. He was supposed to go on at 8:30 p.m., but it's almost 10:00 and he still hasn't hit the stage. His manager says he don't feel like it and the fans can wait. This show is full of teens and young adults and it's Tuesday night, Tee. People have to go to work tomorrow. They're already starting to ask for their money back. My assistant was supposed to handle this show, but he says he can't get Blak to even open the door to his dressing room. Tee, right now I'm barely breaking even on this thing and with the new baby coming, the last thing I need is a loss."

I hear somebody scream his name in the background. It must be his wife, Tasha.

"I'm coming baby!" he shouts. "I'm at the hospital and Tasha's in labor right now. Tee, I gotta go. Please say you'll handle this for me. I need you!" he pleads.

"Eric, you know I gave that up. And isn't he that rapper with that song 'Me, You, and Your Girl'?"

"I know, Tee, but I need you. I'm about to have my first son, and I can't leave. If anyone can handle this situation, I know you can. Tee, PLEASE! I'll pay you. Name your price."

"Only for you, Eric. Consider this your baby shower gift." I say.

"I love you girl! Now, I'm paying him $10,000 for this show. I gave him half and he's supposed to get the other half when he gets off the stage. You might be able to use that as leverage."

I hear another ear piercing scream in the background.

"I'm coming, honey! I gotta go. Bye."

I hang up the phone, apply my lotion, and put on some clothes. Super Tee is on her way to save the day! Some of these artists irritate me. They get a hit and a little money and start thinking they're God's gift to the world. They start making crazy demands and mistreating the very people who made them famous in the first place. This kid better be ready to get on stage when I get there. He's making me miss my beauty sleep.

As I drive to the Mid-South Coliseum, I reminisce on my last show with Eric. It was at the Pyramid Arena with this artist called Blaze B. Eric and I spent a crazy amount of money on publicity and sold the place out. The night started out great. Excitement was everywhere and the fans couldn't wait for us to begin the show. The opening act was a local R&B singer named Torrey. Blaze B took the stage and rocked the house! He performed about five songs with no problem, and it looked like it was going to be an incident-free evening.

If you did those kinds of shows, it was understood that violence could occur. As a promoter, you had to make sure your security was more than adequate and could kill an intense situation quickly. Blaze B wrapped up with his big hit at the time, "Bust Her In Da Mouf." It's about a guy who suspects his girl is cheating and in the song he's talking about what he's going to do to her if he catches her. Before the song was over a fight erupted between a couple in the audience. Witnesses said the man hit his wife in the jaw and then proceeded to kick her unmercifully. Security pulled him off of her and held him for the police and that poor woman was rushed to the hospital by ambulance. We found out later that the couple was having problems because the husband had recently caught her kissing another man.

The wife was hurt pretty bad. Her injuries included a concussion, fractured skull, a broken jaw, and broken ribs. The damage to her jaw was so severe that they had to do reconstructive surgery and wire her mouth shut to insure proper healing. Can you imagine taking your meals through a straw for weeks? Her husband was sentenced to six months in jail for assault. After he was released, the couple divorced. They had two children.

I recognize that it wasn't totally my fault. I didn't write the song, I wasn't the one caught cheating, nor did I beat the wife up. What I did do was create a venue for a song about violence toward women to be heard. I put it on stage. I gave it a spotlight, a microphone, and an audience.

I went to see the woman in the hospital. Her name was Monique. She looked so helpless lying there with her purple, swollen jaw and a bandage around her head. She even had a black eye. I stood over Monique and prayed for God to heal her body, and I promised him I would never do another show with artists that promoted negativity again. Eric wasn't happy I ended our business partnership, but he said he understood.

I know all hip hop artists aren't violent, vulgar, or demeaning. I love Common, Talib Kweli, Mos Def, and others like them, but at the time hard core hip hop was what was hot here in Memphis. If you want to make money in the promotions business, you better bring the artists people want to hear.

I enter the Mid-South Coliseum parking lot, and drive around to the gated area in the back they use to securely transport performers and their equipment into the facility. There are several people there I used to work with. Danny, Eric's protégé, runs up to me panting. He was a teenager when he started working with Eric, but now he's an adult with facial hair and everything. Although, it's hard to tell by the way he's behaving.

"Tee, I'm so glad you're here! I don't know what to do. Icy Blak is in the back getting high with a bunch of freaks, and he won't come out. The audience is starting to get hostile and people are asking for their money back. I got 3,000 people in there and they all paid 30 bucks to be here. I have threatened Blak with everything I have, but nothing's working. He won't come out!" He ends in a high pitched squeal that I would expect from a prepubescent girl, not a grown man.

"Calm down, Danny. Help is here," I say in my best I-can-do-anything voice. "Show me where he is. Some things just require finesse and a woman's touch, especially when there's a man involved." I give him a reassuring wink and a pat on the back.

I follow Danny to the largest dressing room in the facility. A security guard and the building engineer are standing by the door.

"He won't unlock it, so I was about to have the building engineer let me in so I can try to talk to him. Then, someone told me you were outside, so I decided to wait for you," explains Danny.

"Good idea. Now, what you're about to witness stays between me and you. You hear me, Danny?"

He nods his head in a manner that resembles those plastic bobble head dolls. I take off my belt and hand it to him. I thought I might have to resort to some of my old tactics, so I dressed for the part. I had on my House of Deréon skinny jeans and a matching tank top. I work out at least three times a week, and I look darn good, if I do say so myself. I could give any of those 20 something-year-olds you see in the music videos a run for their money—any day. I bet they don't have a washboard stomach. I give my breasts a firm lift to make sure they look perky, instruct the building engineer to open the door and tell security to keep the corridor clear. I tell Danny to get whoever is supposed to be performing with this guy ready to go on stage.

The building engineer opens the door and a wave of cannabis-scented air hits me in the face. I never could stand the smell of that stuff. I try not to make any noise as I walk across the floor, but five-inch stilettos aren't known for their stealth capabilities. I see Icy Blak's personal security standing by the door. To my surprise, it's my childhood friend Beef. We lived on the same street and used to ride our bikes together. He was given that name in high school because of his body builder physique. He's only 5'6", but it's all muscle. He doesn't appear to have changed much since I saw him two years ago. What's he doing here? I thought he was doing security for Earth, Wind, and Fire. I give him a quick hug and a peck on the cheek.

"When did you start working with teenie boppers?"

"EWF is taking a break right now, and I needed a little extra money. I got five kids, Tee. I don't like rolling with these baby ballers, but it pays the bills," he says.

"How old is this kid?"

"Sixteen, maybe 17. He's what you call an emancipated minor. The word is he divorced his parents last year and thinks he's grown. Can't nobody tell that kid nothing. Been in here three hours. He told me to stay over here by the door and make sure nobody comes in."

He's a baby. This is going to be easier than I thought.

"Thanks, Beef. You know why I'm here, so please don't get in my way. Eric paid a lot of money for this boy to be here, and he's got to go on stage now or none of us will be getting paid. Where is he?" I ask.

"I know better than to mess wit chu, Tee. Somebody needs to put this boy in check. I woulda' done it, but like I said, I need the check. Walk around the corner. You'll see him."

I give Beef another hug, and walk softly towards my target. I take about five steps and see this skinny kid in the corner with four females around him. Most of them aren't wearing much of anything. They all looked to be about 21 or younger. Blak is in the process of taking a blunt from one of the girl's hands and putting it to his lips when he spots me. There's low music playing in the background, so I begin to move my body to the beat. I keep it simple. Nothing raunchy. My hips swing from left to right, and Blak sits up to get a better look. This kid is really handsome. He's has dark skin and thick lips. He's shirtless. What he does have on is a pair of designer jeans, a pair of icy white, shell toe Adidas, and a black New York Yankees hat cocked to the side. He smiles at me. Two adorable dimples pop out and say hello. I see why he has the girls going crazy. I would be in love with him, too, if I were a teenage girl. As I make my way towards him, I notice the girls all giving me who-are-you looks. I pay them no mind, because I'm here for the boy. As far as I'm concerned, they are all little girls; I'm a full-fledged woman. There's no competition at all.

I inch towards him and say is a low, seductive voice,"I heard there was a party in this room, and I came to see if I could join you?"

"Aaaaw man. An old chick," announces Blak to no one in particular. "Yeah, I like old chicks. Every old chick I been with has taught me some freaky, nasty stuff I never done before."

Who is he calling old? I'm only 30.

"Come over here, momma. Y'all need to respect your elders and move!" he orders the girls.

All four of them step back to let me through. But they stay close enough to view the action.

I bend over and whisper in his ear, "Blak, baby, aren't you supposed to be doing a show?"

"Yeah, but it can wait until after I do you. Take off dem clothes, momma. Let me see what chu workin' wit." His breath reeks of weed.

"I need you to go do your show, baby? Do it for momma," I say softly.

"Why do you care whether I do my show or not? I'm chillin'. I'll do it, but not right now. You need me to help you wit des jeans?"

"But what about your fans?"

"The fans can wait. Do you need me to help you wit dis shirt?"

"Naw, but I do need you to do your show. I'm the woman who's paying you. And if you don't get your narrow behind out of this room and on stage, I'm going to take back the $5,000 I've already paid you and sue your behind for breach of contract, which clearly states that you will be on stage no later than 9:00 p.m., and it is now 10:30!" By the time I reach the end of my statement, I am screaming at the top of my lungs.

"Huh? What you talking 'bout, momma?" Blak screeches in a high-pitched voice similar to the one Danny used earlier.

I grasp him by one of his large, diamond stud adorned ears. He screams but I continue to hold his ear tightly as I guide him to his feet and lead him to the door. His jeans are several sizes too big and they fall down to the floor, revealing a pair of Spongebob Squarepants boxer shorts. Blak struggles to walk while pulling them up with one hand. I don't care if his penis pops out. I'm not letting his ear go, and he is coming out of this room.

"Hey, get off me, woman! What cha doin'? Security!"

"I'm protecting my investment. Scream all you want. Nobody's coming to help you. I run this!"

As Blak and I pass Danny, I reach for my belt and continue to lead him by his ear to the area near the side entrance of the stage.

"That hurts! Stop! I'm sorry! I'll do whatever you want. Just let my ear go," he begs.

"You're going to get your scrawny behind on stage, or I'm going to take my belt and whip you," I threaten.

"Okay. Just let me go."

I believe him and release his ear. Blak turns and heads in the opposite direction. I block him with my small 140 pound frame. He's about three inches taller than I am, but we're almost equal in size. I can probably take him if I have to.

"Where are you going?" I demand.

"Back to my dressing room. I'm not doing a show at all now, and you ain't getting your bills back! Now move! Don't make me call you the b-word cuz I will!" His breathing is heavy and his eyes are red and narrow. He defiantly looks down his nose at me, and his dark, thick lips are curled into a menacing a snarl.

I'm usually pretty good at judging people. I know from that statement that I have this kid pegged right. He's one those rich kids, parading around like he's hood. I bet he grew up in the suburbs and went to private school.

"Is that so?"

"That's so," he responds, sticking his face in my face.

Dang, this kid's breath is foul. Does anybody have a mint or some gum?

Okay, he asked for it. I hold him by the arm with one hand, and I use my other hand to give him a hard whack on the butt with my belt. He wasn't expecting that. Before he could fully comprehend what was going on, I kick him in the back of his knee and watch his body buckle due to lack of adequate support. He let go of his jeans and tries to use that hand to keep himself from hitting the Coliseum floor. His jeans slip down exposing his underwear again. I aim my next blow for the Sponge Bob face plastered across his behind. I guess I am his momma tonight, because I'm about to tear him up.

"I told you to get your behind on stage!"

"Stop B---!"

WHACK. Blak stops mid-word as another blow connects with his body. His thin underwear is no protection. He struggles to stand up. His entourage is running down the hall in our direction. *Lord, please protect me. I can't whip all of these boys*. I continue to give this prima donna what he deserves. I whip him exactly the way my momma used to whip me, with words interjected between each stroke.

"I'm a lady … WHACK … and you will always … WHACK … address me as a lady. Now do … WHACK … as I tell you to!" I squeak out. This whoopin' stuff is hard work. His entourage of about five young men surround us, but, amazingly, no one jumps in to help Blak or break us up. It appears they're all here to enjoy the show before the show. *Thank you, Lord.*

"Are you gon' do it?" I stop and hold the belt high as if I'm going to hit him again.

"Yes ma'am!" Blak screams.

"You gon' do it now?!" I yell, holding the belt higher.

"Yes ma'am!"

I know he's more embarrassed than hurt. No young man wants his boys to see him getting treated like this. I let my arm drop to my side, but continue to hold the belt tightly in my hand. I instruct him to stand up.

I must look a mess. I'm sweating, and I can feel small strands of hair sticking to the sweat on the sides of my face and neck. My chest is heaving up and down as I catch my breath.

Blak stands and pulls up his pants. He rubs a spot on his thigh where one of my strokes landed. For a moment, I feel the twang of guilt. I normally feel this way after disciplining my niece or nephew. Blak is also breathing hard, sweating and looking at me like he wants to give me some of what I gave him. I hold my belt securely in my hand in case he decides to try.

"I hope I didn't hurt you too bad, but you're acting like a spoiled brat and you're costing someone I care about a lot of money. This isn't all about you, Blak. You're not just an artist; you're an investment.

"All those people in the audience came to see you, and you're disappointing them. Your fans made you famous and rich, and putting on a good show is how you say thank you. You have one minute to compose yourself. Then, you go on stage and give these people the show they've been waiting on. You're supposed to be a star, right? You're supposed to be a professional, right? Act like it. Professionals never let the audience know when things aren't going right. Go out there and make momma proud," I instruct.

Standing in front of me is a scared, embarrassed little kid who is only pretending to be a man. The scowl on his face slowly changes to a boyish grin and those million dollar dimples pop out again to greet me.

"Yes, ma'am. I will."

A stage hand hands him the mic. I pat Blak on the back and watch him walk toward the stage, pulling his sagging oversized pants up again. That boy really needs a belt.

As soon as the crowd sees Blak, they start screaming.

"I'm sorry for making y'all wait so long, but y'all look real good tonight. Where all my sexy ladies at?" he says.

Thousands of young ladies scream. He begins doing a song about some new dance called the Wind It Up. Six girls wearing fitted pants and baby doll shirts run past me onto the stage and start winding it up.

The show isn't half bad. I must be getting old, though, because I can't understand most of what he's saying. But the audience knows every single word. One song is about a crush he had on a girl. Another is about the usual bling, cars, and poppin' bottles with models. Unfortunately, he's using profanity, but I have to admit that the kid's actually pretty good. He has great interaction with the audience, and his beats are tight.

He transitions to the next song and screams out, "I love women! Hey, where my ladies at who love women as much as I do?"

Again, loud screams emanate from the crowd.

"It's time for some girl on girl action here. Show me what you can do," he says.

Several girls in the audience begin to rub and kiss on each other. Some even begin to pull off each other's clothes. Then, Blak raps:

You say you like girls.
Well mommy, I do, too.
Let me see you do your girl,
While I do you.

I turn and walk away in utter disgust. I can't believe I brought him on stage to encourage lesbian behavior. This is unbelievable! Don't these girls have any home training? You don't pull your clothes or anybody else's off in public! This show is supposed to be PG-13, not Rated R. There are teenagers in the audience. If this gets out, it could mean big trouble for Eric. I have to stop this and fast. If I cut Blak's mic off and cancel the rest of the show, we'll have to give him his money and refund the audience theirs.

Think fast, Tee. What can you do to stop this before we have an audience full of nudists and live porn?

I got it! I run down the steps and ask Danny where the bathroom is. He tells me to go down the hall and make a right. I have no intention of going to the bathroom, but I needed an excuse to disappear. I head down the hall, but instead of making a right, I make a left. Mounted on the wall at the end of a dead end hallway is a bright red fire alarm that reads, "Pull in case of fire." I don't hesitate to pull it. The alarm rings loudly, and five seconds later the sprinkler system sprays cold water from the ceiling onto everyone below. People start screaming and I hear Danny on the mic instructing everyone to stay calm and walk to the nearest exit. That ought to cool their hot behinds off.

The fire department arrives and inspects the building. Of course they determine that there is no fire. One of the firemen informs me that the performance area is drenched and that it would be in our best interest to end the concert. I couldn't agree with him more. I instruct Maurice, the head of security for tonight, to shut it down. This party is over.

Chapter 9

Everybody's Got A Story
Michael

"The next morning, I awoke to find Becca in the kitchen making her delicious Belgium waffles. The smell made my mouth water. Michelle was on the couch watching cartoons. I decided to make the best of the situation and enjoy their company for the time being. After the DNA test, I planned to place them in an extended stay hotel until Becca could get a handle on her situation. I felt sorry for her. If Michelle was mine, I couldn't have them staying on the street.

"Michelle bounced over to me and gave me a big hug. She insisted that I sit next to her while we ate. The three of us had light, kid-friendly conversation over breakfast, and then we all got ready to go to the DNA testing center.

"The DNA test went smoothly. A nurse swabbed my mouth and Michelle's and told us we would have the test results back in a week. I gave strict orders not to give the test results to anyone but me. Next, we went to the mall and I purchased Becca a cell phone so we could easily stay in touch.

"I couldn't help stopping in the toy store and buying Michelle a few things. I must have dropped off at least $700. It was obvious she didn't have very many toys. She behaved as if she was scared to touch them. Once Michelle realized that she could play with every single toy with no fear of being reprimanded, she put her hands on everything she could: Barbies, teddy bears, toy cars, hoola hoops, board games. You name it, she probably touched it. I enjoyed watching her and helping her explore her new surroundings. I got a small glimpse of what it was like to be a dad that day, and it was a blast!

"It took a while to persuade Michelle to pick out a few items so we could leave. She wanted everything. I took her to a nearby park to play with her child-sized Jeep. She looked so cute, pretending like she was revving the engine. Becca and I took a stroll around the park. We were careful to keep Michelle in our sights at all times. We needed to talk.

'How are you feeling?'

'Better. I was really afraid of how you would react to the news. I wanted to tell you as soon as I found out that I was pregnant, but I didn't want to face you. I still remembered the look on your face and the tone of your voice when you put me out. I had never seen that side of you before. Until then, you had only shown me kindness.'

'If she's mine, I'll be the father she needs. You have nothing to worry about. If she's not, I'll still help you get on your feet so you can take good care of the two of you.'

'I'd appreciate that. It's been hard, Michael. I'm a high school drop out and I don't have any real skills, so I can't get a good paying job. I never told you about my child-hood, did I?' she asked.

'No, I don't recall that conversation.'

'Well, I think I should. It might explain a few things. When I was 15, my parents died in a car accident. I had amazing parents. I called us the interracial Huxtables. My African American dad was an OB-GYN, and my Caucasian mom actually was a lawyer. We had so much fun together. My dad was smart and hilarious. My mother was quite the professional and the homemaker. They both had demanding jobs, but they always made sure they had time for me and my little brother, Cameron. Each day was full of laughs and love.

'We didn't have a lot of family and after they died, no one offered to take me and Cameron in. Child Services threatened to break us up and put us in different foster homes. I couldn't bear the thought of losing him. He was all I had. So, I convinced my 25-year-old cousin, Preston, to take us in. He really didn't want to, but I begged until he said yes. He agreed under one condition: I had to do everything he said. I was thinking he was going to turn me into Cinderella and make me do all types of manual labor. If that's what it took to keep Cameron with me, then I was more than willing to do it. Unfortunately, that wasn't what he had in mind.

'At 15 I was fully developed. I could easily pass for 18 or older. Grown men were always hitting on me. I guess Preston noticed the way men looked at me and he saw an opportunity. He turned me into a child prostitute. He sold me out to the highest bidder on a regular basis, and I wasn't cheap either. He had friends with money who were willing to pay, and I went for anywhere between $300 and $500 a night.

'Between the age of 15 and 17, I must have been with at least 50 or more men. My cousin never touched me, and to make himself feel better about what he was doing, he was always buying me expensive gifts. As a teenager I was wearing diamonds and gold, Chanel, Gucci, Louis Vuitton, Dooney & Bourke, MCM, Girbaud, Cross Colours, Exhaust, or whatever was in style at that time. I even had a fur coat. For a while it was enough. It didn't seem like such a bad life to me, because

I was the envy of all the kids at school. But I didn't have very many friends. I purposely kept to myself. I didn't want anyone getting close enough to me to figure out what was going on. I was so scared of someone splitting me and my brother up. My only escape when I was with those men was to close my eyes and let my mind wander to a different place. By the time I got back from Paris, Rome, Italy, Hawaii, or whatever grand trip I had mentally taken, it was over.

'One of my regulars was a really kind man named Paul. The first night I was with Paul, we didn't do a thing. We just sat and talked for a couple of hours. He told me I was smart and pretty, and that he planned on being around a long time. He said that it was important that we were friends if we were going to be lovers. The next week when he came back, we did have sex and he was really gentle with me, unlike some of the others. But when we were finished, Paul told me that if we were going to make love I needed to be an active participant. Just lying there with my eyes closed wasn't an option. Making love. That's what that sicko actually called it. I was a kid. I didn't know anything about love. But I was happy to have him because finally I had a friend that I didn't have to lie to. Paul brought me books and tapes with all types of sexual positions and tips on how to please a man. He called it my homework. And because Paul was so kind and gentle towards me, I learned everything he wanted me to learn. I wanted his approval. I wanted to make somebody proud of me and feel like I mattered. He acted like he really cared about me. I remember telling him I was having trouble in math. On a few nights, he told me to bring my books, and helped me with my homework. By the end of the school year, I could rock a man's entire world in 10 minutes, and I had an A+ in Algebra.

'Two months after my 17th birthday, my cousin announced that Paul had given him $30,000 for me to go and stay with him for the next six months, but there was no way I was going to be somebody's personal whore 24/7. I liked Paul, but he was still a pedophile. I knew that I could be in serious danger if I had to stay with him unsupervised. I ran away the same night Preston told me about the money. I packed me and Cameron some clothes, stole $40,000 out of Preston's safe and his silver, 1993 Camero. I had never seen so much money, and I knew it was money he made from pimping me. So, essentially it was my money.

'I had no idea where we were going. We ended up in Dallas, TX. I sold the car and bought another one. I got myself a fake I.D. and an apartment, and I finished raising Cameron myself. He was about 12 at the time.

'When the money I took ran out, I started dating rich men who could take care of me and Cameron. I only dealt with married men. That way we didn't have to live with anyone. I was enjoying my freedom. If a man started acting all crazy and being possessive, I would threaten to ruin his life by telling his wife and he would generally leave me alone. If things didn't work out, I went and got another rich boyfriend. Dallas was full of rich men who didn't mind paying to have an attractive woman on their arm. My sugar daddies were always giving me money or expensive gifts like jewelry, clothes, and electronics. Sometimes I sold them and put the cash in the bank. By the time I was 19, I had a BMW courtesy of a car salesman I was dating and more clothes than Sachs Fifth Avenue.

'Eventually, I tried to develop some real relationships with single, available men. But I didn't know how to have a healthy relationship. I had been taught that sleeping with a man was how you earned your keep and got the things you wanted. So, that's what I did. I never got what I wanted, though. I wanted love.

'There was one ray of sunshine in my life: Cameron. He was a great kid: smart, funny, and handsome. Eventually, he graduated from high school. I tried to get him to enroll in a university, but he wouldn't. My brother is real good with his hands, so instead he went to a technical school and studied auto mechanics, refrigeration, and air conditioning. That boy can fix anything.

'While he was in school, he fell for this girl who worked in the admissions office. When she got pregnant, she convinced him to marry her. My brother had told her all about me, and after they got married she told him he could no longer have anything to do with me. She didn't want a whore in her house and around their baby. Can you believe that, Michael? I slept with all those men to keep us together and, later, to provide a life for us. Then, he meets some woman and he kicks me to the curb. I never even got to see their baby!

'Up until that point, I was the only family he had. He was the only man who had ever loved me unconditionally since my dad. I needed him, and he left me. We haven't spoken in 10 years. Before I had Michelle, raising him was the one thing in my life I was truly proud of. I hit rock bottom when Cameron put me out of his life. It felt like my heart had been ripped out. I started using any drug I could get my hands on to numb the pain. I didn't want to feel anything.

'I was out of control. I decided to leave Dallas and moved to Miami to try and start over. Then, I met you.

'You were wonderful. You were kind, gentle and caring. You gave me love. I felt good about myself when I was with you.

I knew you knew I was on drugs. I never asked you to buy me anything, because I wanted you to respect me. I would go to parties and get some from friends instead, but I was trying to quit. I was doing it because I wanted to be with you. I knew that in order to be the woman you deserved, I had to be sober. That last week we were together, I hadn't done anything all week and I felt really good.

'I wanted to tell you about my past, but I was afraid you wouldn't be able to accept it. In the end, my past caught up with me, and I was right.

'I loved you, Michael and I still do. If Michelle is yours, could we try again? Couldn't we be a family? I don't do drugs no more. I started again when we broke up, but when I found out I was pregnant, I quit cold turkey. I wasn't gonna mess my child up like that. Have her with all types of health and mental problems because her momma was a junkie. Not my baby! I even stopped having sex. Nobody really wanted a pregnant lover anyway. After she was born, I had no desire to continue to have sex with men for money. I wanted to set a good example for her. I'm trying really hard to be a good mother. I know I don't look like I used to, but after I had her I couldn't lose the weight. The stress of being a single parent with no job and no money started to weigh heavy on me. I could get some plastic surgery, and I bet they'll make me look good as new. Say something, Michael!'

"Dr. Foster, I couldn't believe what I was hearing. This woman had been through so much, and now she was standing there begging me to love her. She was even willing to go through an extreme makeover just to make herself more pleasing to me. She was on the brink of tears. I didn't want to hurt her feelings, but I knew we couldn't be together. There was so much hurt and pain behind those beautiful green eyes. I had to choose my words carefully. I said,

'Becca, right now I'm working on me. After I hurt my knee, I wanted to kill myself. But instead I turned to God and he helped get me through. You do have skills. You have people skills. If you didn't, you wouldn't have been able to get what you needed from others as easily as you did. Yeah, sex played a part in it, but it was also your ability to communicate and your wonderful personality that made them keep coming back. You're funny, and you have a way of making any man feel like he's the luckiest man on the planet. We'll find a way to make that work for you. I'll help you find a job with a decent salary. You can even go to school, get your GED, and go to college if you want.

'I can't give you the world, but I can give you the love of Jesus Christ. He's loved you from the day you were conceived. Ask Him to come into your heart. He doesn't care about your past. He loves you unconditionally. He knows what you've gone through and he's been waiting for the opportunity to make it all better. Ask Jesus Christ to come into your heart and wash all your sins away. He will. Let him in, Becca.'

'I don't know how. I want to stop hurting. Will you help me, Michael?'

"That woman was hurting and needed the peace that only our Heavenly Father could provide. I told her, 'All you have to do is confess your sins and ask him to come in.' I took both her hands in mine and said, 'Close your eyes, bow your head, and repeat after me. This is what we call the sinner's prayer.'

"She bowed her head, and I recited the sinner's prayer. '*Father, I come to you in prayer, asking for the forgiveness of my sins. I confess with my mouth and believe with my heart that Jesus is your Son, and that he died on the cross so that I might be forgiven and have eternal life in Heaven. Father, I believe that Jesus rose from the dead, and I ask you right now to come into my life and be my personal Lord and Savior. I repent of my sins and will worship you all the days of my life. Your word is truth. I confess with my mouth that I am born again and cleansed by the blood of Jesus. Amen.*'

"Becca repeated each word. When she opened her eyes, they were full of tears. But she was smiling. I gave her a hug and told her I wanted her and Michelle to go to church with me soon. I no longer wanted to put them in a hotel. So many people had already pushed her away. A week wasn't so long. I would know soon enough if that little girl, who had now abandoned her expensive toy car to swing on a hard plastic swing, was mine."

Dr. Foster has a big smile on her face. She looks as if she's about to cry herself. I figured with her being a therapist that she would have heard almost every story in the book by now.

"Dr. Foster, I appreciate your listening to me, but do you have anything to say? I've been talking for a while."

"Not at this time. This is the part where you talk and I listen in an attempt to get to know you better. Doing so will allow me to figure out the best way to help you," she says.

"Oh, okay. Well, please excuse me while I go to the restroom."

"By all means. When nature calls, you better answer."

Chapter 10

I Am My Brother's Keeper
Tee

After Danny announced that the concert was over, I go stand outside near the back door of the Coliseum to make sure that all of the performers get safely to their vehicles. Eventually, Icy Blak and his entourage exit the building. Right behind them, are the girls who were in the room with Blak when I arrived. They are all half-naked.

I give Danny the okay to give Blak his check for the balance of his money. Out of nowhere, a big guy in a tight shirt appears. He introduces himself as Felix, the manager, and takes the check from Danny. I start to ask him where he's been this whole time, but I decide not to waste my breath. He is not a true manager or else he would have instructed his client not to bite the hand that feeds him by refusing to do a show because he would rather have sex and get high. Luckily, Blak is still all smiles.

"Okay, momma. Show's over. Tell me, what did you think? Was it professional enough for you?" I want to tell him how strongly I disapprove of that last song, but something in my spirit tells me to hold my tongue.

"You did a good job. You've got talent, Blak." He continues to grin, showing those adorable dimples.

"You mean it?"

"Fa sho," I answer, giving him a fist bump. He also gives me a tight hug and picks me up off the ground. I can't help but laugh. All that hard talk earlier was truly a façade.

"Thanks, momma."

One of the guys from the entourage says, "Yo, Blak. The vans are here. We takin' these freaks back to hotel. So, let's go."

Not on my watch! A couple of these girls look under-age.

"Young man these ladies will not be leaving with you tonight. I suggest you get on the van," I say. I walk over to the young ladies he was referring to.

"Excuse me, ladies. I understand you have been invited to go back to the hotel. Well, I'm paying for this van and that hotel and you are not welcome. Whatever plans you thought you had with these young men are cancelled. I would appreciate it if you would get in your cars and leave now."

"Excuse you," says a red bone chick with a curly afro puff. "You ain't my momma. You can't tell me what to do. I ain't ready to go home. I'm staying wit Baller Blak tonight. You go home!"

"Oh really," I say mimicking her attitude. I tried to be nice.

"I don't know who you're talking to, but the only place you're going is home. You're so confused that you don't even recognize help when it's here. I'm trying to keep you from catching a STD or getting pregnant by a man who doesn't care anything about you. Did you have sex with Blak today?"

"Not yet. I was about to when you came in blockin'." Her answer is followed by the rolling of her eyes.

This poor, misguided girl really thinks that sleeping with a celebrity is some type of noteworthy accomplishment. He probably won't even remember her name afterward.

Blak and his entourage are standing about three feet away listening. I instruct him to come close to me. He saunters over, still grinning.

"Yes, momma."

"What's this girl's name, Blak?" He looks at her momentarily before shrugging his shoulders.

"I don't know."

She opens her mouth to tell him, but I throw up my hand to signify stop.

"Don't say a word. I'm not talking to you."

She closes her mouth and sticks out her pink, lip-glossed bottom lip.

It looks like I'm going to have to embarrass somebody else tonight in order to get my point across. Others hear the commotion and gather around us, including Blak's entourage.

"Does anybody here, other than her friends, know this girl's name?" I ask. They all either say no or shake their head to signify no.

"So, young lady, let me get this straight. You're about to give your body to one or more men, who care so little about you that not one of them has taken the time to learn your name." Red bone doesn't say a word. She continues to stand there with her lip poked out, looking very childish.

I turn toward the girl standing next to her. She has on a pair of skin-tight jeans and a shirt with a deep, plunging neckline and slits on both sides, exposing her breasts. She has a large tattoo of a candy cane going down her right arm. She is also tall and very attractive. Her hair is in a short chin-length bob. She could have easily been a model. She should be at home resting up for her next photo shoot instead of hanging out in an arena trying to get with rappers.

"How old are you sweetheart?"

"I'm 18. That means I'm grown," she answers nastily.

"Did you have sex with Blak today?"

"Yeah. Not that it's any of your business, nosey heifer."

Calling me names is not a good idea. "Blak, what's this girl's, I mean, this grown woman's name?" I ask.

"I think she said it was Cheryl or was it Shanice? Momma, I was so high when I was doin' her, I'm surprised I remember my own name. Hold on. Shantae. That's it Shantae," he announces.

"What's your name, grown woman?" She opens her mouth to say something but closes it. She begins to cry, instead. The tears come quickly, and she uses a hand with long, multicolored fingernails to wipe them away. One of her faux eyelashes comes half-off.

"It's Candace," she chokes out. "But everyone calls me Candy."

"Not everyone, baby girl, 'cause Blak just called you Cheryl, Shanice, and Shantae," I say softly.

More tears try to escape her hazel eyes, but she blinks them away.

"You told me you thought I was special. You said I was the type of woman you could see rolling around with you in your Lamborghini," she whines to Blak.

"And you were dumb enough to believe me," he replies grinning.

I am not amused. I really want to say something, but once again, something in my spirit tells me not to reprimand him. I continue to talk to Candy softly. I want her to know that even if she doesn't care that she is being used and then discarded, I do.

"You gave yourself to a man who doesn't know anything about you. Not even the simplest thing like your name. Don't you see something wrong with that?"

One of the guys in the entourage yells out, "I got next!"

"Did you hear that?" She nods her head yes. "You're just a vagina to these guys. You're better than that, baby. You are a human being. But most importantly, you are a child of God. He didn't create you to fulfill some man's groupie pleasure. He wants more for you. I want more for you. Do you still want to go back to the hotel with them?" She shakes her head no.

"Good. I'm glad."

The girl standing next to Candy is short, thick, and curvaceous with a wide gap between her two front teeth. Her hair could best be described as a bad weave in an obscure shade of orange that resembles a wet mop, thanks to the water from the sprinkler system. She has on a mini-dress that is two-sizes too small. It barely covers her behind. I spy several stretch marks and pockets of cellulite that resemble cottage cheese. Behind her, stands a gangly young man who is attempting to put his hand beneath her dress. She wriggles to the left and swats his hand in an effort to prevent him from doing so.

I am still holding my belt and like a ninja hurling a Chinese star, I whip it around and hit that mannish boy across the hand. He howls and puts the injured hand underneath his shirt while dancing around in a circle. The crowd laughs.

"She does not want you touching her. So don't!" He does his injured hand dance over to the van and climbs in. I continue with my interrogation.

"What's your name and how old are you, young lady?"

"I'm Patrice, and I'm 20 years old ma'am. Thank you for what ya done," she says in a deep southern bassy drawl. She's not wearing any shoes and she is looking at her feet. I can tell she's afraid I am about to embarrass her, but there is no need. I've made my point. I'm not trying to hurt anyone. I only want them to understand that the choices they are making could be detrimental to their emotional, physical, and mental well-being.

"Patrice, sweetheart, you should look people in the eye when they are speaking to you." She slowly raises her head, and I smile to let her know she has nothing to fear.

"Where are your shoes?"

She points to a young lady in a pair of shorts so short I can see her ashy behind hanging out the bottom. "Do you know the rest of these ladies?"

"Yes ma'am. We're friends. We came together."

"You mean to tell me you all came together to sleep with the same man? You can't be serious?"

"No ma'm. We wanted to meet him, but when we went back stage, things kind of headed in that direction. We only wanted to have some fun."

"Did you know that Blak is only 16?" Her bottom jaw drops in disbelief.

"I could have you arrested right now for having sex with a minor.

"I didn't do anything, miss."

"That's good, but you shouldn't be here, young lady. Why would you want to sleep with a stranger? Especially, if he wants you to share him with your friends and judging from the way his boys are acting, he's willing to share you with his." What if one of you gets pregnant? A man needs to have more than money to help raise a child. And if you're having sex with multiple men, how would you know who the father is? What if you catch a STD? Does HIV, herpes, gonorrhea, Chlamydia, or genital warts sound fun to you?

"I never thought about it that way."

"You should. You are your best asset and, you must always protect your assets. Who drove?"

"I drove," she answers softly.

"And where are you keys?"

"She has my keys, too." I look at her friend and tell her to hand them to her. She digs them out of her pocket without hesitation. She's looks extremely uncomfortable. I guess she thought she was next, or maybe it's those tiny shorts riding up her behind.

"I'm tired," I announce. "It's time for everyone to leave. Ladies, please go get in your car and go home. I don't ever want to see you at another concert unless you're in the audience. I will remember your faces, and I promise I will have security escort you out." They each stand there looking like I deflated their birthday balloons, but no one utters a word of protest.

"I'm talking to each and every one of you. I want a response. I better not ever see you backstage at one of these concerts again, trying to get with the artists or their entourage. Do you hear me?"

"Yes, ma'am," they all say in unison.

Dang, these kids are making me feel old. They're treating me like I'm a senior citizen. I wave Maurice over toward us and ask him to have someone escort the ladies to their car. I give them each a hug. Patrice is the only one who returns the hug. She wraps both arms around me, and gives me a warm embrace. "Ma'am, can I have your number? Sometimes, I need somebody to talk to," she says.

"Of course, sweetheart. My name is Tee. Call me anytime." I reach into my back pocket and give her one of my business cards.

"God loves you," I call out as they walk away. "Now, you need to love yourselves! You deserve better than a one night stand! Wait for a man who loves and respects you! And put some clothes on! If you want respect, you have to act and dress like it!"

"And to the rest of you," I say to the small crowd, "You go home, too. There is nothing to see here. They disperse as well.

I turn around to look for Daniel. I don't have to look far; he is standing directly behind me smiling.

"That was really nice of you to talk to those girls, Tee. I see that kind of stuff all the time. Some girls will do anything to get with an artist."

"Some things you can't ignore, Danny. That could have been me if I hadn't been taught better. Behavior like that could have life-altering consequences. By the way, good job tonight."

"Thanks. I couldn't have done it without you," he says. "I have to make sure I carry a belt to all our concerts from now on." He takes his arm and acts like he is striking something with a belt.

I laugh and inform him that I am now turning this situation back over to him. I ask him to please make sure everyone gets on their vans and heads to the hotel. We've all had a long night. My head is hurting and so are my feet. It's hard to believe that I whipped Blak in heels. Now, all I want to do is pop an ibuprofen, soak in my foot spa, and go to bed.

"Hey! You gon' leave without saying good bye, momma." I turn around. Blak and Beef are standing there like they have no place to go. Why aren't they headed to the hotel too?

"Sorry, Blak. I'm tired. It's past my bedtime. It was nice meeting you. I'm sure Beef will make sure you get wherever you need to be," I respond drowsily.

"You remind me so much of my big sister," he continues. "She died of breast cancer last year. She was the only person who could keep me in line. You were right back there. I'm sorry I've been so disrespectful to women, but I felt I was justified because them freaks coming after me ain't bout nuthin'. So, I treated 'em like nuthin'. They ain't want me, Isaac Blackston. They wanted Icy Blak, platinum rapper. So, I felt like they were gettin' what they deserved for being a bunch of groupie garbage."

"Well, you're wrong, Blak. Every one of those girls is somebody special. If they were your sister, would you want someone to treat them the way you did? Birds of a feather flock together. So, if you're constantly in the company of garbage, as you say, what does that make you?"

"Dang, you takin' me to school tonight. Don't take this the wrong way, but I wanna stay with you. If I leave with the fellas, the only thing they're gonna do is pick up the girls who are waiting for us in the lobby of the hotel and take them to the room. It happens all the time. You hungry? Let me take you to breakfast," Blak suggests.

I forgot about the girls that wait in the hotels.

"Hold that thought." I run over to Maurice. He is now near the vans watching everyone board.

"Hold on, Maurice. Please send two guards over to the hotel to clear the lobby before the vans arrive. Tell the bus driver to take the scenic route to give you some time."

"I like the way you think," says Maurice. "I won't even charge you extra."

"Thanks. Just like old times, huh Maurice?"

"Not exactly. If it was like old times, you would be going home with me. You still look good girl," says Maurice. He looks at me lustfully.

"You're right. It's not like old times." I head back over to Blak. I forgot we used to date. I'm so glad I don't live that life anymore.

"Isaac, I've got a better idea. Why don't you and Beef spend the night at my house? I'll cook you breakfast before you leave to catch your plane in the morning."

This kid is begging for somebody to care about him. Where is his manager, anyway? It looks like he took the check and left. I guess I'm his manager and his momma tonight. How do I get myself into these things?

Chapter 11

Fly the Friendly Skies
Michael

The Captain announces that we are about to land in Memphis. He instructs everyone to return to their seats and fasten their seatbelts. Dr. Foster and I exchange information and agree to meet up before we leave the city, if possible. All I want to do is check into my hotel room and get some sleep.

The landing is smooth. Departure from the plane goes swiftly. I find my luggage in baggage claim, and I call Peter to let him know I'm on my way to the hotel. I don't have anything to do until my afternoon visit at a children's hospital tomorrow. I have a special surprise for this group that I know they're going to love. Hopefully, I can get some sleep without having another nightmare.

Chapter 12

Today Is A New Day
Tee

I awake to the sound of my alarm at 6:00 a.m. like always. Only this time I wasn't in bed by 11:00 p.m. and I didn't get my customary seven hours of sleep. Beef decided Blak would be safe with me and returned to the hotel. He and I didn't make it to my house until about 2:00 a.m. Sleep or no sleep, I have events to plan.

I begin my daily ritual of spending time with the Lord. I call it my quiet time. I usually start things off with morning prayer. I thank Him for my blessings. I pray for my family and friends, the sick and the shut in, Blak, and the girls and the guys I met last night. I asked the Lord to order my steps so that I can be a positive influence in Blak's life. I know our paths crossed for a reason. I always pray for myself last. As I focus on myself, my eyes become two hydrants gushing liquid sadness.

Lord, You told me that if I dedicate my life to you, you would give me the desires of my heart. I don't mean to sound ungrateful but I desire someone to share my life with. If I'm the reason my relationships keep failing then show me myself so that I can improve and become the woman you would have me to be. Prepare me, Lord. If this is not my season for love, then grant me patience, because whoever you send, I know he'll be exactly who I need when I need him. Give me strength to continue to abstain from sexual immorality, because Father I sure do get weak sometimes. Forgive me for my sins, those known and unknown. Amen.

I wipe my tears and open my Bible to read a word from the Lord. I begin with I Corinthians 6:15–20.

"Do you know that your bodies are members of Christ himself? Shall I then take the members of Christ and unite them with a prostitute? Never! Do you not know that he who unites himself with a prostitute is one with her in body? For it is said, The two will become one flesh. But he who united himself with the Lord is one within spirit. Flee from sexual immorality. All other sins a man commits are outside his body, he who sins sexually sins against his own body. Do you not know that your body is a temple of the Holy Spirit, who is in you, whom you have received from God? You are not your own. You were bought at a price. Therefore, honor God with your body."

I turn to Romans 13:14.

"But put on the Lord Jesus Christ, and make no provision for the flesh, to gratify its desires."

Lastly, I read Psalms 34:17-18.

"The righteous cry out, and the Lord hears them; he delivers them from their troubles. The Lord is close to the brokenhearted and saves those who are crushed in spirit."

I close my Bible and open my thoughts and meditation journal. After Jarvis and I broke up, I began penning positive thoughts to help me keep that energy in the forefront of my mind throughout the day. I write down.

Remember your purpose is to live a life that is pleasing to God. You will be rewarded for your faithfulness, but you must be patient. God hears your cries. Blessings aren't delivered on your time, but on your Heavenly Father's time who loves you dearly.

Things always look a little brighter after spending time with the Creator. I shout, "Thank you Lord for one more day!" Enough of this pity party! My life is good. I have more important things to worry about right now. I have a young man in my house whose problems are much bigger than my lack of a man. *Lord, I need you to help me, help him.*

Chapter 13

Poor Little Rich Boy
Tee

After selecting a white Yves St. Laurent pants suit and gold top to wear, I head to the kitchen to make Blak and myself some breakfast. I whip up one of my specialties and place it in the oven to bake to perfection.

My quiche is almost done when a yawning Isaac Blakston enters my kitchen in a pair of basketball shorts, a t-shirt and white socks.

"Good morning, momma."

"Good morning, Blak. Do you mind calling me, Tee? I am nobody's momma."

"Okay. What's up with breakfast? Whatever you cooking smells good."

"It's called a breakfast quiche. So the smell of food wakes you up."

"Yeah. I wanna tell you thanks for last night, even though you did embarrass me in front of my boys. You got some strength. You gave me a lot of things to think about. I think I need to make some changes."

I wasn't expecting that from a spoiled hip hop star. I tell him you're welcome and set the table for our meal. I'm glad he feels like talking.

"It's been a while since someone seemed to have my best interests at heart. Everybody thinks I'm a dumb young'un, but I'm not. I can tell my manager only cares about making money off me, and so do the people at my label. My boys only hang with me because I'm rich. Did you notice when you were whipping my tail that not one of them tried to stop you? And I pay for all of them to go on the road with me. My life may seem glamorous to some, but it's hard having to live up to the image my record label created for me. Half the stuff they feed the media about me is lies. Like my age, I'm not 16. I'm actually 19. I didn't divorce my parents. I didn't have to, because it was only a couple of months until my 18th birthday when I left. I guess you could say they divorced me, though." There was a definite sadness in that last statement.

I notice that Blak's English has improved this morning along with his attitude.

"What do you mean?"

"Both my parents are super saved. I mean, Jesus is their best friend. When I first started doing rap, they didn't have a problem with it because I was rapping about kid stuff, school, girls, stuff like that. I even had a song about the Lord. But when I got signed, my label wanted me to do music for the streets. It's like they wanted to make me the new Lil Wayne with a touch of NWA or something. I knew my parents wouldn't approve, so I hid it from them. I would make G rated songs and let them hear it so they would think that was what was going to be on the album. But when the album came out, I couldn't hide what I was really doing. All the songs on the album were about violence, drugs, money, and sex. And I was cussin' a lot. I didn't necessarily want to do those songs, but the label told me if I wanted to be a star that's the kind of music I had to make. My parents were so disappointed in me. They told me I was letting the devil use me, and they were constantly putting my music down. At the time my single, 'Born to Bust' was #1 on the charts.

My parents weren't even proud of my accomplishment. The record label bought me an Escalade and an iced out watch, so I thought they were crazy to ask me to stop making music. I moved out of the house, and we've barely spoken since. Last time I saw them was at my sister's funeral. I really do miss my parents, though." Blak takes a sip of the orange juice I put on the table before continuing.

"This music I'm doing, it's not me. I don't know who I am any more. The stuff I say in my songs, I've never done most of it. I don't tote no guns, I never sold drugs, and I only started having sex with all these women because I was getting offers all the time and after I kept turning them down people started asking if I was gay. I had an image to protect. I was a good kid. I'm tired of being used as a money making machine. I think my Felix is stealing money from me. I don't know how much I'm making, how much I'm spending, or how much I have in my bank account. My sister used to handle all that. Momma, I mean Tee, I don't know what to do. I can't talk to anyone at my label. They're all friends and I don't know who I can trust. I'm under contract so I can't just quit! I feel trapped."

Blak looks angry, frustrated, and sad simultaneously. I go to his side and put my hand on his shoulder.

"I'm going to do whatever I can to help you. You have taken the first step to resolving this by admitting that you need help. God placed me in your life for a reason. Now, eat your breakfast. I have to run to a meeting, but when I return, we're going to sort this mess out together."

Chapter 14

There's A Killer on the Loose Tee

I hated to leave Blak, but I still had that meeting with Michael Stokes' manager, and I couldn't miss it. I'm not into sports much. In all honestly, I hate football. But athletes draw a crowd, especially among single women and rich old men who like to reminisce about their days on their high school or college teams. Michael Stokes is handsome, single, and well worth the $15,000 I am paying him to come speak. I have a sold-out event with 800 people attending for a price of $100 a plate. I also have corporate sponsorships to the tune of $100,000. Needless to say, this event is already a success. His manager, Peter Parker, and I are scheduled to have brunch at The Croissant Club, a restaurant located inside the exclusive Lamonte Golf Course. I plan their annual Christmas ball, and this past year they gave me a free membership to say thank you. I use it as often as I can.

I arrive a little early, and the friendly hostess seats me at a table by the window. I order a cappuccino and enjoy the sight of the beautifully manicured greens. Several men and women are milling about in stylish golf attire with their shiny clubs packed in sturdy bags or zooming to another area of the course in carts. My mind shifts to the conversation I had with God earlier this morning. I really have nothing to complain about. I begin to count my blessings. My Grandma Mae taught me to do this as a child. Whenever I was down she would say, "Tee Baby, count your blessings. Someone with no feet would love to be able to wear your shoes."

One, I'm healthy. I had a complete physical two weeks ago and my doctor said I'm in excellent condition. He told me my almost daily ritual of walking Chestnutt seems to be helping to keep everything in working order. Two, I have wonderful, supportive family and friends who love me and want the best for me. Three, I'm financially stable. Last year, I purchased my first home and now I'm investing. My financial planner, Cynthia, and I outlined a plan that could make me a millionaire when I retire, if I stick to it. I've got a nice portfolio of stocks, CDs, and an IRA. I even raised my monthly contribution to the company match 401(k) to help me save more money. She suggested that I consider purchasing more property, and I've looked online at a couple of multi-family units. Four, I have a good-paying job that I enjoy and --"

"Excuse me, miss. Are you Tina Long?" Standing to my left is a handsome man in a blue pinstriped suit. His face is clean-shaven with smooth skin the same shade as my cappuccino. He's attractive with hard features and a muscular jaw line, but that smile of his could use a dentist. His teeth are terribly uneven and stacked on top of one another like they are in a competition to occupy any extra space within his mouth.

"Why, why-- yes I am," I stammer.

"I thought so. I'm Peter Parker, Michael Stokes' agent and manager. I'm sorry if I startled you. You look like you were deep in thought."

"No interruption, Mr. Parker. I was just counting my blessings. Please have a seat."

"Only if you promise to call me Peter. Mr. Parker is my father."

"Deal," I say, and flash him the your-wish-is-my-command smile I give to all my clients. He is about to sit, but I stop him and say, "I probably should have told you to keep standing because our first stop is the buffet. Follow me, Peter Parker."

We make our way to the buffet table, which is filled with delectable breakfast treats. I grab two white porcelain plates and hand one to Peter. We move slowly down the serving line, adding whatever our hearts desire. Since I ate earlier, I select some fruit: cantaloupe, melon, and strawberries. Peter selects a plain bagel and generously applies some strawberry cream cheese. I notice the wedding band on his left hand. This one's taken.

"I see you're a healthy eater, Tina. It's obvious that you take good care of yourself. If you don't mind me saying so, you look lovely this morning," Peter says admiring my ensemble. "Those colors bring out the glow in your skin."

"I don't mind at all. Thank you." I always enjoy a compliment. I am in front of Peter and it is obvious that he is looking at my behind as we make our way back to the table. Men will be men. We sit down. I ask Peter to bless our food. He looks surprised, but honors my request.

"Dear Lord, thank you for the food we are about to receive. Bless the land that produced this food and the people who receive it. Amen."

"Amen," I chorus.

"I haven't done that in quite some time, Tina. I'll have to remember to do it more often."

"Good. Now, what was so urgent that you had to meet me in person to discuss?"

He laughs, showing that jagged smile, "You like to get right down to business. I admire that. Time is money. Well, for one I like to see who I'm dealing woth. And B, I wanted to discuss some security issues with you." I smile at his mistake, but I don't make mention of it.

"Okay, but I thought you had already defined Mr. Stokes' security needs in your contract. I will have two armed guards as you requested."

"Since we signed the contract, we've had an issue to surface. Unfortunately, Michael has acquired a stalker that is requiring us to use additional security. This is of no cost to you since I am informing you at the last minute. I took the liberty of having someone from our private security detail go down to survey the venue, and he suggested four additional guards. I will try to make them as inconspicuous as possible, but please know that they will all be armed and ready to protect Michael at any sign of danger. If danger becomes imminent, Michael will have to leave regardless of whether or not he has delivered his speech. In the event that he does have to leave before speaking, you will receive a refund of your money minus travel expenses," Peter says and takes a bite of his bagel.

I put my fork down and give Peter Parker my full attention. This is serious. The man is a football player. A big, strong football player. And did he say there's a chance he might have to leave? That would ruin my event.

"Oh, goodness. This person must be dangerous if you need four additional guards?"

"We're not quite sure about the level of danger at this time, but I'm not taking any precautions. I'm not at liberty to give complete details because we are trying to keep this out of the tabloids. I trust you will keep this information in confidence. Now, please excuse me but I have another appointment in 30 minutes and it's on the other side of town. Thank you for the breakfast, Ms. Tina. It has been quite a pleasure meeting you. Will I see you later today for our hospital visit?"

"Yes, I'll be there. Wait a minute, please. Michael's situation causes me great concern, and I need to know if my guests will be safe during the Gala. We have a full guest list of the who's who of Memphis. They trust me to provide safe, quality events."

"I assure you, your guests will be fine. Our security is excellent and will adequately handle any situation that arises. Many of them previously worked for the Secret Service. Think of it as you do when the President comes to town. His security is a concern, but you know his people can handle it," Peter assures me. "Here's my card. Call me should you have any further questions."

I have plenty of questions, but I'm sure he won't answer most of them, so why bother.

"Mr. Stokes and I will see you at the children's hospital at 2:00 p.m." Peter rises from the table, shakes my hand, and heads for the exit without finishing his bagel.

Dang. Who could be after Michael Stokes? A bookie, a crazed fan, former lover, his baby's momma? It couldn't be a woman. I don't think a woman could intimidate a 6'4", 243 pound former football player so much that he would need six body guards. This stalker must be a man and he must really love or really hate Michael. I decide to keep this to myself. No need to alarm my client or my company. I'm sure everything will go off without a hitch, but I have to call my sister and tell her!

Chapter 15

Baby Love
Michael

I sleep in late, watch TV, order room service and then head to the gym inside the Madison Hotel to work out for a bit. No one is there except Dr. Foster. I didn't know she was staying here. We could have shared a cab from the airport. She is in a pink short set and running shoes, walking at a brisk pace on the treadmill. I wave and head over to the free weights. After completing a few reps, I step on the treadmill beside hers.

"Hello, Michael. You look well this morning," she says with a slight pant from walking.

"I feel well, Dr. Foster. I actually got some rest last night. How are you?"

"I'll do, for an old woman. Can you walk and talk?"

"Why yes, ma'am, I can."

"Do you mind continuing with your story? Your life is quite fascinating. The faster you finish, the faster I can help you," she says with a look of sincere interest.

"I don't mind at all. I believe I stopped right after I told you about Becca being a child prostitute."

"That first week with Becca and Michelle was amazing. I couldn't help but fall in love with Michelle. She was such a well-behaved little lady. At the same time she was a total kid. The way she looked at the world with her childish innocence was wonderful. She became my shadow, and I took her everywhere: the zoo, the movies, Chuck E. Cheese. I couldn't get enough of seeing her laugh and smile. I became addicted to the random hugs I received throughout the day. Becca told Michelle I might be her Daddy, and Michelle decided right then and there that I was her father. She wouldn't call me anything but Daddy. I tried to get her to stop just in case I wasn't her father, but she wouldn't. I must admit that I kind of liked it.

"Michelle wasn't the only one who seemed to be forging a place for herself in my life. Becca started running my house and me like we were hers, but not in a bossy, controlling way. It was in a helpful, concerned way. She made us three delicious, healthy meals each day. She washed and ironed my clothes, and cleaned the condo from top to bottom each day. She made sure I went to my doctor and physical therapy appointments and took my medication and vitamins.

"I tried to be a help to her, too. I encouraged her to look for a GED program to attend. I even talked her into making an appointment to see a counselor to help her deal with her molestation issues. I knew I shouldn't let Becca and Michelle get comfortable in my home, but I couldn't help it. After being alone for so long it felt good to have someone to come home to. However, I couldn't shake this uneasy feeling that something wasn't right.

"The day finally came to find out if Michelle was mine or not, and I decided to go get the results by myself. I sent Becca and Michelle to the salon and to do a little shopping, and I went down to the DNA testing center. After signing in, they sat me in a cold room with nothing but a table and two chairs in it. I felt like I was in the interrogation room of a police precinct. The head of the facility came in and introduced himself as DNA Doug. Doug looked to be of Middle Eastern descent. He was relatively short and wore black glasses that reminded me of my fifth grade teacher, Mrs. Taylor. Whenever Mrs. Taylor had something sensitive in nature to say, she would slide her glasses down to the tip of her nose and peer over them. It always gave her a look of nerdy compassion. DNA Doug was doing that now but all I saw was a nerd. No compassion. I could tell it was all business to him. He sat down across from me, opened a manila file folder and gave me the news.

'Mr. Stokes, your case is highly sensitive. We ran the test several times to make sure our results were correct. You are not Michelle's father, but we think someone related to you might be.'

'What? Why would you think that?'

'The DNA is very similar--so similar we believe that someone in your immediate family is that little girl's father. Is that possible?'

"I was about to say no but I remembered the dis-traught look on Becca's face when I told her Maxwell was still in high school when we met. My mind then raced to the dimple in Michelle's chin. My brother has a dimple in his chin. It's just a coincidence. My 20-year-old brother can't be the father of the child I wanted to be mine. Becca couldn't have slept with my little brother, could she? That would make her a pedophile.

'Mr. Stokes. Did you hear me? Is it possible that someone in your family could be Michelle's father?' DNA Doug asked again.

'I don't know. Could you please leave me alone? I would like to use my cell phone to do some investigating.'

'I understand, Mr. Stokes. This can't be easy news for you. If you do have an idea about who the father might be, we would be happy to perform the test for you. I'll leave you now. Hit the buzzer on the wall or come to the front desk when you're ready to continue.'

"I sat there for several minutes with my feet planted solidly on the floor, wondering how to begin the conversation I was about to have."

The alarm on my cell phone goes off to alert me that I have an hour before my visit to the hospital. "Sorry, Dr. Foster, but we will have to finish this later. I must get ready for my next engagement."

"You are not going to leave me in suspense over the parentage of Michelle, are you?" she asks with a raised eyebrow.

"Afraid so, Doc. I told you. I don't want to leave out a single detail. I can't rush the story just to satisfy your curiosity," I say with a sly grin.

Chapter 16

The Prodigal Son
Tee

As I drive back home to Blak, I call my friend Lee Fletcher. Lee and I met in college, and he's now a very successful entertainment lawyer who represents several high-profile, multi-million dollar clients. After graduation, I hooked him up with my friend Gwen. They hit it off beautifully and now, they are happily married and living in Manhattan with their three children. My girl is living the good life, thanks to me. She hasn't had a job since she popped out the first baby. She is always rocking the latest fashions, and everything in her closet is name brand or custom made. Best of all, she has a good husband. They both said if I ever needed anything to let them know. I think this is the perfect time to call in a favor.

Luckily, Lee answers. I tell him about Blak's situation and ask if he can do anything to help. He says he has dealt with such a case recently, and he would be more than happy to consult and possibly represent Blak on the matter.

"He probably has two options: He can ask to be released from his contract or try to negotiate with them. I suggest the latter first. He has to go in there adamant about what he wants, and tell them if they want him to continue to be on their label they have got to let him have more creative control. If he is suspicious that his manager is stealing from him, he needs to be able to prove it. If he gave him access to his accounts and authorization to pay his bills, then his manager should have receipts for every dime of his money that he spent on his behalf. Tell him to print out his bank records, and let's see if we can figure out where the money's going. Have him call me when he gets a chance. I'll do what I can," says Lee. I thank him for the advice, and promise to have Blak contact him soon.

I locate Blak in my den playing video games—the ones I keep to help entertain my niece and nephew when they come to visit. I greet him, and hand him my cell phone. He puts it up to his ear, thinking that it is a call for him. When he realizes that no one is on the other end, he gives me a puzzled look.

"Call your parents. It's time for you to go home."

"You read my mind. I was thinking the same thing," is all he says before dialing the number. He puts the phone on speaker so I can hear.

A gentleman with a deep voice that reminds me of Lou Rawls answers the phone.

"Hey Pop," Blak says, sounding a little nervous.

The Lou Rawls-like voice responds, "Hello, Isaac. Let me get your mother."

"Pop, don't go. I want to talk to you. I want to come home. I don't want to make this music no more. I miss you. I'm not happy and I think my manager is stealing my money. I feel so alone, like nobody cares about me. I need you---and Mom."

There's a brief silence. Lou Rawls' voice now has a quiver.

"I miss you too, son. If you're serious, come on home. Your mother and I have been praying so hard for this day. God told me you were coming home, and I've been waiting. Whatever it is we'll handle it together. No

one is going to take advantage of my boy, not while I'm
around. Now, you hurry up and get home. I'll make sure
your mother has your favorite meal waiting on you when
you get here. We love you so much, son."

"Thanks, Pop. I love you, too. I'm going to catch the
first plane I can. I'll call you with my flight info when I
have it," says Blak happily.

"Alright, son. I'll be waiting to hear from you."

We hear Mr. Blakston shout, "Irma, prepare the fat-
ted calf. The prodigal son is coming home! My boy is
coming home!"

Blak is all smiles. He hits the button to hang up the
phone.

"You hear that, momma. My Pops ain't mad no more.
He said I can come home! I gotta book a flight because
the record label told the private jet to leave me when I
didn't show up this morning. I don't care. I'm going
home! Oh, before I forget, do you like younger men? For
an old chick, you're HOT!"

Chapter 17

Man of My Dreams
Tee

Blak was able to book a flight to Chicago that left in three hours. I gave him Lee's information and instructions before dropping him off at the airport. I insisted that he wait until he was home with his parents to call him. I also politely let him know that I thought we were better off as friends, because he has more than enough on his plate right now. I figured that was better than telling him that he doesn't have a snowball's chance in Hades of getting with me.

It's beautiful outside. The sun is scorching hot, but the heat doesn't seem so bad today. The clear blue sky, full green trees, lush grass, and colorful flowers in bloom all seem add a little more joy to my day.

I arrive at Mercy Children's Hospital at about 1:30 p.m. Whenever I plan an event, I try to have my high profile guests come in early to do some community service, and Mr. Stokes will be paying a special visit to some ill children today.

While I was in college, I volunteered here to fulfill my scholarship's required community service hours. It never felt like work to me, and I developed a great respect for the hospital and its staff. They do a great job of treating the ones and keeping their families abreast of their condition and treatment options. Being here can be heartbreaking, though. Most of these children will recover from their ailments, but some of them, no matter how hard the staff tries, aren't going to make it. When I was volunteering regularly, I tried my best not to get attached to any of the children or their families, but you get sucked in. How could you not care for a child, especially a sick one? Some of them are so sweet and loving that you have to love them back. I remember the first time a patient I was close to died. Her name was Tabitha. She was five years old and had an inoperable brain tumor. She was at Mercy for five months, and she fought until the very end. The night she passed, I was right there next to her bed, crying with the family. That night I vowed I would do all I could to bring joy to children of this hospital. That way, the children who don't make it will have good memories before they go to their final resting place.

I am standing in the lobby of Mercy with the head of marketing, Lindsey Carter, waiting for the famous Michael Stokes. The children will be so excited to have him in their midst. At 1:50 p.m. Peter Parker and Michael Stokes enter the building accompanied by two armed guards. The guards are dressed in casual attire, khaki pants and polo shirts, and each of them is also brandishing a shiny gun strapped to their sides in leather holsters. Even the attention getter of men with guns couldn't overshadow the awesomeness of Michael Stokes, though. That man's pictures don't do him justice. He is gorgeous! He swaggers inside the building dressed similar to his guards in khaki shorts and a polo shirt but no amount of clothing can hide his finely tuned body. No doubt a beautiful byproduct of hours in the gym. His handsome face is donned with a pair of Cartier sunglasses, and he is carrying a very large backpack. I'm usually not taken aback by attractive men, but this man is breathtaking. He is a real live Adonis. His lips are perfect. His brown eyes are perfect. His bald head is perfect. Instead of Michelangelo creating David, he should have been fashioning Michael Stokes. Someone this exquisite needs to be immortalized for generations to enjoy. It's taking everything in my power not to stare at him. I step forward to greet them.

"Good afternoon, Mr. Parker. You're punctual. I like that." I extend my hand to gently shake his and then turn to Michael. "Hello, Mr. Stokes. I'm Tina Long with Innovations Marketing & Events. This is Lindsey Carter, head of marketing here at Mercy Children's Hospital."

Michael says, "hello ladies." And gives us both a firm handshake.

Lindsey chimes in, "Gentlemen, it is good to see you. We are honored that you have agreed to visit with us today. However, we cannot allow armed guards with visible guns in the hospital unless it's an emergency. We have ill children here and the last thing we want to do is upset them or their families. Would you happen to have jackets?" Each of the guards responds that he does not have a jacket.

"It seems we have a dilemma here. Would you be willing to relinquish your guns while in the hospital? I assure you that this is a secure facility."

"Mrs. Carter, I'm Peter Parker, Mr. Stokes' agent and manager. I understand that your concern is the residents of your facility, but my concern is for my client, and it is necessary that he be properly guarded at all times. And--"

"It's okay, Peter," interrupts Michael. "Tell the guards to wait here in the lobby."

"What? No way, Mike. You know the danger."

"I said have them wait in the lobby. I'll be fine. As a matter of fact, you stay here, too." Peter is about to object again, but Michael gives him a don't-test-me look.

As much as I am enjoying this show of male bravado, I need to get this visit started. I still have some things to do before the private reception for the Gala sponsors tonight.

"Mrs. Carter, is it possible for you to have one or two of your security guards here at the hospital to accompany us?"

"I would be happy to, Tee. Let me set you guys up in visitor orientation, and I'll make it happen. Follow me, please."

Michael and I head to the viewing room to watch a short film on the history and purpose of the hospital and the dos and don'ts while visiting. We leave Peter in the lobby sulking. The guards, on the other hand, seem relieved to have a few moments off, and they quickly settle into the lobby chairs. At the finish of the film, Lindsey still hasn't returned, so I decide to strike up a conversation with Mr. Superstar.

"Thank you for being so accommodating, Mr. Stokes. I was worried for a minute that you would have to cancel your visit. The children are looking forward to seeing you."

"No problem, Tina. Do you mind if I call you, Tina?"

"Actually, I prefer Tee."

"Ok, Tee. I love children, and when I heard about the awesome work Mercy does, I really wanted to come. I get tired of being trailed everywhere I go. Peter means well. He's like a brother to me, but he can be a bit overbearing. Also, he's not good with children at all. I welcome little breaks like this where I get to do something worthwhile in the company of a beautiful, intelligent woman," he says and flashes me one of the nicest smiles I have ever seen. Peter should see his dentist. I smile back.

"Thank you, sir. Do you have any children of your own?"

"Not yet. I promised myself I would do everything I could not to have children with anyone but my wife."

"Oh, so you're married?" I hope he can't hear the disappointment in my voice.

He picks up his left hand and waves it in front of me.

"No, I'm not. I was speaking in future tense. What about yourself?"

"No, I'm flying solo these days and I have no children," I share.

"Solo? Come on now. I know someone like you must have someone special."

"No, I'm still on the market. And what do you mean someone like me?"

"Beautiful, intelligent, caring…and that's just what I've picked up in the first 15 minutes of meeting you. I'm sure there's more to discover. I'm also single."

Lindsey enters the room with two guards wearing suits. Her timing couldn't be worse.

"If you're ready, Mr. Stokes and Tee, please follow me," she says.

She escorts us to the game room where about 20 children are playing. Michael enters the room and one boy who looks to be about 8 years old shouts, "Puppy dog tails and toe nails. It's freakin' Michael Stokes!"

The children run towards us. It is a beautifully chaotic sight with children of all different sizes, ages, and nationalities. Their ailments range from minor to life-threatening. I see little girls wearing wigs and several of the boys have on baseball caps. A tale-tell sign that they are undergoing chemotherapy. A couple of them are even in wheelchairs and one is on crutches. Sometimes seeing ill children knocks the wind out of our guests. Many are overcome with compassion and it takes them a few minutes to compose themselves. Michael doesn't flinch. He distributes hugs, fist bumps and high fives to the group. He asks them their names and where they're from.

Lindsey is a stickler for order. She claps her hands three times and says in a loud voice, "All right children. You know better. Let's all go sit down on the listening circle so each of you can meet our guest of honor."

Several "awwws" echo through the room, but they all obey and walk or wheel to the other side of the room where a big red circle is painted on the floor. Those who are able to, sit along its lines. After every child is settled, Lindsey places a chair at the top of the circle for Michael. He walks over to the chair, picks it up, and sits it outside the circle. He then, takes off his backpack and positions himself on the floor with the children. He also instructs them to move closer to him so they can all hear. He finishes asking each child his or her name and allows each of them to ask him questions as well.

After the Q & A he asks, "Who here would like for Michael Stokes to read a story?" The children yell out "me" in unison. He reaches into his monstrous backpack and pulls out a book. The colorful cover reads, "Victory Is Mine," written and illustrated by Michael Stokes.

I whisper to Lindsey, "This wasn't in his press kit. I had no idea he was releasing a children's book. This man is fine, athletic, loves children, and can write and draw. This is too good to be true. If he can cook, I'm going have to take him home to meet my momma."

"Tee, if I wasn't married, you'd have to fight me for him," Lindsey laughs.

Michael begins reading his book. Each page contains beautiful, colorful illustrations. As he reads, Michael turns the book around so the children can see the pictures.

His story is about a little boy who wants to run in the annual regional relays. Several towns in the area compete against each other to see who has the strongest and the fastest men. Everyone tells the little boy that he is too small and weak to run in the big race. The boy keeps insisting that they let him join the relay team. Eventually, the team captain complies to silence him, but he has no intentions of actually letting him compete. The little boy doesn't know that, though, so he works hard and never misses a day of practice. On the day of the race, one of the relay members becomes extremely ill. This leaves them one man short. In order to stay in the race, they have to let the little boy run in the race but they decide not to put him in until the last leg of the race. When it is finally his turn, his team is so far behind the others that no one expects them to win. The little boy isn't very fast, but he's smart. Because he is smaller than everyone else, he is able to take a short cut through the bushes when everyone else has to go around. Thanks to his ingenuity, his team wins!

At the conclusion of his story, Michael puts the book down and looks at each of the children.

"The little boy in this story was me. When I was younger, I was small for my age. I was also anemic, so I stayed sick. Like you, I had to go to the hospital. I actually had to go a lot. People were always telling me what I couldn't do because of my illness. But my parents told me that I could do anything I wanted to do. As I grew older, my health improved. I started working out and playing sports, and I discovered that I had talent. I participated in basketball, football, baseball, and track, but I enjoyed football the most. In my senior year of high school, I was named one of the top players in the United States. My athletic ability allowed me to attend the University of Miami on a full scholarship. It was a great experience and, thanks to my coaches, I became a better athlete. I won a Heisman Trophy. And the next thing you know, I made my dream of playing professional football come true. The moral of my story is this: If you believe in yourself and you're willing to work hard, you can make your dreams come true, too.

I know you're sick right now, but try not to let that deter you from your dreams. I'm a firm believer that there is always a way. Your illness may limit what you can do, but if you look hard enough, there is something you can do that will bring great joy to you and others. Explore different things. You may find that you can draw, sing, or play an instrument. Maybe you're a comedian and can make people laugh. God has blessed each of us with some kind of gift. I encourage you to find yours. For years I focused so much on football that I forgot how much I loved to write and draw. Now that I don't play football anymore, I've picked up my colored pencils again, and I'm drawing all the time. I drew all the pictures in this book myself. Did you like them?"

"Yes," the children cry out in unison.

"Who would like their very own Michael Stokes book to take with them?"

"Me!" they shout.

"Great! Line up and I'll give you one."

The children run to line up in front of him, almost toppling each other over. Each child smiles as he or she hugs Michael and receives their own autographed copy of his book. The fact that the book isn't even in stores yet makes owning it even more special.

Michael then spends time with about 15 children who are too ill to come to the game room. He also gives them autographed copies of his book. By the time we return to the lobby, I am almost in tears. It was such a beautiful sight to see that big man taking the time to express concern and entertain ill children. I don't think the day can get any better, but Michael proves me wrong. He takes out his checkbook and writes a check for $100,000 to the hospital. Lindsey and I jump up and down with delight. I am so moved that I jump right into the arms of this incredibly handsome, talented, sensitive man and plant a kiss right on his lips. I realize what I've done, and try to slip away from his arms but Michael pulls me closer to him. I breathe in his scent and revel in the strong masculinity of his arms. I feel my face flush from embarrassment, and I can't bring myself to look up. I know he's looking at me. Did I do what I think I did? This is most unprofessional. I can't continue to avoid his gaze. I have no choice but to look up.

Michael looks into my eyes and says, "That's the best thank you I've ever received. Would you like to have dinner with me tonight?"

His breath smells like spearmint gum. I wonder if his mouth tastes as good as it smells. Lindsey, Peter Parker, the guards, and several others are staring at us. Lindsey has her hand over her mouth, trying to stifle a giggle. How can I get out of this one without losing any cool points?

I slowly pull myself away from him and say in a low voice, "Excuse me, I don't know what came over me. Thank you for your donation and thank you for the invitation. But did you forget that you have a reception with the Gala sponsors tonight?"

"Yes, I did. Beautiful women with incredibly soft lips tend to do that to me," says Michael. He is looking deeply into my eyes.

I am in full blush and shut-yo'-mouth mode. I take another step back and smooth out my pants. I have to regain control of this situation.

"Please try to arrive by 7:30 p.m. at the McKeller Room of your hotel. I have some very generous, high profile donors who are dying to meet you. I must leave now. I have to attend to some unfinished business. I'll see you in a few hours. Lindsey, will you please see that our guests get to their automobiles safely?"

She nods.

"I look forward to it," he replies.

I finish my thank yous, give Lindsey a hug, a smile, and a wink and exit the hospital. Once I reach my Denali, I deactivate the alarm, open the door, and climb into the driver's seat. I glance around to make sure that no one is within earshot and begin screaming like a little girl who just kissed her crush. Michael Stokes asked ME out!

I glance at the radio clock and it reads 4:30 p.m., which means I don't have much time. I have to get home and get ready for tonight's event. Now, more than ever, I have got to look GOOD. No, better than good. I've got to be FAB-U-LOUS! Today is turning out to be a REEEEEEAAALLLY good day.

Chapter 18

Whose Is It?
Michael

I enter the lobby of the Madison Hotel and notice Dr. Foster sitting in a multicolored chair listening to a gentleman playing a jovial jazz number on a shiny, black, baby grand piano in the center of the room. She is moving her head and tapping her foot to the beat.

"Good evening, young man. Glad to see you. I was thinking about our conversation earlier, and I can't wait to hear what happened next. Have you had enough storytelling for one day or are you ready to continue? If you're tired we can do it some other time, but I sincerely hope you want to continue."

I decide to end her suspense.

"No. You're in luck, because I'm in a talkative mood. I would really like to get your take on things as soon as possible." I have a seat next to her in an identical chair.

"That's good to hear. I'm ready when you are. You stopped just as you were trying to figure out who could be Michelle's father other than you."

"Well, there I was in the DNA lab after hearing that Michelle was not mine, but possibly a family member's. There was only one male family member Becca had access to, and I was going to get to the bottom of things right away. I pulled out my cell phone and called my baby brother.

"Maxwell answered with his usual happy-go-lucky, 'Hey, big brother.'

'I haven't heard from you since you left home. How's the life of the injured and unemployed?' he joked.

'I'm good, Maxwell. How about you?'

'I'm great. I had a math test today. I'm sure I aced it, which should put me on the dean's list this semester. I'm so happy you sent me to that college prep charter school. So many of my classmates are stressing, but I'm not even breaking a sweat!'

'That's good. Glad to see you're not wasting my money by partying and flunking out. Max, I need to ask you something, and I need an honest answer. Do you remember Becca? The mixed chick I was dating when you were living with me.'

'Yeah, I remember that broad. What about her?' he asked dryly.

'What did you think of her?'

'I thought she was cool at first, but after she hurt you I hated her.'

'Did you think she was pretty?'

'I won't lie to you. I thought she was sexy as a mother until …'

'Until what, Max?'

'Until she showed her true colors. What's with all the questions about Becca? She's been long gone.'

'Hold on. It will all make sense in a minute. One more question. Did you sleep with her? And don't lie to me. I really need to know the truth.'

"There was a long silence, a heavy sigh, a deep breath, and then an answer. 'Yeah, Mike. I did,' he said slowly. 'I didn't mean to. It only happened once, the night you told her to get out. I heard you yelling at her not to be there when you got back. I felt sorry for her and went in your room to check on her. She was in there crying and pulling her things out of the closet and the drawers. I didn't know what she had done, but I figured it must have been pretty bad 'cause you were really into her. I asked her what all the noise was about, all she kept saying was, "He don't want me no more, Max. He don't want me no more." I sat her on the bed to get her to stop crying and I went and got her some tissue. After she blew her nose and dried her face, she started looking at me all funny. Then, she kissed me. The next thing I knew, she was on top of me. She kept calling me Binky and telling me to let her stay. When it was over, she realized it was me, not you, and ran in the bathroom. I didn't know what to do so I went back to school. I sat in the library and pretended to do homework until it closed.

When I got home, she was gone and you were in the bed asleep. I could tell you had been somewhere and gotten yourself twisted. I could smell the liquor on you from the doorway to your room. I decided not to tell you. She was gone, so it didn't matter anyway.'

'That's where you're wrong, Max. It does matter. Becca is back and she has a four-year-old daughter. Her name is Michelle. Becca told me she was mine, but I received the results from the DNA test today. She's not mine. But the doctor said Michelle's DNA is so close to mine that he thought a family member could have fathered her. You are the only family member Becca met. I need you to take a DNA test so we can know if she's yours.'

"I was so mad that I could have punched a hole in the wall. Becca had taken advantage of a 16-year-old. She was more messed up than I thought! How could she? I know she thought he was an adult, but he was my little brother!

"Maxwell went ballistic. 'Michael, quit playin'! You funny. I'm being Punk'd, right? Okay guys, you can come out now. Ashton Kutcher, you got me. Laugh, Michael! Why aren't you laughing!' he screamed.

'Because it's not a joke, Max. I need you to take a DNA test as soon as possible. We have to know who this little girl belongs to so we can do right by her.'

'Do right by her? What are you talking about? I'm only 20. I'm not ready to be anybody's daddy. I'm going to be a doctor. I want no parts of this. I'm NOT taking a DNA test!'

"I think he forgot who he was talking to. I could break his little twig behind in half without even trying. My little brother, the brainiac, was like me in so many ways, but size and strength had never been one of them. 'YES you are!' I yelled. 'I see living with me may not have been the best thing for you, but I didn't help raise a punk. You're grown now. Those running scared days of me fighting your battles are over. We're Stokes men, and Stokes men take responsibility for their actions no matter how messed up they might be. I'm going to find a testing facility near you, and you are going to get there and get tested.'

'And if I don't!' Max challenged.

'You can kiss medical school goodbye, because I'm not spending another dime of my money to put you through school.'

'Nice one, big bro, but I'm on a scholarship,' he retorted.

'You're in undergrad, but I pay your dorm fees and your other living expenses. How much scholarship money do you think you'll get for med school?'

'I can get a job or take out a loan. I don't want to be a daddy. How am I going to care for her? I'm a full-time student. As you stated, you pay my bills. I don't want my baby's momma to be my brother's ex-girlfriend. Mom and Pops are going to kill me, Mike! I just got a girlfriend, and she was specifically looking for somebody with no kids.'

"Max was screaming and he was whining. I hate when he does that. I needed to calm him down so he would actually go take the test. 'I didn't know you had a girlfriend, Max.'

'Yeah, I do. She's wonderful, and fine, too.' His voice went back to its normal pitch.

'I'm sure she's pretty special. This is your first real girlfriend isn't it? Congrats. My lil bro has got him a shorty. You hittin' that?'

'Naw. It's not about that. We're talking it slow. She's still a virgin.'

'Sounds like you found a good girl. Girls like her are special. So, don't rush. I'm happy for you. Look, I know this can't be easy for you to hear, but there's a little girl who deserves to know who her father is. If you are her father, you can't just abandon her and shirk your parental responsibilities. You have to take the DNA test. I'll call you back in a few minutes with the name and address of that clinic. Okay?'

'Okay, Mike. I'll do it, but this baby can't be mine. Everything in my life is finally falling into place.'

'And if I can help it, everything will stay in place. You're my brother. You are destined for greatness. I'll call you back in a few.'

"I hung up and pushed the button on the intercom by the door and asked for DNA Doug to come back in. I asked if he could conduct a test in Los Angeles. He told me he had a colleague there with a facility similar to his. Max could take the test there and they would ship his sample to Miami. I called Max back, gave him the address and number, and told him to get his butt down there by the end of the day to take the test. DNA Doug told me that under the circumstances he would put a rush on the test, and we should have the results within the next three days. I already knew they would be positive, but I needed to have it medically confirmed.

"I wanted to call Becca and tell her to get out of my house again, but because of Michelle, I couldn't. How can you put a child out? Instead, I went home and packed my bags while they were still out. I wasn't ready to face her. I'm still new to this Christian thing, so I have to be careful when it comes to my emotions. I left early for my speaking engagement in Ft. Lauderdale the next day and checked into a hotel. This was not what I expected. I was supposed to be celebrating fatherhood, not running away from my own home. I left Becca a note saying the test was inconclusive and they needed a few more days to determine paternity.

"Dr. Foster, I hate to do this to you again, but it's time for me to get ready for my event tonight. If I get some more free time before I leave, perhaps I can meet up with you somewhere and talk some more."

"That's fine, son. You've had quite a bit going on in a short amount of time. Before you go, tell me how you are sleeping. Do you have nightmares like the one you had on the plane frequently?"

"Actually, no. Those just started on the plane. I was able to rest last night but for the past few days sleep has been hard to come by. The stress of having someone trying to kill you can have that affect."

"I'll give you a prescription for a sedative next time I see you."

"Thanks, Doc."

"You're very welcome. I hope you have a good event tonight."

"I'm sure I will."

I think about Tee's soft lips. When she pressed them against mine, my entire body tingled. I haven't felt that way during a kiss in a while. I'll definitely be on my A-game tonight.

Chapter 19

If I'm Dreaming, Don't Wake Me
Tee

I pull up to the Madison at exactly 6:30 p.m. The valet and my intern Samantha are standing on the curb. I hand my keys to the young man in a black uniform and Samantha walks with me to the McKeller Room. Samantha attends Memphis' only HBCU, LeMoyne-Owen College. She's got a good head on her shoulders. She's organized and follows directions well. She's a little short in the creativity department, but I'm working on that. With the right guidance, this girl is going to be one heck of an event planner. Samantha also has a beautiful personality. She always has a smile on her face and a kind word. Sometimes when I'm tired, she's all I need to remind me why I do what I do. This job is more than a paycheck for me. It's my way of giving back. Quite a few of the events I plan are to assist charitable organizations whose missions range from reducing birth defects to providing adequate care for the elderly. Mentoring Samantha is also a good way to give back. She briefs me on the day's events as we walk. The room looks nice. I compliment her on the excellent job she has done setting up the room to my specifications.

Every good event planner knows that you must make your high dollar sponsors feel extra special, because without their deep pockets the organizations they support wouldn't be able to function properly. This is an intimate gathering of 50 or so people. I have prepared gift bags filled with donated items from local vendors and a mouthwatering, Cajun-inspired buffet. The menu includes blackened catfish, chicken and seafood gumbo, étouffée, crawfish, and more for their dining pleasure. The guests dig in as soon as they arrive.

At 7:30 p.m., Michael Stokes walks in with Peter Parker and one guard. To my relief, he is wearing a suit coat, so this time there are no exposed guns. I have no intention of giving my guests the slightest hint that something is wrong. Michael looks fantastic in his brown slacks and beige dress shirt. He makes his way around the room, introducing himself and initiating small talk with the guests. Will this man ever cease to amaze me? Oftentimes, the guest speakers come in, head straight to their table and make the guests walk over to them. There are times when I have had to put in a special request for our guests of honor to unglue themselves from their seats to mix and mingle with the people who are helping foot the bill for them to be there. This man is acting as if this is his personal party, and he has to play the gracious host.

Halfway through the reception, I formally introduce Dr. Abel Martin, the Chair of the Board of Directors of the receiving agency, the I Will Live Foundation. He says a few words and invites Michael to do the same. Michael stands and gives a mini speech about how important HIV/AIDS research is, and how honored he is to play a small part in this event. He even relays the details of his earlier visit to Mercy, expressing how important it is to have people like our sponsors, who unselfishly give of their time, their talent, and their finances.

Somebody pinch me because I must be dreaming. This man knows exactly what to say and do. There has got to be a major flaw somewhere. I wonder what it is.

At 9:00 p.m. Samantha and I begin wrapping up. I thank Michael and inform him that his duty has been done for the evening. He is free to leave. He decides to stay and talk football with some of The University of Memphis' biggest boosters, who in turn invite him to join them for a drink. He politely declines, stating he had already agreed to meet a friend.

The remaining guests leave. Michael approaches me and whispers in my ear.

"Do you have to go? I would love to go somewhere and talk if you have time."

"I-I-I think I can arrange that," I stutter out. "Give me a few minutes to finish up here." What is it about this man that makes me lose my cool? I'm around attractive men all the time.

Samantha and I box up the table decorations and left-over gift bags and take them to my truck. After loading up my truck, I tell her what an excellent job she did.

"Coming from the most talented event planner in the city, that means the world to me, Miss Tee. I want to be just like you," she says.

I give her a stern look and say, "I don't want you to be like me young lady."

Her face falls into a frown. "Why not? You're my inspiration. You don't think I can?"

"Of course you can, but I want you to be better than me. The true sign of a good protégé is when she can take what she's been taught, add her own style to it, and surpass the accomplishments of her mentor. You're a talented young lady, and you will do well in this business if you're willing to put in the work."

She smiles. "I am? I mean, I will. You're the best! I won't let you down, Ms. Tee. Good night. And don't look now, but I think somebody's waiting on you? If you don't mind me saying so, you two look cute together."

"Actually, I do mind. He's a client Samantha. It's business. Nothing more, nothing less. It's acceptable to socialize with clients, because they can be the best business card you've ever had, but always remember not to cross the line."

"Okay. I understand, but technically he's talent, Ms. Tee, not the client." I had to admit she was right. I was paying him, not the other way around.

"Young lady, don't you have a party or something to go to?"

"I sure do."

"Well, go get ready and get out of my business."

"Oh, I'm sorry. I hope I didn't offend you. I was only kidding," she says wrinkling her forehead.

"Good night Samantha. Drive safely."

I decide to let her worry for a little while. That will teach her not to comment on my personal life. Michael is peering out of a large glass window in the lobby of the hotel. He's not even trying to hide the fact that he's staring at me. I try not to get excited but it's hard not to get a little excited about someone that handsome and personable.

I ask the valet to park truck again and return to the hotel to join Michael for a quick drink in the hotel lounge. We sit down at the bar, and he orders a Coke. I opt for cranberry juice. I would have figured him for a Jack and Coke man.

"Shall we take our drinks back to my room?" he asks. I knew he had a major flaw. Just like every other man, he's only after one thing. Well, Ms. Tee is not having it!

"I'm sorry if I gave you the wrong impression earlier Michael, but I don't go to hotel rooms with men I barely know. If that's what you're after, please don't waste your time on me. I'll leave so you can begin your search for someone to enhance your evening. It has been a pleasure meeting you," I curtly say and dismount my bar stool. Michael places his hand around my arm to stop me from leaving. As I halt my steps, I wonder why MacKenzie hadn't done the same. I wanted him to ask me not to leave. I miss him already.

"Whoa, that's not what I meant at all. Please forgive me if I gave YOU the wrong impression. I only wanted to go to my room so we can talk. No disrespect intended, but being who I am makes it hard for me to hold a decent conversation in public without someone interrupting."

A slim, white man with glasses and sandy brown hair walks up beside us and says, "Michael Stokes, is that you? Oh my goodness. Can I get your autograph, man? The game isn't the same without you, man. It's a shame what happened to your knee."

"See what I mean?" Michael says, before addressing his fan. "Sure, man. I miss the game myself. Who do you want me to make this out to?"

"Percy. My name's Percy Smith."

"Nice to meet you, Percy."

He didn't have a thing to sign. So Michael scrawls his name on a cocktail napkin and hands it to him. Percy is clearly in awe. He carefully takes the napkin and holds it to his chest like a treasured heirloom.

"Thanks. You don't know how much this means to me. I see you're busy, so I won't talk your ear off. I'm sure you've got better things to do." Percy then looks me up and down like I'm dessert.

I give him a look that clearly says, "Kick rocks." Instead of moving on, the perv lowers his framed eyes to my breasts and lets them linger a little too long for my taste. He then licks his lips like a lion getting ready to enjoy a tasty meal. I roll my eyes at him. He gets the hint and begins backing away but never averts his eyes from my bosom. At least he is leaving. Good riddance. Michael rises from his seat and steps between the two of us. He looks like a giant next to the small man.

"Percy, please respect my guest and behave like a gentleman," Michael says sternly. Percy's eyes are now fearfully focused on Michael. He takes a deep breath and gulps.

"My apologies, man. I didn't mean any harm. I was only admiring your taste." Without looking at me he adds, "Miss, I'm sorry if my actions were inappropriate. You look lovely this evening. You two enjoy your drinks. I must be going." He clumsily trips over his own feet and stumbles to the floor.

"Careful." I say. "I'd hate for you to hurt yourself." Without acknowledging my comment, he quickly gets up and runs away as if he is being chased. Michael and I both laugh. How sweet. He defended my honor—sort of.

"I see what you mean by interruptions. But I wouldn't feel comfortable in your room. Follow me. I think I know a place where we can have a little privacy."

I lead Michael to the elevators. As the doors close, a hand reaches in causing them to reopen. It's one of Michael's guards.

"Isaac, I almost forgot about you."

"I didn't forget about you, Mr. Stokes. I know you probably want some private time with your lady friend here, but I was instructed to stay with you. But I'll hang back," Isaac says, looking stoic. He needs to start buying his clothes in a bigger size. His jacket is so tight, he can't button it.

"This is another reason I wanted to go to my room. Security stays everywhere with me except in my room. Okay, Isaac. Come along, but hang back, waaay back," Michael laughs and leans back like the rapper Fat Joe in his "Lean Back" video. I laugh as the doors close with the three of us securely inside. I look at our reflection in the shiny mirrored walls inside the elevator. Samantha was right; we do make a handsome couple.

I take them to the Madison's rooftop. The view from up here is spectacular. It's a little cooler tonight than it had been the past couple of evenings. There's a small breeze blowing, giving our heated city some much needed relief from the elevated temperatures. The breeze dances around my legs, making the bottom of my skirt lift slightly. It feels good. I feel good. Better than I have felt the past two days.

The sky is littered with stars surrounding a bright crescent moon. Below them sits the M bridge that separates Memphis from Arkansas and serves as a passage way over the Mississippi River. It is completely lit, illuminating the waters below. The lights from the cars scurrying across the steel structure only add to the ambience. The horn blares from a barge slowly moving through the murky waters. There aren't very many people up here on the hotel rooftop. Tomorrow, it will be crowded with party goers or lovers trying to enjoy the view. One kissing couple is here now. We move toward a row of chairs lined against the railing on the opposite side of the roof. Love is in the air, and I don't want to disturb their flow. Michael and I take a seat. Isaac walks to another section of the railing.

"So, Tina Long, you seem to know a lot about me, but I know very little about you. Tell me about yourself."

"Please, call me Tee. I'm not one for talking about myself, so if you want to know something specific, you might want to ask, Mr. Stokes."

"Beautiful and mysterious. Okay then, how old are you? What college did you attend? Do you attend church? And in a fight would you rather be Superman or Batman?"

"I'm 30; I am a graduate of The University of Memphis; I attend Faith Persists Christian Church, where I sing in the choir and plan singles ministry events; and I would rather be Superman, because he had real super powers. All Batman had was a bunch of fancy gadgets. Without them he would be nothing. Perhaps, I'd be Wonder Woman. That way I could use my magic lasso to make sure you never tell me a lie. Now, it's my turn."

My plan is to ask why he needs so much security, but I decide to save that one for later. I'm enjoying this moment and don't want to ruin it.

"What's the most outrageous thing a woman or a group of women have tried to do for you or with you?

"I had a very interesting experience last night and I'm curious to know what lengths women have gone to, to get your attention. I'm sure Michael has some juicy stories to tell."

"Nice question, but I've learned not to air my dirty laundry because most women can't handle it. Ask something else."

"I've never been one to judge a man by his past. We've all got skeletons in our closet. Tell me, what is it?" I insist sweetly.

"Tee, I understand your curiosity, but I want to introduce you to the man I am now, not the man I used to be. Besides, we're supposed to be talking about you," Michael reminds me.

"Fair enough. What else do you want to know? Compared to the life I read about in your bio, mine is pretty boring. I work, go to church, and hang out with friends and family when I can. By the way, I love your new book. You were absolutely amazing today at the hospital."

"Thank you. I'm very proud of my book, and I'm glad you enjoyed it. Did I tell you that you look lovely tonight? I can't believe that some man hasn't snatched you up."

"Why do men always say that when a halfway attractive woman tells them she's single? I get approached regularly, but very few of them are the type of man I'm looking for. I don't have a shortage of dates, Michael Stokes. I have a shortage of potential mates, which makes it kind of hard for someone to snatch me up."

"And what type of man are you looking for?"

"I'm looking for Mr. Righteous, not Mr. Right. Someone who's like King David and loves God with all his heart and strives to please Him. I'm a godly woman, Michael, and to get with me you've got to be a godly man. There seems to be a severe shortage of those these days," I inform him.

"You do know that David was a whoremonger right? Women were his weakness. He slept with Bathsheba knowing she was married to another man and after she told him she was pregnant, he had her husband put on the front lines so he could be killed in battle. That way, no one would ever find out the baby was his," Michael says.

"That's true," I say. "But when David realized his errors, he always repented and he never stopped giving God the glory. After God allowed the child to die, David accepted his punishment and then praised God for being God. There's no such thing as a perfect man. It's one thing to make a mistake while pursuing righteousness. It's another to refuse to even try."

Michael is smiling. I wonder how many more questions he has.

"You say you are a godly woman. From that statement, is it safe to assume that you don't have sex."

"You assume right. The next time I have sex, it will be with my husband."

"How long has it been?"

"Three years."

"That's a long time to go without doing the do, Tee."

I brace myself for at least one of the questions that usually follows my revelation. Do you masturbate or do you participate in oral sex? Men can be so crass when you tell them you're not getting any. They all assume you partake in some other type of stimulation. Then, there's that horrible joke—so, you're cel-a-bit. Well, I'll buy-a-bit.

"I'm going on a year myself. That's one of the reasons I'm not in a relationship right now. It's hard to find a woman who understands that my main focus is getting closer to God and establishing a new career. When I found out I couldn't play football anymore I fell into a deep depression. I thought my life was over. It was God and the love and support of my family and Peter that brought me out. God showed me that it wasn't the end. It was a new beginning. He has allowed me to reinvent myself and do something else wonderful with my life in order to motivate and inspire others to pursue their dreams. I don't even have to go to a million practices or suit up. The best way I know how to say thank you is to live according to His word."

I smile and shake my head. Did he say what I think he said? He's not getting any either! I celebrate silently within. On the outside I'm calm, but on the inside my stomach has butterflies and my heart is doing cartwheels. Go team celibacy! Go!

"I know exactly what you mean. It is hard to find someone who understands your decision to abstain," I say.

"So maybe two saved and celibate people can keep each other company from time to time. But I ask that you be patient and cautious with me."

"Why?"

"As fine as you are, I think I would have a hard time keeping my hands to myself."

"I'm not only sexy, but I'm sassy. So you better be-have or I'll have to hurt you," I say, playfully holding my fists up in front of me.

"Down, Lennox-Lewis-in-a-skirt. I'll control my hormones. Just don't try to sample the chocolate and then walk away like you did today. I know I'm irresistible, but kissing like that could be misconstrued as teasing."

"My behavior earlier was a sign of extreme emotional bliss brought on by your generous donation to one of my favorite institutions. Nothing more, sir. I realize that women throw themselves at you on a regular basis, but I assure you that I will not be one of them. Now, as much as I am enjoying our time together, I have a long day tomorrow and I must get some rest."

"I understand, Ms. Long. I'm tired myself. Let me and Isaac escort you to your car."

"That won't be necessary. I gave it to the valet. Why don't you go ahead and go to your room so you can have some privacy and rest that handsome head of yours."

"As you wish, my lady. But don't do me any favors. I really don't mind."

Michael gestures to Isaac that we are leaving, and the three of us walk back to the elevator. Isaac is careful to give us as much privacy as one can give in an elevator by stepping in last and turning his back to us. Michael places his hands around my waist and draws me near. This time I don't attempt to pull away and briefly nestle my head in his chest. He smells even better now than he did earlier today. Neither of us says a word. This is one of those times when words are unnecessary and would contribute nothing, that moment when you think you have met someone nice who may be able to contribute something positive to your life. I find myself wishing the ride down were longer.

The elevator slows to a stop. I say, "It was a pleasure meeting you, Michael Stokes. Sweet dreams."

"Then, I'll have to dream about you, pretty lady. See you tomorrow." He kisses me on my cheek.

The elevator doors open, and Isaac steps to the side to let me pass.

During the drive home I silently pray:

I'm not going to get my hopes up, Lord, but I want to say thank you for reminding me that all men aren't dogs. There are some men out there with good hearts who want to be good men. Even if this isn't the man you have predestined for me, this one meeting has shown me that all is not lost. Please keep Michael close to you and allow him to continue to prosper, remembering to put you first in all he does. Keep him safe from his predators. He's got a lot of work to do for you. Amen.

Gosh, darn it! I forgot to ask him who was stalking him! His good looks keep distracting me.

Chapter 20

Burn Baby Burn
Tee

The next morning I am humming. I hum songs by Marvin Gay, Luther Vandross, Rachelle Ferrell and Will Downing. I hum as I take my shower and get dressed. The only time I stop is during my quiet time. I thank God again for the life he allows me to lead.

I hum as I drive to the office. I hum while I wave at Herman. I hum on the elevator, and I hum as I walk down the hall to my office. What a wonderful morning! The sight in my office confirms that it truly is. On my desk are three dozen pink roses in exquisite crystal vases with a bright pink bow tied around each one. The note attached to the first vase reads,

These are symbolic of our blossoming friendship. Thank you for a wonderful evening. I am looking forward to seeing you again tonight.

Regards,
Michael

I hum "The Closer I Get to You" by Roberta Flack and Donny Hathaway as I arrange the vases around my office. I leave one on my desk, and place one on the credenza near the window. I am contemplating where to put the last vase when Katty Kathy, our friendly office hater and gossip enters my doorway. That girl has a knack for placing clouds over anyone's sunny skies, and it's all because she's jealous. If she spent more time doing her job instead of minding other people's business she'd probably get a promotion.

"Roses from two different men in six days? Somebody must be very busy. Are those for services rendered?"

Oh no she didn't! That girl has some nerve. I decide to ignore her. She stands there awaiting a response that I have no intention of giving. I return my attention to deciding where to place my flowers. Maybe she'll suddenly disappear. Something even better happens. Sandy appears in the doorway and bumps Kathy to the side with the forceful thrust of her wide, curvaceous hip.

"Kathy, move your boney behind out of the way before the cheap perfume you're wearing makes the petals on Tee's roses wilt. You wish someone would send you roses for services rendered. All you get are VD positive test results from your gynecologist."

Kathy gives Sandy a dirty look and extends her middle finger before walking in the direction of her cubicle.

"What aisle did you say the vaginal anti-itch cream was on at the Walgreens on the corner?! I hear you're a regular down there!" Sandy shouts after her. I slap my thigh while laughing.

"Sandy, you are too crazy! Stop before you get me fired."

"I am not about to let Katty Kathy ruin my baby sister's high. I never liked that girl anyway. She knows not to mess with me. You see she didn't respond. I'm sure she remembers the way I went off on her at the company Christmas party last year. Did she really think she could get away with flirting with my husband in front of me?

I don't know who these roses are from, but if he can keep you beaming the way you are, then he can't be all bad. Tell him I said, 'Thank you.' After what happened between you and MacKenzie, you need a pick me up. And who are you fooling? You are the top money maker in this place, so no one is about to fire you."

"Sho' you right," I say and give my sister a high five. "What are you doing here?"

"I took a break from the restaurant to handle a little business downtown today. Since I was in the neighborhood, I decided to stop by to see you. Can you dip out for breakfast?"

"I wish I could, but my Gala is tonight, and I need to get down to the venue to make sure all the details are being taken care of."

Edgar sneaks behind Sandy and taps her on the shoulder, startling her.

"Is this the baddest woman to ever put on an apron or pick up a skillet that I see?"

"It sure is," answers Sandy. "How are you doing, Edgar? You look like you're losing weight."

"I am. You know Marva can't cook. Lately, the only think we've had is beanie weenies. Before that it was canned soup. You wouldn't happen to have some friend chicken in your purse or a little pecan pie in your cleavage would you?"

"Of course not, boy, but what I do have is an invitation to breakfast since my sister here can't get away."

"Sold! To the woman with the junk in her trunk. You got yourself an Edgar escort for breakfast."

"Great! You can tell me all about Tee's new man."

"New man? Ms. Tee didn't tell me about a new man. You've been holding out on us? You scandalous woman. Let's go Sandy, so we can talk about her behind her back."

"There's no new man. These were sent by the speaker for tonight, Michael Stokes, to say thank you."

"Honey, I knew you were good at your job, but these roses say I want to be all up in your business and your pudding pop," says Edgar. "You gots some splainin' to do, missy, when I get back from feeding my face."

"And you better tell me before you even think about telling this diva, bye," adds Sandy.

My life would be truly boring without those two. I need to get to the venue to make sure my centerpieces were delivered this morning, like I requested. I head towards the elevators, Katty Kathy steps from behind a partition and walks directly in my path. What does she want now?

"I hate to be the bearer of bad news, but I was recently informed that the Crystal Ballroom is on fire." The ugly grin on her face reminds me of the devil.

"What? Where did you hear that?"

"The news. The Crystal Ballroom is in flames, darling. Isn't that where you are holding your big, fancy, shin dig tonight? If I were you, I would leave and go find out for myself."

I locate my cell phone inside my Gucci purse and attempt to call the ballroom several times. No one answers.

The ballroom is also downtown so it only takes me a few minutes to drive there. Katty Kathy was right. Two fire trucks are blocking the entrance to the parking lot, but it looks like the worst is over. The Crystal Ballroom has been doused with water, remnants of the spray spill down its walls onto the grounds surrounding the building. Most of the fire has been contained but a couple of firemen continue to water the smoldering building to insure that all the flames are extinguished. The staff and several onlookers are outside gawking at the charred back entrance to the kitchen. I park on the street and get out of my truck to get a closer look.

Leigh, the head of client services, is standing on the sidewalk with her co-workers. Her parents run, Taste This, one of the more popular catering businesses in the city. She's only 21, but she practically cut her teeth on a dinner napkin. There's no denying that she is more than qualified to run the entire catering department of this fine facility. She talks very fast and if you don't listen closely, you'll miss something. Leigh sees me, gives me a tight hug and begins speaking in her usual run-everything-together manner.

"Tee, I think I saw the light today. My life flashed before my very eyes. I was in the kitchen with the head cook, Salvador, when the stove burst into flames. They came out of nowhere. It was like fireworks or something. Salvador, being the calm soul he is, ushered the whole staff out of the back door. Luckily, no one got hurt. Everything happened so fast. The kitchen is burnt crispier than Flavor Flav. It got part of the ballroom, too. I'm so sorry, but I don't think we'll be holding anybody's gala in there tonight. That wouldn't be a good look anyway. You want your steak well-done, not your ballroom. I'm sure we can reschedule you once the repairs are done. Tee, I almost lost my life today! Oh my God! Oh my God! Oh my God!"

This poor child is scared silly.

I take Leigh to the ambulance on site, and tell a female EMT with a gold tooth that she is hysterical and a little oxygen might do her some good. She assures me that she will take good care of her. Leigh reluctantly transfers from me to her, but I stay close by to make her feel better. Then I call her father, Herb, and he informs me that he heard about the fire and is on his way. He also thanks me for looking after his daughter. Bless her heart. In less than 15 minutes, Herb is on the scene soothing his only child's fears. Good fathers are priceless.

Chapter 21

Fire and Desire
Tee

I have no choice but to admit defeat. I will not be having a grand Gala this evening. That sucks! I return to my office and call the florist, the executive director of the I Will Live Foundation, and anyone else directly connected to the execution of this event to tell them the news. Then, I sit down at my computer, write a brief media alert announcing the cancellation, and e-mail it to all the local media outlets. There's a knock at my door. Without looking up, I tell whoever it is to "Come in."

It better not be Katty Kathy, because I'm not in the mood for her antics. Every evil thought I am having dissipates after I see Michael Stokes standing before me, looking quite handsome in stylish orange golf attire and his 1,000 watt smile.

"I see you got the flowers I sent you. I hope you like them," he says.

"I love them. Roses are my favorite. What are you doing here?"

"Well, hello. Nice to see you, too."

"Forgive me, Michael. I am happy to see you. I'm just a little disappointed right now."

"I heard that the venue for the Gala was badly burned. I figured you would be devastated, seeing how consumed you are with your events. I thought you might need some cheering up."

"Cheering up is definitely in order."

"Look on the bright side. The fire happened before your event rather than during."

"You're right."

"What if the fire had broken out while you had hundreds of attendees in the room? Someone might have gotten hurt, or worst, killed," Michael says.

"You're right, again. I'll have to reschedule the event but what am I going to do about you? I already paid you for tonight's appearance."

"Don't worry about it. We'll coordinate our schedules and I will come back when you need me to. I won't even make you pay for my flight and hotel accommodations. That way you can give the money you save to the charity."

"That's very kind of you. How can I ever repay you?"

"That's easy, pretty lady. Allow me to take you out for a late lunch."

"Deal." I realize that I haven't eaten a thing all day. I've been so busy I neglected to eat.

"Great! But please allow me to go back to my room to shower and change. I've been playing golf and really want to get out of this outfit." Michael flashes that smile again.

"How about I meet you in the lobby of your hotel in an hour," I suggest. "That will give me time to finish up here."

"An hour is fine. Now, don't go changing your mind. I would really like to spend some more time with you before I leave in the morning."

"Why?"

"You seem like someone I should get to know. See you in an hour."

"For someone in danger, you sure don't act like it. You've been golfing, and I see you are here without Isaac." I say in hopes of getting him to confide in me.

"I ditched him to come see you. Security was Peter's idea. I'll tell you more about it during lunch. See you in one hour, Ms. Long." Before I could blink he was gone.

Chapter 22

Lunch for Two?
Michael

Tee is beautiful and sexy. Her skin reminds me of rich mocha lattes. I love the way her hips move as she walks. If I had to guess, I'd say she was a size seven. Not too big, not too small. When I had my arms around her last night, it felt right. I'm even attracted to that slightly hard exterior she has. I can tell she's sweet, though. Women like that have usually been hurt a time or two.

I shower, change and go to the lobby to wait for her. To my chagrin Peter is there, too. It's obvious he's peeved about something. I figure it has to do with me sneaking out to see Tee.

"Mike, I need you to go to your room and pack your bags. Becca has been here. Since the event is canceled, we can leave," he says.

"Whoa, Pete. We haven't had an incident the entire time we've been here. What makes you think she's been here?"

He holds up a black Ken doll and a white Barbie doll covered in what is supposed to be blood. They have miniature knives stuck where their hearts would be if they were alive. There is a note pinned to Barbie that reads,

Til death do us part. Lose the nappy head. You're mine. You're staying on the 10th floor, right?

I had another nightmare last night. It was the same one I had on the plane. The sight of those mini knives makes my heart beat a little faster. I can't let her intimidate me.

"Who is she talking about, Tee? This is going too far. Becca is NOT going to tell me who I can and cannot see. How did she find out what floor I'm on? The rooms were booked under aliases," I say.

"Evidently, she thinks she can. This was delivered to the front desk about an hour ago. They said a blonde brought it in at around noon. I checked the surveillance tapes. It's her, Mike. She even looked up at the camera and waved. You need to leave. You remember what happened in Atlanta. You're not going to die while you're under my charge."

"Becca must be spying on me. This is crazy! I'm not afraid of her. I'm not leaving."

"No, she's crazy. You should be afraid and yes, we are leaving. Someone has to look out for your safety, because evidently you think this woman is playing. This is serious. What was that stunt you pulled today, leaving without telling anyone? She could have wacked you off and no one would have known where to find your body. She tried to kill you once. What makes you think she won't try again? I have arranged for a car to take us to the airport immediately. Go get your bags." He can't be that upset over some dolls.

"Peter. I'm not ready to leave. Let's stick to the plan and leave in the morning."

"If you don't leave now, I'm going to quit," shouts Peter.

"Peter, you can't quit. I'm more than a client.. I'm your boy. You wouldn't quit on your boy, would you?"

"That proves how serious I am. Get your things and let's go, or today is my last day as your agent and manager."

Peter has been guiding my career since I entered the draft. I can't let him quit. I need to call Tee and tell her that we have to postpone our plans. This is some bull!

Chapter 23

Parting Is Such Sweet Sorrow
Tee

"Innovations Marketing & Events. Tina speaking."

"Hey, Tina. It's Mike. I'm glad I caught you before you left.

"Hello. Michael I was about to leave for your hotel. Are you ready?"

"Unfortunately, my plans have changed, and I have to leave Memphis now. There's been an emergency."

"What? Is everything okay? What happened?"

"I'd rather not get into it right now. My flight leaves in a couple of hours, so I have to get to the airport. I am truly sorry about this. I can think of nothing better than to spend time with you. Please forgive me. I promise to make this up to you. I owe you an amazing first date. Okay?"

I'm confused. This man cancels on me and doesn't even give me a sufficient reason as to why. Does this have something do to with his stalker?

"It's not okay, but I'll give you the benefit of the doubt. You can ask for a first date when your schedule permits. Hopefully, I'll be available."

"Don't be like that, Tee. Believe me when I say that no one is more disappointed than me. I promise to give you a first date to rival all first dates. I'll send details soon. I like you, Tee, and I'm going to take the time to get know you. Unfortunately, I have a few personal issues I need to resolve first. Talk to you soon, pretty lady. I gotta go now."

"I hope your situation improves. Goodbye."

Two events cancelled in one day. This is worthy of a short day at the office. Maybe I'll go see my sister. She said she was heading home after running her errands.

Chapter 24

The Ties That Bind
Michael

Tee sounded so disappointed. This madness with Becca has got to end soon. Peter, Isaac, and I arrive at the airport in record time. We approach the ticket counter. Dr. Foster is there, too. It's uncanny how we keep ending up in the same place at the same time.

"Hello. It's funny how we keep bumping into each other, young man," she says.

"It was thinking the same thing. Where are you headed, Doc?"

"I'm going to visit my sister is Akron, Ohio for a little while. We haven't seen each other in two years. It's about time we had some time together."

"Yeah, you're right. You're long overdue for a visit. That's where I'm headed. Are you leaving on the 4 p.m. flight?"

"I sure am. Don't tell me. You are, too."

"Yes, ma'am. Perhaps we can finagle some seats together so I can finish my story. After the day I've had, I need to talk to someone."

"Why wait until we're seated on the plane. We have a little time before the flight. Let's find a quiet section near our gate and resume our conversation there."

"Sounds good to me. See you at the gate."

Me and my two amigos get our tickets and make our way through security. Peter is headed back to Miami. I give him some dap and a hug and tell him not to worry.

He tells me to call him when I land and instructs Isaac to watch me like a hawk. Isaac and I walk to our gate. Dr. Foster is already seated waiting for me. She is eating a strawberry ice cream cone, being very careful not to soil her jeans or her white ruffled blouse. I really want to tell her all my troubles. I need someone to help me make sense of this mess. I seem to have met a wonderful woman but Becca had to go and ruin our first date.

I make my way over to Dr. Foster and have a seat. Isaac sits nearby.

"Dr. Foster, I really appreciate you taking the time to help me. I know I've been all over the place with this story, but I'm almost finished. Maybe you can give me some advice about how to end this so that no one gets hurt. I want Becca to resume being a mother to her child without some unhealthy attachment to me."

"Perhaps, she can but right now you are my patient. I need to know what's going on with you before I can begin to help her."

"I understand. Well, here's the next chapter of my saga. Within 48 hours the test results came back, revealing that there was a 99.9 percent chance that Maxwell was Michelle's father. I called my brother with the news. He was shocked and extremely sorry. I told him I forgave him for sleeping with Becca, but he had to accept responsibility for his child. I booked us flights to go home to Akron for the weekend. We had to tell my parents, so we could face this as a family. I never went back to my condo. I lied and told Becca that I had more business to attend to and stayed in Ft. Lauderdale for the next two nights waiting for Friday to arrive. I talked to my brother several times to make sure he didn't try to chicken out on me and miss his plane.

"Friday, my brother and I arrived in Akron about the same time. He looked like he hadn't had any sleep. I let him know everything was going to be okay.

"We took our parents out to dinner to break the news. I wanted to do it in a public place because I figured my mother would be less likely to make a scene. Vanessa Bell Stokes is an evangelist and a deacon's wife. She's very into appearances and would never do anything to embarrass herself in public. Or, so I thought. I chose their favorite steak house: The Bistro. While we ate our expensive steak dinners, Max updated my parents on college life. They stated several times how proud they were of him and how nice it's going to be to have a doctor in the family.

"We ordered dessert, and I delicately told my parents about the situation with Becca and Michelle. After my mother heard me say that my ex-girlfriend had a baby by my little brother, she clutched the crucifix dangling from her neck with both her hands and shouted, 'Jesus, keep me near the cross!'

"Then, she took out the bottle of holy oil that she keeps in her purse, poured a small amount into the palm of one hand and used the fingertips of her other hand to fling droplets at me and my brother. I thought you were supposed to rub it on people's foreheads and pray for them, not ruin $2,000 Italian silk suits. If that wasn't enough, she also stood up and started speaking in tongues. I couldn't understand most of what she said, but the part I could decipher was something about deliver them from their heathenous, fornicative ways, hell bound … better women selections, a managé trios and a child molester.

"My father, came to where my brother and I were seated and instructed us to stand. We did as we were told. Next, he told us to get down on our knees for prayer. That was asking too much. I wasn't about to kneel in prayer in the middle of a five star restaurant in front of a room full of strangers and high profile politicians. I'm almost sure I saw the mayor and a couple of city councilmen over in the corner booth. My father is a tall man and when we didn't move, he placed a hand on each of our shoulders and began pushing us down. Max and I tried to resist, but my mother came and pinched both of us in our sides like she used to do when we were disobedient as little children. With her pinching and my father pushing, our knees went jelly. Before Max and I knew it, we were both on our knees on The Bistro's marble floors. I guess neither one of my parents thought about the fact that I had a bad knee. Or they didn't care. I could feel the whole restaurant watching us. Our father still had one hand placed firmly on our shoulders to make sure we didn't move. He bowed his head and said a low prayer. I was thankful he did it quietly so the whole restaurant wouldn't hear our business. What I didn't appreciate was him calling us whoremongers and asking the Lord to give us a double portion of sense and self-control. He even prayed for the temptress who had unknowingly defiled his youngest son. Oh I forgot, he asked the Lord to forgive me for being a poor example.

"He prayed and my mother ran around the table chanting, 'Deliver my family from Satan, Lord!' over and over again. I had seen her break out in a Holy Ghost sprint in church from time to time, but never in a restaurant. At first my brother and I were looking at each other. I closed my eyes and bowed my head to try and ignore the multiple sets of eyes balls that were looking at us. I was also praying that no one would recognize me, but I knew better.

"My father only prayed a few minutes, but to me it felt like hours. When he finished, he patted me and my brother on the back and said, 'Get up, boys. Dessert's here. The Lord told me everything is going to be fine. So let's eat. That crème brûlée sure looks good.'

"We rose from the floor and sat down in our seats. I was beyond embarrassed. Our waiter was a young white man with blonde hair named Timothy. When I opened my eyes he was standing in front of our table, holding our desserts. His face was extremely red, and he had a smirk that kept appearing then disappearing. I gave Timothy an angry look. He got the picture, set down our desserts and ran to get away from our table before he was overcome with laughter. I wanted to leave, but I could tell that my father wasn't going anywhere before he finished his dessert. I may be a grown man, but I know better than to walk out on my parents. My mother sat back down in her chair next to him and began eating her strawberry cheese-cake. Her brow was moist from running around the table. Her black wig was now on crooked with her gray hairs protruding from underneath it. I had ordered the seven-layer chocolate cake. It no longer looked delicious, but I had to do something to distract my thoughts from what had taken place. I wished the earth would open up and swallow me whole.

'Now, Michael Jr., what's my grandbaby's name?' my mother asked with a smile and her sweetest voice. Did she really expect me to hold a conversation with her as if the last 15 minutes had never taken place?

'Boy, your mother asked you a question. Answer her,' my father ordered.

"I told her Michelle and angrily broke off a piece of seven-layer cake. I bit down so hard on the fork I could hear my teeth clash against the metal. I didn't taste a thing.

'Michelle. That's a nice name. No doubt she was trying to select a name that was close to yours. Too bad that Jezebel had the wrong father. I have half a mind to file molestation charges against her. But I'll wait until I meet her to decide about that. Son, how could you date such a loose woman? I thought we taught you better than that? The Bible says that a woman with no discretion is like a gold ring in a pig's snout. Looks like you found just that. You even brought her around your little brother. Michael Jr., this is as much your fault as it is Maxwell's. When we sent Maxwell to you to get a good education, we didn't mean sex education. Sunday, I want you both to go to church and stretch yourselves out face down across the altar and ask God to forgive you. I'll tell the pastor to say a special prayer for you, too.

"I want to meet my grandbaby as soon as possible, too. We got to love on her and love on her real good. I agree with your Daddy on this one. Everything will work out fine.'

"I think that was the only time I had ever wished I had been born to atheists. For the duration of our dinner, Maxwell sat in silence, fuming. He never even touched his red velvet cake. We didn't leave for another hour, because my father decided he wanted another crème brûlée and some coffee to wash it down."

Chapter 25

The Poison Apple
Tee

"You told me it was over!" screams Sandy.

"It is over. I haven't seen her since I fired her. I promise," says her husband, Patrick.

"You're lying. I saw your credit card statement. You got Sheniqua an apartment and you've been paying her bills for months. You don't do that for a woman you never see."

"Baby, it's true. I have not seen her since I fired her. Sandy, please calm down. Let me explain."

The arguing in my sister's house is so loud I can hear it from the driveway. What in the world is going on in there?

"Calm down? In counseling you promised no more secrets. You did it again. I'm the mother of your children. I don't deserve to be disrespected like this. I gave you everything! Leave, Patrick. I don't want your explanation. I'm sure it's more lies. I need to clear my head and think about whether this marriage is worth salvaging. I refuse to deal with anymore deception."

"Sandy let me explain. Please. I know this looks bad, but it's not what you think!"

"I said get out!"

I get out of my car and walk to the door. The yelling is momentarily replaced by the sound of glass breaking.

"Woman, are you trying to kill me?" Patrick shouts.

"That wouldn't be such a bad idea right now. Leave if you value your life, boy! You're despicable. You've been sleeping with that woman and you know it. Get out of my house, Patrick! NOW!"

The door opens and I take a step back to avoid being smacked in the face by their security door. Patrick exits looking very distraught. He is usually well maintained, but today he looks like a mad man. His face is unshaved and his hair is uncut and uncombed with small pieces of lint in it. His plaid shirt and jeans are a wrinkled mess. The two of them must have had quite an afternoon.

He yells over his shoulder, "I'll pick the kids up from school and take them to my mother's tonight with me. When you calm down, maybe we can talk about this like adults. It's really not what you think. I love you baby, and mark my words, I'm coming back home."

He doesn't see me standing there and almost bumps into me.

"Oh, hey Tee. How long have you been here?"

"Long enough," I reply.

"I see. Well, you being the good Christian woman you are, I'm sure you won't judge me too harshly for my actions, especially without hearing both sides of the story. Will you do me a favor?"

"Depends on what it is."

No matter how much I like my brother-in law, my loyalty will always belong to my big sister.

"Pray for me and my marriage. I won't lose my wife. She and the kids are my life."

There's no way I can deny a request for prayer.

"Of course I will, but you need to pray for yourself."

"I will. But Tee, I need you, too. I am going to throw my wife a surprise birthday party. She told me she always wanted one and she's going to get it. Even if it's the last thing I'm able to do for her. Will you still help me put this party on tomorrow night?"

"Patrick, under the circumstances I don't think I should."

"It's not what you think, Tee. I'll call you late tonight and explain everything. Just hear me out, okay?" He looks so sad.

I nod. I want to know what's going on for myself. Maybe I can help.

Patrick thanks me and gets into his black Range Rover. I see him wiping tears from his eyes before he drives away. That man really does love my sister. I'm just as sure of that as I am that I love her.

I walk into the house and carefully step over shards of glass on the floor of the foyer. They appear to be from two pictures of Sandy and Patrick that used to be on the bookshelf in the living room. One of the pictures lies torn in half among the glass and the other is crumpled into a ball. Sandy is sitting on the living room floor, hugging her knees and a red decorative pillow from her red and white couch. The pillow matches my sister's swollen eyes. She appears to have been crying for quite some time.

"What's wrong, Sandy? What happened?"

"Life isn't fair, Tee. We spend our lives looking for the man of our dreams, and when we find him, our dream life turns into a nightmare. You remember those stories Momma used to read us when we were little? Those fairytales with the knights in shining armor and princes on white horses who come to rescue the damsels in distress. They defeat the evil witch or ogre or whatever, and then the two of them ride off into the sunset. The story always ends, 'and they lived happily ever after,' right? I don't think there's such a thing as a happily ever after, Tee. Those stories are just lying to little girls, getting our hopes up so life can let us down. I remember the jewelry box we shared as little girls that would play that song from the cartoon "Cinderella" when we wound it up. I can't remember the name," she says.

"It was 'Someday My Prince Will Come,'" I say softly while smoothing out my sister's hair.

"Yeah, the 'Someday' song. I loved that song. I used to wind up that jewelry box every day and listen to it over and over. I was so devastated when the handle broke and it wouldn't play anymore. Well, that's how I feel now, like the handle just broke off my life. Only instead of it being broken and useless, it's spiraling out of control. What happened to my prince, Tee? It's bad enough my husband cheated on me with his receptionist and we've been going to counseling to work things out. But now I find out he is still sleeping with her. I love my husband, and I've been trying to get past the adultery. But it's hard. That home wrecker had the nerve to call my house today. She asked when Patrick was going to pay her cable bill, because her kids are bored watching regular network television. She told me he has been taking care of the woman he really loves for months." Her body is shaking with emotion and tears continue spill from her weary eyes.

"That she-witch is expecting me and my husband to take care of her. She's not even ashamed of the fact that she slept with a married man. What's wrong with these women, Tee? Don't they have any integrity or self-esteem? They would rather share a man than get their own." She hands me one of several papers that are strewn all over the floor.

"After she called, I got on the computer and pulled up Patrick's credit card statement. Tee, look at it! He has all types of charges for Babies R Us, utilities, and phone. Tee, he even paid the deposit and first month's rent for her apartment with our money. Can you believe that? I'm his wife, the mother of his children, the woman who worked long hours helping him get his dental practice up and running. Do you remember when I made all my employees go get their teeth cleaned at our office when business got slow? And this is the thanks I get? I feel so stupid. He told me he was through with her. Word to the wise, baby sister. If your man ever cheats on you, leave him. Don't stay, because at some point he'll make you regret you did. Why aren't I enough, Tee?" Sandy wails and then buries her head in the pillow.

My sister has been through so much and sacrifices a great deal for her family. She works hard all day at the restaurant and them comes home to be mother and wife. She barely has time for herself, but she never seems to mind. Sandy has always found great pleasure in taking care of the people she loves. The words to comfort her don't come easily. So, instead of talking, I get down on the floor, wrap my arms around my only sibling, and hold her while she cries. Through thick, through thin, through men, she will always have me. I guess Patrick's canine tendencies have resurfaced. Unfortunately, my sister is the one who's feeling the bite. After sitting on the floor for about an hour, I coax Sandy to get up and go to bed. A nap might do her a little good.

I go to the kitchen to fix myself something to eat, because I still have yet to eat. Dirty dishes and cookware are all over the counter and brimming in the sink. I put a pepperoni pizza in the oven and get to work cleaning up.

As much as I love my sister, I'll be the first to admit that money has changed her. At times, she has bouts of bourgeois, and indulges in frequent spending sprees in an effort to keep up with the Joneses--who happen to be the other rich people in her expensive gated community. I don't think there's a house on the block that's below $800,000. Her spacious home in Collierville is a far cry from the two bedroom duplex in North Memphis where we were reared. Now that my sister can afford almost anything she wants, she seems to want the world to know it. Her home is a massive display of wealth. Large flat screen TVs in almost every room. Remote controlled and voice activated gadgets that do everything from microwave food to massage your back. I've seen her purchase some hideous clothes, shoes, and purses because of the name on them. Her most recent error in judgment is this ugly, scrawny, hairless, rare breed of cat she purchased for $1,500. When she told me how much she paid for the grey, putrid thing, I told her she was crazy. Not only is the thing ugly, but it is bad as can be. Sandy has already sent two cushions from her leather sectional to be reupholstered, because Ms. Tiara—that's her name—decided to sharpen her expensive little claws to them. But it's her money, so who am I to tell her how to spend it.

I have to do something to stop this wound from getting infected with depression or a fit of where's-my-gun rage. I know, I'll call the girls. There's no way I'm going to let my sister sit here in this house feeling sorry for herself. The girls always cheer us up.

The girls are a group of women we met at a monthly gathering we attend called LNO, Ladies Night Out. LNO meets once a month for food, fellowship, and fun. We're all college educated women between the ages of 28 and

45 who have achieved varying degrees of success and who love to have a good time. About six of us have become really good friends, and, occasionally, we meet outside of the LNO gatherings. I pick up the phone, call the girls, and explain that we need to have an emergency gathering at my sister's house tonight. Lenora, Lenise, Tiffany, and Teresa all agree to come. Each one of these women is a complete character. If they can't cheer Sandy up, no one can. Let me see what I can whip up, because this pizza won't be enough. The girls love to eat.

Chapter 26

And The Walls Came Tumbling Down
Michael

Dr. Foster is quietly and attentively listening to my story, as usual. The flight attendants announce that it is time to board our plane. We do as instructed. I use my charm and celebrity status to persuade a cute flight attendant to upgrade Dr. Foster's seat to first class so she can sit in the empty seat next to mine. Being considered one of America's greatest wide receivers certainly has its privileges. Once we are coasting smoothly in the air, I resume my tale.

"My parents and I decided it would be best to bring Becca to Akron to tell her the news. The whole family wanted to help her and Michelle. After I told them about Becca's childhood, they even apologized for their emotional outburst at The Bistro. I was shocked when they volunteered to let the two of them stay at their house until she got on her feet. I was also relieved because I didn't think continuing to have them live with me in Miami would be a good idea. I arranged for them to fly in the very next day. Becca begged me to tell her the paternity results on the phone. The only thing I would tell her was that I received them and I wanted her and Michelle to meet my family as soon as possible. I knew she wouldn't come if I told her the truth. I really had to use my acting skills for that one, because I still wanted to shake the demon out of her for sleeping with my little

Max. However, I had to think of my niece. Now that she was in my world, I wasn't going to let her go.

I met them at the airport and during the drive to my parent's house, Becca talked excessively about how she knew I was the father; she was going to make everything better; and by the time she was finished, I would forget she ever hurt me. I kept driving my mother's Mercedes and my only comments were 'really' and 'okay.' Michelle was in the back in the booster seat I purchased for her, playing with her doll. I hated that she overheard Becca's babbling. I really wanted to tell her exactly what I thought of her."

I pause. A flight attendant is now making her way down the aisle taking drink orders and handing out pretzels. I ask for a Coke and Dr. Foster requests a Sprite. She pours our beverages into clear plastic cups and hands them to each of us. I drink a little.

"My parents, Maxwell, and my baby sister Tomeka were assembled in the living room, along with our pastor, Rev. Jenkins, and his wife, Bertha. My parents wanted them there in case we needed a mediator. When my mother laid her eyes on Michelle, she looked at her like she was the most amazing thing she had ever seen. It was a very touching moment.

'That's my grandbaby. Look at my beautiful grand-baby. Come give your grandma a hug,' she cooed.

"At first Michelle looked a little confused, but then it was as if a light went off in her little head. She smiled, ran to my mother and said, 'I got a daddy and a grandma! Yeaaaaaaaaaah!' and fell into her arms. My mother swept her off her feet and swung her around in absolute joy. My sister went over to hug her new niece.

'You sure do, precious. And you got a granddaddy and an Auntie Tomeka and an uncle.'

"I noticed that she craftily left off the name on that one. I looked over at Becca and she had tears in her eyes. Telling her the truth wasn't going to be pretty, and I knew it. My mother started crying while she kissed every inch of Michelle's little face. My father never moved from his place in the corner, but he was misty-eyed as well. This was their first grandchild, so I guess they had the right to be a little emotional. My brother looked at Michelle for a few minutes and then, walked out of the room. I didn't see how I didn't notice it before, but Michelle possessed several of his features. She had his forehead, his chin, and that crooked little smile of his. We share the same nose and ears, which she also has, but the cheeks and shape of her eyes were definitely Becca's. I started to follow him, but I decided to let him be for a few minutes.

'Everybody into the dining room,' my mother ordered. 'This is a cause for celebration. My grandbaby and her mother are here. Becca, I hope you like turkey 'cause I fixed a big one. Where are my manners? Relax, you're with family now. Would you like to freshen up?'

'Yes, ma'am, if you don't mind.'

'Michael, Jr., show her where the restroom is.'

"I took Becca to the bathroom and then went to find Maxwell. He was sitting at the desk in the room we shared as children with his head in his hands. 'Michael, I got a kid. I don't think it really hit me until I saw her. I got a kid and she's beautiful. What kind of father am I going to be? I still feel like a kid myself. What am I going to do?'

'You're going to be her father, Maxwell. The good thing is you've got plenty of help. Now, come to dinner and spend some time with your daughter. She's amazing,' I said.

"We walked into the dining room, everyone except Becca was already seated. Michelle ran to my side, grabbed my hand and pulled me toward the table. 'Sit by me Daddy,' she said.

"Max gave me an angry look. 'Why is she calling you Daddy?'

"I forgot to tell him about that earlier. I tried to tell him in a low voice that we would talk about it later, but Becca had heard his remark. 'Why shouldn't she call her father Daddy, Maxwell?'

"Maxwell still had some major resentment towards Becca, and he wasn't going to miss the opportunity to hurt her feelings. 'Because he's not her father. I am, Rebecca!'

"Becca froze and the room went silent. It was so quiet, you could have heard a moth gnawing at a wool sweater. We were supposed to tell her after dinner. Why did he have to go and ruin our plan to enact his own vengeance? All eyes were on Maxwell and Becca. Becca was the first one to speak.

'What the hell is going on here? Michael, I thought you got the test results back and they were positive.'

'They were positive. They positively showed that Max is Michelle's father, not me. I know you slept with my little brother, Becca. So, please don't try to deny it.'

"In an effort to protect Michelle, my mother told Tomeka to take Michelle to her room. Tomeka tried to take Michelle by the hand, but she ran over to her mother. I'm sure she didn't understand what was going on, but she could tell something was wrong. Fear showed on her sweet little face, and she had run to her mother for comfort.

'It's okay, baby. Go with Auntie Tomeka, Becca said while hugging her. Mommy has to do some grown up talking now. What did I tell you about grown up conversations?'

"Michelle looked up at her mother and said in a whisper, 'They are not for children's ears to hear.'

'That's right. Go with Auntie Tomeka. Everything is okay.'

"Michelle walked over to my sister. She scooped up her niece and ran out of the room as fast as she could. Becca slowly looked around the room. Her eyes rested on Max as he stood in the corner, glowering like a child who had his favorite toy taken by the neighborhood bully.

'So I assume everyone in here knew that bit of information except me," said Becca. "You all probably think I'm some kind of whore, don't you? I'm not proud of the things I've done, but I'm still a good person. I'm saved now and this isn't supposed to be happening. Coming to God is supposed to make everything better.' She seemed to think we ambushed her.

'Becca, this is a Christian family and we practice forgiveness here. I admit I'm not thrilled that my youngest son has a daughter by his older brother's ex-girlfriend, but it's a fact we all have to accept. Now, my concern is the well-being of my grandbaby. I no longer care about the circumstances under which she got here. She's here and she's everything I've always wanted and I am grateful for her. Thank you. We want to help you and Michelle. You're family now, and we don't turn our back on family. Open your eyes child. God is working this out for you,' my mother said.

'Help me? How the hell are you going to help me? I'm 35 years old and I have a child by a 20-year-old. I don't want Max to be my baby's daddy. I don't even know Max. In my eyes he's a little boy. I'm a grown woman. I have grown woman needs. I'm going to have plastic surgery so I can be beautiful again. Max doesn't have a dime to pay for it. He can't pay for clothes, private school, ballet, gymnastics and doctor's visits. I bet he's still on your insurance! I am in love with that man over there, Michael Stokes, Jr.!'

"She rose from her chair and walked over to me with tears in her eyes, yet again begging me to love her.

'I want you, Michael!' She choked out. 'I want to raise my child with you. You know I never let a man touch me after I found out I was pregnant. I haven't had sex in over four years. I had plenty of offers, but none of them were good enough because they weren't you. I didn't mean to sleep with Max, but when he came to console me, he reminded me so much of you that for a moment, I thought he was you. Michael, tell me we can work this out. Tell me we can be a family. You can adopt Michelle as your own. I know you love her, and she loves you too. You were the best thing to happen to me in a long time. Michael, I want you and nobody else will do. Please forgive me and marry me. Please.'

"I was speechless. How do you tell a woman at her wits end that you don't love her and you never really did? Becca reached for my shirt, pulled me to her and placed her face close to mine. Her beautiful green eyes were full of sadness.

'Tell me you want me, too. Michael, please tell me you want me, too.' She clenched my shirt inside her tightly balled fists. I continued to stand there in silence. She searched my face for any kind of emotion. I wasn't going to lie about wanting a future with her. Our time had passed. The only feelings I had for her now were pity, regret, and respect for her as Michelle's mother. I could at least give her that.

'Say it!' she screamed and began beating me in my chest. 'Say it, Binky! Say you want me, too! Please, Binky, please. Say you want me, too!'

"I've had women say they wanted to be with me before, but never like that. I had no idea what to do, so I continued to stand there quietly with my hands by my side. Her pounds against my chest hurt, but I was willing to temporarily withstand the pain if it made her feel better. My dad decided to step in and take control of the situation. I was grateful for his assistance. I'm normally only good at handling high pressure situations if there's a ball in my hand. He came over and pried Becca off me. She was crying hysterically and screaming like she was being abused.

'No, God. This can't be happening to me! I'm supposed to be Mrs. Michael Stokes!'

"All of a sudden, she went mute and her body went limp. In the middle of her hysteria, Becca had fainted. My father caught her as she descended to the floor. He then picked her up and carried her upstairs with my mother following closely behind. Max, Pastor Jenkins, First Lady Bertha, and I remained in the dining room.

'Poor girl,' said Lady Bertha.

'Poor girl,' repeated Max angrily. 'That whore ruined my first time and all anyone can think about is her. Did you hear her? She asked my brother to adopt my child. She basically said I wasn't man enough to be Michelle's father, and all you can say is poor girl. I hate that woman.

Michael, if you want Michelle you can have her. I'm not spending another minute in this house with her or her slut mother.'

'What do you mean your first time? You had plenty of girls before Becca. What about all those women I caught you with in my house?' I asked.

'I wanted you to think I was getting some. Back then, I wanted to be like my big brother. I saw you with a bunch of women, so I wanted to show you I could get women, too. I never slept with any of them. Becca was my first and instead of being with me, the whole time she was wishing it was you. Why do all the good things keep happening to you and I get the leftovers? You got the body and the athletic ability. She's right. That should be your baby. You should be the one straddled with child support for the next 14 years. I used to look up to you, but I see now you're nothing. You're as foul and as lonely as she is. I'm going back to school where I don't have to live in your shadow.'

"Max ran upstairs and soon reappeared with his luggage.

'Son, you shouldn't leave in anger. And you shouldn't turn your back on your child. With God you can get through any situation,' said Pastor Jenkins.

'With all due respect, Rev., this isn't your concern. According to that child, I'm not her daddy anyway, so what difference does it make?'

"Max was really making me mad. He needed to man up.

'Then, Becca was right,' I told him. 'You're not a man. You're a little boy. You hate me? After all I've done for you. Everything I had I was willing to share with you. I was thinking Becca took advantage of you, but you knew what you were doing that night, didn't you? You wanted your big brother's woman, you saw a chance to have her, and you took it. The entire time you stayed with me you were always jealous of me, even though I gave you everything you wanted. How many of your friends were driving a BMW at 16? You are so ungrateful.'

'How would you like to go through life being compared to the great Michael Stokes,' he shot back. 'Every school I went to, I had coaches begging me to try out for their baseball, football, track, and basketball teams to see if I had your athletic ability. I tried out at first, but I never told you. Imagine their disappointment when they realized I was an intellectual and not a jock. Those women you saw me with were only with me because they wanted to meet you. That's why I never slept with them. I knew they wanted you and not me. And you're right, I wanted to find out what Becca had that had you kissing her behind. I used to hear you screaming Becca's name all times of the day and night. I finally get away from you and meet a woman who wants me for me and this happens. I'm in this mess because of you. Yes, I hate you. I don't need your money. I can make it without you. I'm glad you busted your knee. Now you see how we mere mortals do it. How does it feel not to be a god anymore? Not to be making headlines every week? Are you tired of people telling you how good you used to be yet? All hail! The mighty King Michael has been dethroned by his own decaying body!'

"He was really asking for it. 'This isn't about me, and you know it. Max, grow up and accept responsibility for your own actions. You're in this mess because you slept with my ex. You weren't even smart enough to use a condom! Stop trying to pass the blame and stop whining.

You sound like a female. Before you leave, see if Tomeka will let you wear some of her panties,' I yelled.

"Maxwell reared back his head, and spit in my face. I was going to knock his front teeth down his throat, but Pastor Jenkins intervened and pinned me against the wall. He was pretty strong for an old man. Maxwell saw his opportunity to make an exit before losing his ability to breathe. He opened the front door and disappeared into the evening.

"I wasn't about to fight my pastor, so I let him hold me to the wall without a struggle. Pastor Jenkins relaxed his stance when he thought he had given Max enough time to get away. I wiped my face and tried to calm down. I couldn't believe my brother had behaved that way. We were raised in the same house by the same parents. They worked hard to provide for us. We were taught to excel and to try to make good decisions, but when we messed up we were expected to accept responsibility for our actions. What made Max believe that because he was not ready to be a father, he had the right to walk away? I thought his body had been invaded by aliens."

"Pastor Jenkins and his wife tried to calm me down but as far as I was concerned their mouths were moving but nothing of value was being said.

"My father came downstairs and announced that they had revived Becca and she was resting in the guest room. He inquired about Max's whereabouts.

'Your son decided he wasn't ready for fatherhood. He left to go back to school where his only concern is studying for his next test and cuddling with his new girlfriend,' I answered.

'What? He left?'

'Yeah, Pops. He left.'

'Go get him, Jr., and tell him I said get back here.' I very rarely defied my father, but this time I couldn't do what he asked.

'No, sir. If you want him, you have to get him your-self. Right now, I can't stand the sight of him. I'm going to check on my niece, and go to bed. I have a flight to catch in the morning. I have speaking engagements in Rhode Island and Atlanta, a golf tournament in Florida, and then I have to travel to Memphis. I'll be gone for about a week.'

'Okay, son. It's probably best you leave for a while. Don't worry about Becca and the baby. They'll be fine with us. Both of them need someone to show them some love, and we got more than enough of that in this house. Don't stay away too long.'

I was furious. 'Yes sir,' was all I could manage to say. I ran up the steps to read Michelle a bedtime story."

Chapter 27

Food, Friends, and Fellowship
Tee

At about 7:00 p.m. the girls begin to arrive. First were the identical twins Lenora and Lenice, although they don't look very much alike these days. Lenora is married with three kids and with each child it became harder for her to lose the weigh. She filled out so much that she no longer resembles Lenice, who is single and model thin with no kids, unless you count her Chihuahua Webster, who goes almost everywhere she does. They are also distinctly different in personality. Lenora is mild mannered and generally good-natured; Lenice is loud, brutally honest, and hilariously sarcastic. But I don't mind. Every woman needs a friend who will tell it exactly like it is, even if it means occasionally hurting your feelings.

I open the door, Webster waltzes his tiny self in, followed by Lenora with a huge chocolate cake, and then Lenice with a bottle of White Zinfandel.

"We brought comfort food," says Lenora, "and drink," finishes Lenice. "Where's the brokenhearted?"

"She's in her room taking a shower and putting on some clothes. She said she didn't want any company, but I told her she didn't have a choice. Take it in the kitchen. I cooked some fettuccini alfredo with garlic bread, so I hope you're hungry."

"Girl, that stuff is fattening," says Lenice.

"You could use a little fattening. Maybe you could get a man," I tease. "You know in the South they like a woman with a little junk in her trunk."

"Ain't that the skillet calling the kettle black, my single friend? Besides, you know I don't need a man. They are nothing but trouble."

Lenice is also one of the I-N-D-E-P-E-N-D-E-N-T types who will educate anyone who will listen about how she doesn't need a man. I love to tease her about it because you never know what she's going to say.

"Besides, honey, men like my boney behind. Look at my sister. That's what you get when you get a man—a whole lotta assets. It's hard to believe we used to be the same size."

"Hold on, Twin. All this lusciousness came from bearing your niece and nephews, who adore their auntie I might add," countered Lenora.

"And Lords knows I love them. But after they spit on my silk blouse, pee on my satin sheets, and wipe boogers on my linen napkins, I'm more than happy to send Ms. Nasty, Mr. Nastier, and The Booger Man back home to you. That's another thing: Men get you…knocked up. No boyfriend for me. Me, Webster, and Bob are doing just fine."

"Bob? Did you get a new bedroom buddy," I inquire.

"Honey, she doesn't have a man. Bob stands for battery operated boyfriend. You can find her at home with a cold, electrical appliance, while I'm at home being stroked by a living, breathing, warm, well-endowed man. And he loves all of this!" Lenora takes her arm and makes a huge circular motion around her wide derriere for emphasis.

I laugh and head back to the front to see who's ringing the doorbell. I open the door and in waltzes the biggest diva this side of the Mississippi. Ms. Tiffany Tate. She put the "B" in bourgeoisie, but under that $80 tailor made bra, that's pushing up her large breasts, is a heart of gold. By birthright Tiffany is a member of Memphis' rich political circle. The Tates have been involved in politics here in Memphis for over 70 years, but Tiffany wants no parts of it. She once told me she had been privy to too many underhanded, back door deals to ever run for an office.

Her exact words were, "I want to die with a clear conscience. In politics, to get anything done, one hand has to wash the other and if you're washing your hands with filthy people, you're gonna get a little dirty too."

I always thought that statement was flawed, coming from a woman who has been seeing a married man for over a decade. She even bore his namesake. Tiffany is also the epitome of a southern belle. Her strong southern accent leaves no doubt what region she is from. I always thought it was cute, though.

She greets me with an embrace and a, "Hi, sugah. Hurry up and shut the door before you let those mosquitoes in. I absolutely abhor those little blood suckers. I brought Sandy some tea. A good cup of chamomile tea always calms my nerves when I've been upset, especially when it's by a vile man." Her dialect reminds me of Scarlett in "Gone with the Wind."

"Thank you, sugah!" I say mimicking her. "We're all in the kitchen."

Lenice can't stand Tiffany. She said she never felt that Tiffany was genuine, and that she was putting on airs. I never thought she was putting on airs; she was Tiffany being Tiffany. Lenice is always throwing verbal jabs and Tiffany refuses to be anyone's punching bag. Some nights

I end up playing referee between the two. I hope tonight isn't going to be one of those nights.

My sister enters the kitchen smelling like honeysuckle body wash and looking less than rested, thanks to the puffiness around her eyes. Before she can take two steps Lenora, Lenice, and Tiffany all encircle her with a group hug.

"Okay, ladies. Don't start asking me a bunch of questions like how I'm doing, because you're going to make me start crying all over again. I'm doing as well as can be expected for a woman who found out her man is still having an affair. Something smells really good. Is that fettuccini? Tee, pass me a plate."

I hear the front door open and Teresa appears dressed in her police uniform and an attitude.

"Don't you know it's killers, murders, and rapists out here? Here you are, sitting up in the house with the doors unlocked. You better be glad I'm off the clock, or I would give you a stern lecture about safety. Hand me a glass and pass me that bottle of wine."

Teresa is a police officer and a lush. For years we've all wondered how she manages to keep her job. According to her, she only drinks when she's off. She once told me that after seeing the worst of humanity, in order to get up the next day and function properly, she needs a little something in addition to the joy of Jesus. I tried to talk her into getting some help. She told me to shut up and mind my own business, because she wasn't hurting anybody but herself. I never mentioned it again after that, but I do whatever I can to curb it a little bit. She is the poster child for a functioning alcoholic.

At 42, Teresa is the eldest of our group. She also has the longest running relationship. She and her sweeter-than-pie husband, Zachary, have been married since they were 19. What they have is what every woman longs for, everlasting love. The door bell rings, again.

I also invited my manicurist Cassie. My sister and I have a standing appointment with her every Thursday night, but since Sandy is in crisis, I invited her over to the house. A little pampering might do her some good. Cassie gives the best hand and foot massages but she isn't exactly known for having tact, though. Her tongue can get sharper than the clippers she uses on my nails. She walks into the kitchen carrying her portable station and almost trips when Ms. Tiara runs across her foot.

"Aw, how sweet of you to rescue a cat from the Humane Society. It must have been burned really badly in a fire. It's as bald as a baby's bottom," says Cassie.

"What? Don't insult my cat like that. You country bumpkin, that cat is a purebred of the highest proportions. It's called a Sphinx," Sandy sneers.

"You mean you paid good money for a naked cat? Girl, I swear the more money you get, the more you waste. There are eight cats in this room and all of them are supposed to be covered in hair, or at least have the ability to grow it. Yours ain't supposed to look like a kindergartener's any more than that cat is supposed to look like it's strung out on drugs and freezing its behind off." Everyone but Sandy is overcome with laughter.

"You are so nasty," says Sandy.

"No, I'm real. I may not be rich yet, but I know a bad decision when I see one. And buying a cat that I'm sure you paid way too much for, that's going to scare all the kids on your block, is one. I bet your own kids don't even play with that thing."

Unfortunately, she's right. Nicole and Donovin think Ms. Tiara has a disease and won't touch her. Even Webster, the Chihuahua, isn't interested in her and he usually barks at anything that moves.

I look at my sister and shake my head. "Hush, I told you when you bought that thing that it was funny looking. So don't get mad because someone else has confirmed my statement."

I don't mind helping sooth my sister's wounds when she has a real injury, but what Cassie said wasn't even a scratch. Sometimes she can be way too sensitive over nothing.

"Shut up Tee before I forget I like you. I didn't come into my own kitchen for a cat fight, especially one about a cat," retorts Sandy.

"Tee, why did you invite these two?" Teresa asks pointing at Lenice and Cassie. "They're not exactly the comforting kind. And why do you two always act like you're on your period?"

"What? I haven't said a thing," defends Lenice.

"But you will, mamacita. It's only a matter of time. Pass me your glasses. You two need this wine more than I do."

While Teresa distributes the wine, I fix her a plate of piping hot pasta. "You're not supposed to drink on an empty stomach, and I know you haven't eaten, so take this, too."

"What day is it?" she asks reaching for the plate.

"Monday. Why?" answers Lenora.

"A *Girlfriends* marathon is about begin. Come on. Let's take this in the den."

We all watch one of our favorite female-centered sitcoms, periodically making comments. After viewing four consecutive episodes, we have all cleared our plates twice, emptied our glasses, and enjoyed Lenora's chocolate cake. Cassie has worked her magic on all who desired her services and is packing up her portable station to leave.

"We need more positive black families on television," comments Tiffany. "All these single women shows are depressing to me. They always make us act like puppies in heat. You don't have to sleep with every man you date."

"What do you know about positive black families? You're the other woman? You kill me talking about the demise of the black family when you're contributing to it. You're dating another woman's husband. I don't understand why you're here," hurls Lenice. "You couldn't possibly have sympathy for Sandy's situation. Women like you are the reason she's hurt. That's what's wrong with men now. The world is full of dumb women with low self-esteem who don't mind borrowing someone else's man. Then, there's the ones who choose to turn a blind eye to the fact that their man is cheating, because they don't want to be alone. Men act the way they do because we let them. If more women would tell men with wives and girlfriends to go home, they'd be faithful because they wouldn't have anyone to cheat with. And if more women would kick a brother out when he cheats, they would suffer the consequences of their actions and think twice before doing it again. I am alone in my bed because I refuse to let another lying, cheating, low down, good for nothing man enter my life and stomp on my heart. Check yourself sweetheart. You're pathetic."

I bet Lenice was waiting for a reason to unleash her verbal AK-47 on Tiffany and her statement about black families gave her one. Here we go again! Where's my referee whistle?

Chapter 28

Watch Your Back
Michael

It's nice that Dr. Foster enjoys my storytelling since we are on day three. We took a break so she could go to the restroom. However, I don't feel like we're making any progress.

I sit on the plane and thank God for his generosity. This time a year ago, I was playing football with a $22 million contract and lucrative endorsements deals with Nike, Gillette, and Gatorade. The world loved me and I loved it back. I was spending a ridiculous amount of money on clothing, cars, jewelry, and women, but none of it had any significance. After I got injured, I thought life was over if I couldn't play for thousands of cheering fans. But God showed me that my life can have even more value. And he continues to show me favor. I retained my endorsement deals, and I've got speaking engagements booked for the next three months. I enjoy what I do. I especially like talking to youth and showing them that they can do just about anything. God is good. Now that I have Michelle, I have something new to strive for. Even though she isn't mine, I plan to make sure her life is smooth sailing from now on. She'll never have to sleep in another car again.

Dr. Foster returns to her seat and I once again, re-sume the story of my life.

"My engagement in Rhode Island went well. I spoke to a group of students at a local college. My message centered on my newfound theme, 'Life Is Full of Detours, So Be Prepared to Travel Rough Terrain.' After taking pictures and signing autographs, I went to the airport to catch a plane to Atlanta. I was scheduled as the celebrity guest at a private charity dinner for several wealthy African Americans. My Pops called after my plane landed.

'Son, Becca is gone.'

'What?'

'Yeah, son, she must have left last night while we were asleep. But she left Michelle here with us.'

'That's a good thing. Did she leave a note?'

'Yeah.'

'Well, what did it say?'

'We'll talk about it when you get back.'

'No, Pop. I want to know now.'

'It said,

I'm leaving my baby here for now, but tell Michael that we belong together. If I can't have him no one will. We're destined to be together, and I'll make him see it if it kills him.'

'This woman is crazy. She lies about her promiscuity, sleeps with my little brother, has his daughter, and somehow, in her warped mind, I'm supposed to look past all that and make her my wife!'

'There's something else, son. She stole your mother's ATM card, her Mercedes, and the necklace from Tiffany's that you bought her for Mother's Day. She had already withdrawn $600 from the machine before your mother noticed her card was gone.'

'What! That necklace is worth $20,000! Pop, did you call the police?'

'No, son, I didn't. I was hoping we could handle this quietly. She is the mother of my granddaughter. Can't you call a private detective or something to track her down?'

"Even after he and my mother had been wronged, my father still wanted to turn the other cheek. Well, I wasn't that saved, yet. As far as I was concerned, when I found that woman, she was going to pay.

'Dad, this is not television. This is real life. Call the police and report the car, the money, and the jewelry stolen. Give them my cell phone number so I can provide any information they need to help them locate Becca. Not only did she steal from you, but she threatened my life. I know she's Michelle's mother, but at this point, she's also a criminal. We have to treat her that way.'

'Okay, son. If you think it's best. I'll call as soon as we hang up. But what do I tell Michelle. She's been asking about her mother since she woke up.'

'Tell her that Becca had to leave for a while and that she said for her to stay at the house with you guys and be a good girl.'

'Why don't you tell her? She just walked in.'

"My father put Michelle on the phone.

'Hey, Michelle. What are you doing?'

'I just finished eating breakfast with Grandma and Auntie Tomeka. I had oatmeal with a smiley face in it and cina-nin-nin toast.'

"I couldn't help but laugh at the way she butchered cinnamon.

'Really? I know it was good. She used to make that for me when I was your age.'

'Yup, real good. When are you coming to get me?' she inquired in a very business-like tone.

'I'll be back in a few days. But don't worry. Grandma and Granddaddy will take good care of you until I get back.'

'Okay, but you forgot Mommy.'

'What do you mean?'

'My mommy takes good care of me, too.'

'I know she does, but Mommy had to leave last night, so Grandma and Granddaddy will take care of you until she gets back.' I was hoping that news didn't upset her.

'When is she coming back? I need her. Who's gonna sing me to sleep, help me tie my shoes, and brush my teefs?'

'I know you need her, but your grandparents can help you do all of that for now. I'm sure she'll be back soon. I have to go, Michelle. Be a big girl for me. I'll call you tonight before you go to bed.'

'Okay, Daddy. I love having a daddy. Hurry back so we can play tea party.'

'I love having you in my life, too, Michelle. Now, gimme a kiss.'

'Muuuuuuah! Bye, Daddy.'

'Son, that little girl adores you,' my father said after retrieving the phone from Michelle.

'I know, Pop, but do me a favor. Help me break her from calling me Daddy. That name should be reserved for Max. She needs to learn to call me Uncle Mike.'

'Me and your mother will work on that. Son, be careful. From the sound of Becca's note, she's going to be a thorn in your side. You don't think she would actually try to kill you do you?'

'She's just blowing smoke to get her way. I'll be fine, Pop. Don't worry. Do you need the money she took? I can send you some more if you do.'

'Not at all. We're still spending the money you sent us for our anniversary. You take care of you, right now. I know I don't tell you often, but you make me and your mother real proud.'

'Thanks, Pop. I'll watch my back and you do the same. Becca is not in her right mind, and she may still be in town plotting something.' I got off the phone wondering how any mother could abandon her child like that.

"I met Peter at our hotel in the high-dollar community of Buckhead and brought him up to speed about the recent events. I had previously told him that Becca had resurfaced, and that I was waiting for the results of the paternity test. I never told him the outcome, though. He assured me that everything would be alright after Becca calmed down. I hoped he was right.

"I decided to visit Lennox Mall. I wanted to get a new Ipod, and I needed to get my mind off my troubles for a little while. I figured women watching in the mall might help. The women in the black fashion capital of the United States always have their sexy game on.

"It was nice outside, so I decided to walk. On my way to the elevator, I knocked on the door to Peter's room to see if he wanted to accompany me. He did, but he was on the phone with his wife, and said he would meet me in the lobby after he finished his call. I had the strangest feeling that someone was watching me, but I didn't think too much of it. Peter came down shortly.

'I made the mistake of telling the Mrs. that we were going to Lennox. Remind me to stop by the Fendi store and pick her up some new bag they have,' he said.

"I nodded and together we stepped out into the late afternoon sun. They call that place Hotlanta for a reason. I felt the familiar warmth of the sun's rays beaming on my face. It wasn't long before beads of perspiration began to form on my bald head. As an athlete who played in all of the elements, this was always a welcomed sensation. I prefer sunny heat to overcast skies and cold or wet weather any day. I reached into the pocket of my shirt and pulled out my favorite pair of Gucci sunglasses. We slowly made our way to the curb to walk across Peachtree Rd. I knew we were jaywalking, but neither of us saw a need to cross at the light. At some point, there would be a definite break in the traffic that would easily allow us to get across the semi-busy street with no problem.

That break soon came and we set out in equal stride. Peter and I crossed the first two lanes. A blue Mustang sped out of the driveway of the hotel. We were directly in its path and the car was not slowing down to let us pass. It was actually gaining momentum. This car was going to hit us! Peter was on his cell phone and wasn't paying any attention. I leaped in his direction to get us both out of harm's way. We narrowly escaped being flattened and landed in the middle of the lanes for opposing traffic. It was only by the grace of God that the cars coming from that direction had plenty of time to stop. The Mustang, however, kept speeding down the street.

"Peter and I were basically unharmed. He had torn pants and a minor scratch on his knee. I banged my elbow pretty hard when we fell, but I'm used to getting knocked around. So, I shook it off. Several people ran to us to see if we were alright. I wondered if someone had tried to kill us or if the driver wasn't paying attention? Peter got up and went straight into manager mode, trying to stop a passerby who was taking pictures.

'Sir, please stop taking pictures. Mr. Stokes is not on display. I'm only going to ask you once,' he commanded.

"Peter is a former football player himself. He only played two seasons before being released from his contract. Rather than try to join another team, he went back to school to finish his degree in marketing. After graduation, he joined a sports management company and later formed his own. He still works out regularly and can bench press 500 pounds. He's kind of stocky, and you don't want to mess with him. The man did the smart thing and the put camera away.

"Peter and I collected ourselves and headed back to the hotel. We were sure to cross at the light that time. One of the young men at the valet station approached us. His name tag said Hector.

'Mr. Stokes, I saw what happened. Do you want me to call you an ambulance or the police or something? I can give them my statement if you like.'

'No, I'm fine. There's no need to call the police. But tell me, what would you say in your statement? What did you see?' I asked.

'I saw the driver of the car, sir. Before she got in, she was standing in the grass smoking a cigarette. It was a white woman with blonde hair. She didn't look good, sir. I thought she was ill.'

'Did she have green eyes?'

'I could not tell the color of her eyes, but I saw the way she looked at you when you came out of the hotel. It was the look of someone who wanted to kill. Before I knew it, she had jumped in her blue Mustang and was trying to run you over.'

"Peter pulled out his wallet and took out two crisp one hundred dollar bills. He handed them to the valet. 'If anyone asks you, you didn't see a thing and this conversation never happened,' he instructed.

'Yes, sir. My name is Ling and I don't know a thing. Thank you so much, sir.' Hector ran off to get the keys of a woman driving a Bentley who had been impatiently waiting nearby.

"Neither Peter nor I said another word until we boarded the empty elevator and the doors closed. 'I'm not 100% convinced that was Becca, but I do think we should cancel tonight's engagement, the one in Memphis, the golf tournament, and any others until we are sure that was the doing of an inattentive driver,' said Peter.

'I know it was Becca, and no way. I won't live in fear for anybody.'

'Being cautious is not living in fear, Mike.'

'I'm not going to stop living my life because of her. That's exactly what she wants—for me to be unhappy because she's unhappy. I am going to this event and every other one I scheduled. God has given me an assignment. I can't motivate others to excellence if I'm holed up in my house.'

'Jesus Christ, Mike. If you won't cancel, I'm getting additional security.'

'I can take care of myself.'

'If that were true, we wouldn't have almost been road kill today. I don't care what you want. Besides, even Jesus was smart enough to travel with his disciples. If he needed an entourage to help protect him, what makes you think you don't? Although, it didn't help him much in the end, did it?'

"I hate when he uses Biblical references in jest. It seems so blasphemous.

'Watch yourself, Peter.'

'Okay. Lighten up. It was a joke. When we leave for tonight's dinner we will have armed security accompanying us, and that's final. I suggest you go to your room and get some rest and I would appreciate it if you would stay there until it's time for us to leave.'

"I thought Peter was overreacting but I didn't feel like arguing, so I agreed.

"Did you ever find out what happed to your mother's Mercedes?" asked Dr. Foster.

"Yeah, a couple of days later the Atlanta police raided a chop shop and found it there. The guys they arrested said Becca traded it for the stolen Mustang she was driving."

"The dinner in Atlanta went well, except for me wondering if a killer was in the crowd the whole time. When we returned to the hotel, I was given a note by the front desk attendant removing all doubt in my mind of whether it was her or not behind the wheel of that car. It simply read,

If you want to say alive, you should be by my side.
XOXO

"That was the first of many. I left Atlanta, and did the golf tournament in Florida. I was leaving there when we met. She left a note at my hotel there as well."

I tell Dr. Foster about what happened with Tee in Memphis, bringing her completely up to date on my dealings with her.

"For the most part, Becca's left me alone except for leaving her calling card at the front desk of the hotels I've been staying in. I must say, though, the one she left today of her and me being murdered in effigy has been the worst so far. It's creepy knowing that someone is watching you.

"That's my story, Doc. I'm your normal, average, every day, retired NFL player with a niece who thinks she's my daughter and a crazy ex-girlfriend who is the mother of my niece, who wishes that she were my wife and is trying to kill me because she can't be my wife. On top of that, I met a wonderful woman in Memphis, but I'm afraid to pursue her because I could get her killed. Your thoughts?" I am anxious to get her feedback.

Dr. Foster sits back in her seat. Her expression is quite pensive. When she is ready to respond, she sits up straight and turns her body toward me. I do the same. We are now facing one another.

"You do have quite a bit of irregularity going on. I'm pleased to see that you have a healthy perspective on things. You are not bitter or angry at the loss of your football career. You seem to be handling the fact of your brother and ex-girlfriend had sex and produced a child very well. I find it refreshing that you have removed yourself from the equation."

I give her a puzzled look.

"What I mean by that is you are more upset about their current lack of adequate parenting skills than you are about the betrayal of your trust. The fact that you are willing to take on the parental responsibilities of Michelle shows that you have great character. You are realistic about the fact that your life is in danger, and this may not be the best time for you to pursue a relationship. The fear you have of death is completely natural. It's actually healthy. I would be concerned if you were not taking Becca's threats seriously. Now, what you need to do is work with the authorities to put a plan in place to capture the woman who is trying to kill you. Concerning your brother, my advice is give him some time. You said yourself that the two of you are cut from the same homespun cloth. A man reared the way he was will not be able to turn his back on his child for long in good conscience. This is a lot for a young man to take in at once. He needs some time to process the idea of being a father. Most men have several months during the pregnancy to do this. Maxwell has only had a few days. The key is to continue to let him know that he has a support system.

"Here is that prescription for sleeping pills I promised you. Get some sleep, son. Your weariness is definitely beginning to show. My number is on it as well. Feel free to call me if you need to talk again. Oh good. Our plane is getting ready to land. I can't wait to see my baby sister. Buckle up. Captain's orders. Thanks again for the autographed picture for my grandson. I can't wait to see his face when I give it to him. Do you mind if I take a picture of the two of us with my camera phone?"

I muster a smile for her camera. That's it? I've spent three days telling Dr. Foster all my troubles and all she really had to say was that I got it under control. She only asked two questions and they were about my car and my sleeping habits. I guess it's a good thing that I don't need to be committed to a psychiatric ward. She is right, though. I should devise a plan to become the hunter instead of the prey.

Tomorrow is the official release date of my book, and I have my first book signing at a small African American bookstore near the Akron Art Museum. I can't think of a better place to unveil my rekindled talents than home. I'm hoping for a bestseller.

I wonder what Tee is doing? I need to tell her about Becca, but how do I do that without scaring her away.

Chapter 29

Love Me Tender
Tee

After Lenice's mean-spirited comment, Tiffany's eyes widen. She bats her eyelashes a few times and issues a heartfelt reply.

"I sicken myself, but I've been doing it so long I don't know how to end it. Quincy pays all my bills. Don't you think I get tired of being the other women? I used to believe him when he said he was going to leave his wife so we could be together. After 10 years, who am I kidding? But I'm trapped. I can't afford the life I'm accustomed to on my own. My family has money. I don't. They cut me off financially years ago. I've never had a job a day in my life, unless you count occasionally volunteering at the hospital with Tee. I used to think he really loved me and Quincy II."

Tiffany looks around the room as if she is searching for some understanding. Her small, sweet voice now sounds horribly shrill. It reminds me of something I once heard in a parody of an opera.

"So go ahead and hate me. You couldn't hate me half as much as I hate myself. At least I allow myself to be loved and give love in return, even if it's the wrong kind of love from the wrong man. But you, Lenice, you're so mean. You treat any man that approaches you like he's trying to steal your purse. You're a bitter woman who got her heart broken and some kind of way you came to the conclusion that you have the patent on pain. We've all been hurt, but instead of getting past the pain, you Lenice, you harbor it in your heart, where it festers and spreads like cancer. If you don't stop, it's going to consume you. I'm surprised you have any friends at all, as rude and crabby as you are. I know what my problem is, but have you acknowledged yours?"

Tiffany had said a mouthful. The heated stare from her brown eyes is searing through Lenice like she's attempting to dig a hole into her soul. We all wait for Lenice to respond with her usual rude wit, but she says nothing. Instead, she slowly turns her head toward the large bay window to her right and tightly closes her eyes as if she is trying to shut out a dreadful sight.

The break in this unsisterly conversation is long enough for Sandy to jump in and change the subject. "Did Tee tell you about her new man? I know she didn't, because she didn't even tell me but Edger believes my little sister done snagged herself a retired football player, MVP Michael Stokes!"

"That fine specimen of muscular manhood, Michael Stokes?" chirps Lenora.

"They are one and the same," answers Sandy.

"I don't have a man," I say. "We haven't even been out on a date. He merely said he thought I was nice. Remind me to tape Edgar's mouth shut." I could tell them about what happened earlier today, but I don't want to. Reliving those moments will only dampen my spirits. This cheering up session isn't going as planned. We're supposed to be laughing and forming a Soul Train Line by now. Maybe Teresa can give Sandy some advice on how to handle her situation.

"Teresa, were you ever suspicious that Zack was cheating on you?"

"Tee, please. My husband is married to a cop. I have a license to bust a cap in his behind and a shrink on staff to say I was mentally incapable of telling right from wrong at the time. Zack is a lot of things, but stupid isn't one of them. I don't worry about such things. I prefer to stay prayed up. I pray over him, our marriage, and our son constantly. So far the good Lord has kept all of us intact. Plus, when you go looking for something, you might find it. I don't believe in all this keeping tabs on men, going through his pockets and his cell phone. Calling all times of day asking where he is and what he's doing. I have real crimes to solve, so I don't need to spend my time playing detective at home. Me and my man got us a good thing. I'll admit that it hasn't always been sunny days. Marriage is work, but as long as both people are dedicated to making it work, you'll get through. But we all have our shortcomings. I will tell you girls something I've never told anybody else. About five years into our marriage I cheated on Zack."

That news jolts everybody in the room. Teresa and Zachary are our example of what love is supposed to be.

"I felt terrible and told my baby the same night it happened. He didn't say a single mean word to me or even raise his voice. He asked me if I had a desire to do it again. After I swore to him that it would never happen again, he said that's all he needed. I even gave him permission to cheat on me so we would be even. He took my hand in his and said the most beautiful thing. He said, 'Resa, you were my first, my last, and my only. Another woman doesn't even compare to you. So why would I even waste my time? An eye for an eye just makes us both blind on one side. If I'm gon' see us through this life, I need to have two good eyes.'

"That man has held me up when I felt low and carried me when I thought I couldn't take another step. He supported me when I said I wanted to be a cop. He even helped me learn to shoot straight. The first time I had to kill someone in the line of duty, it was Zack that got me through. I was an emotional wreck. And even though he knows I drink too much sometimes, he loves me in spite of my flaws. So, Sandy, I'm not going to tell you whether or not you should salvage your marriage. We all make mistakes and sometimes we make them more than once. You have to pray and ask the Lord what you should do about that one. But this too shall soon pass."

Teresa had graced us with wisdom gained through experience. She must have seen in our eyes that we were hungry for more because she kept on talking.

"Sandy, you say you love your husband. Well, forgiveness is the greatest gift you can give someone you love. Now ladies, it's been nice, but I'm old and I can't kick it like I used to. Zachery doesn't go to bed until I come home, and when he stays up too late, he's down right ornery in the morning.

"As for the rest of you, all men aren't bad Lenice. You need to release some of that aggression you have. Go work out. I suggest you start with the punching bag or try kick boxing 'cause girl, your attitude is horrible and any little thing sets you off. Stop attacking Tiffany 'cause she is already covered in bruises. Can't you see her relationship is eating her alive? And stop running from love, 'cause it's the one thing we all need to be our best. Everyone in this room has been hurt by a man, but we dusted ourselves off and kept going. This life is meant to be shared with someone special. But I guarantee, a man won't say as much as hello to a woman who's scowling at him. 'Cause if you didn't know it, you exude attitude 24/7!

"And you, Ms. Tiffany Tate, if you want a good man, you've got to be a good woman. You're a queen and you've let Quincy make you his concubine. Makes no sense to me that you would want to have a cheater for yourself. All he's going to do is cheat on you.

"You're a smart girl. You have a degree. I suggest you start using it to take care of you and your son. So what if you won't be able to afford the best of everything right away. Work hard at your career and you'll get there. Never let a man's money be the leash around your neck. Quincy has had you by the throat for years. Quincy II is getting older and it won't be long before he puts it all together. Do you really want to explain to your child that you're the mistress? More importantly, think about the kind of example you are setting for him. How would you like him to grow up to be the kind of man who cheats? Would that make you proud?

"Lenora, I wasn't going to say anything, but as your friend I'm going to tell you that you could stand to lose some of that weight you think so highly of. Yeah, you got a big booty, but the rest of you is big, too. Do it before heart disease, high cholesterol, or diabetes gets a hold of you. I don't want you skinny, but I do want you healthy. Well, that's my two cents."

We all listened without interruption or comment, except Lenora, who simply replies, "I'm working on it." Leniece continues to look out of the window.

"Good night ladies I need to go home to my man. Tee, come lock the door behind me," Teresa instructs.

I can't let her leave without imparting some of her wisdom to me. "Wait, Teresa. I have a question for you?

Where are all the good men? I believe I'm a good woman, but I can't seem to catch a break. Every time I think I've met my prince, he turns out to be a frog. I'm tempted to make a t-shirt that says I'm a good woman. If I wear it every day, maybe somebody wonderful will notice while he's checking out my boobs." I laugh and everyone laughs with me.

"Well that might not be a bad idea, but the only sure place I know to find him is on your knees. I know you've been praying for God to send you a good man, but keep praying. I've watched you over the years, and you've gone from a shy, skinny, bratty teenager to a beautiful, successful young woman who dominates any project she undertakes. If I had to guess, God hadn't sent your man yet 'cause he needed to do some work on you. I'd say he's done an excellent job and your prince will be along soon enough."

"Thanks, Teresa. One more question. Do you think my decision to wait until I'm married to have sex again is old fashioned? Men keep leaving me because I won't sleep with them."

"Old fashioned, no. Righteous, yes. And the root word is R-I-G-H-T. If doing the right thing were easy, then everybody would do it. If a man leaves you because you are striving to be righteous, he is not the man for you. These young people today hop in and out of one another's pants like rabbits in heat. God made sex for the marriage bed. I've been married 23 years. Do you think Zachary would have felt like he couldn't wait to make me his wife if I was giving it to him anytime and anyplace he wanted? He was 17 when met. All he thought about was sex. I let him know I was not put on this earth simply to clear his acne. If he wanted me, he had to do right by me.

All this sexing with no marriage and no commitment is ridiculous. That's not how you get a man. Learn how to cook. Stroke his ego and be a help to him. Learn his heart. Give him love. Make him feel like his life is better with you in it and what you bring to the table he'd be hard pressed to find with someone else. That's how you get a husband, not by sexing him senseless. Sex is only a small part of the relationship. I admit that it is important but it shouldn't come into play until you've learned what type of man he is and that takes time. Now, come lock the door. Good night, ladies!"

Teresa's exit prompts everyone else to do the same. Kisses, hugs, and promises of support are all exchanged as the girls file out of Sandy's home. My sister decides to stay up for a while and watch TV. I think I'll retreat to the guest room. I should still have some clothes here from previous sleepovers. Considering all she's been through today, it would probably be best if I spent the night.

"Tee, I know you meant well tonight, but the next time you want to cheer me up, please don't invite the girls over. The only reason I feel better is because they showed me that they are more messed up than you or I will ever be. On second thought, Teresa and Lenora can come, but leave the rest of them to their pessimistic, unhappy existences," says Sandy.

"I was thinking the same thing, big sister. Don't stay up too late. I love you."

"I love you too, boo."

I turn the corner and head upstairs to relax. Once in the guest room, I take off my clothes, slip between the covers, and think about what Teresa said about praying for a man. Now wouldn't be a bad time to talk to God again.

Father, I know you see me down here. I know you see my tears every time a man tells me he can't date me, because I won't have premarital sex with him. I'm asking you to please bless me with a good Christian man in my life. I don't really care if he has money or incredible looks. I just want a man with a good heart who knows how to love a woman. And in the meantime, help me to avoid the bad selections I've been making out of loneliness.

Lord, bless Sandy and her marriage. Show her what you would have her to do. Bless Patrick and the kids. He made a mistake, but I know he's not a bad man. I'm asking you to help him with his weaknesses, and make him the faithful husband my sister deserves. Lord, watch over my friends and bless them, too. Give Tiffany the courage to stand on her own two feet and not depend on the money of a married man. Soften Lenice's heart. She's been hurt so many times that she's become bitter, angry, and doubtful that love really exists. Blow some kisses her way, so she knows that you love her and you haven't forgotten her. Thank you for placing Teresa in our lives to give counsel. Watch over her as she works to protect the citizens of Memphis. Amen.

My phone chimes to indicate that I've received a text message.

"Hey, beautiful. I made a huge mistake the other night. I'm sorry and I miss you. I came by your office today to apologize in person but you had already left. Please call me. Mac III"

Fat chance! The phone rings. It's Patrick, calling like he said he would. Let's see what he has to say for himself.

Chapter 30

I Miss Tee
Michael

My book signing at The Mental Motherland bookstore is going extremely well! The store isn't large enough to handle the number of people who showed up. The line is out the door and around the block. Friends, fans, and family have come to buy the book and wish me well. I truly appreciate their support.

According to my publisher, 3,000 orders have already come through online. This is a reason to celebrate! But it would be nice to have someone other than family to share my success with. I can't stop thinking about Tee. I only spent a short amount of time with her, but there is something special about her. It's been so long since I've had a special lady to share in my triumphs. I know if she were here, she would be as happy for me as I am, if not more. I have to see her, and I have to see her soon. But how? I've got this crazy woman after me, and I don't want to get her hurt. Wait a minute. If Becca is afraid to fly then I'll have to take Tee somewhere where she won't follow.

Chapter 31

Good Women Unite!
Tee

The next morning I wake up feeling energized, and I have an idea. After my quiet time, I shower, dress, and check on my sister, who is still sleeping soundly. I see an empty bottle of White Zinfandel in bed with her. She'll probably remain that way for a while. I have got to get to work.

I arrive at Innovations and head straight to the graphic design department to see Prodigy. Prodigy is our extremely talented graphic designer. We call him that because he graduated from high school at 15 and finished art school a week before his 17th birthday. He's right where I knew he would be, in his office playing chess on his computer against his cousin Taylor. Each morning he and Taylor get to work early and play a game together. Prodigy says it's like mental push-ups for him and helps to prepare him for his daily task of helping our company maintain its creative edge. They must be working, because since Prodigy joined Innovations two years ago, we have won numerous awards for our print ads and bill board designs. I tell him my idea, and he assures me that he can create a graphic I'll love. I have no doubt that I am in capable hands.

I go to my office and place my "do not disturb" sign on the door and lock it. There is genius at work here, and I don't need Katty Kathy, Edgar, or anyone else ruining my intellectual groove. An hour later, Prodigy emerges with a mock-up of my idea. As usual, he has worked his magic. At that moment, the "I'm A Good Woman" brand is born, and so is the logo for my new line of women's motivational products. I go online and purchase the domain name www.imagoodwoman.com. My joke has turned into my latest business venture. If I'm feeling dejected and lonely, how many other women across the globe feel that way when they're in the dating dumps? I bet there are millions. With these products, we can remind ourselves how good we are rather than waiting for someone else to take the time to tell us or show us. We'll be sisters doing it for ourselves.

I know with my marketing savvy, I can make this work. My church is having a women's conference soon, and that's when "I'm A Good Woman" will make its debut. I bet I can sell t-shirts, mugs, and more, but my ultimate goal is to encourage women who are going through. We all doubt our self-worth from time to time and need a little encouragement. Well, from now on whenever a woman feels that way, I want her to put on her "I'm A Good Woman" shirt and go look in the mirror. I want her to remember all the good things she's done and feel good about herself. Inspiration can come from the most interesting places.

As I am placing the mock-ups on easels in my office, a large white envelope slides across the floor from beneath the door. I pick it up and turn it over to see who it's from. There's no address or return address on the front. Only the words, 'Open Me'. Who am I, Alice in Wonderland? Inside is a round-trip plane ticket to Jamaica and a note:

I promised you a first date to rival all first dates. How about Jamaica, mon? Let me take you on a quick weekend getaway. I know this is your weekend off, because I checked with your assistant. I won't take no for an answer.

Michael

Jamaica with Michael? I've only known him for two days. My sister's surprise party is tonight, and I'm sure I'll be wiped out afterward. We planned it the weekend prior to her actual birthday to throw her off. How dare he assume that I don't have anything to do just because it's my weekend off. Before I call and tell him this invitation is much too forward, I decide to ask Sandy what she thinks. I bet she's still at home hiding from the world. Patrick explained everything to me last night, but I'm not sure I believe him yet. I'm waiting for him to email me some evidence to corroborate his story.

Sandy answers the phone in a very chipper voice. I'm glad she's in a better mood today. I tell her about Michael's invitation and she quickly says, "Go."

"What? But I barely even know him."

"That's true, but what you do know is that you need a vacation. He already knows where you stand on having sex. Go get some wind in your hair and some sand between your toes. And the best part is it's free. If him trying to get in your pants concerns you that much, ask him to get two rooms. For once in your life, stop over analyzing everything and have fun! Be sure to ask him about his stalker. I have to go."

"Sandy, why are you rushing me off the phone?"

"Because I'm busy"

"Busy doing what?"

"None of your business, Tee. Now, get of my phone or I'm going to hang up on you."

"I'll go, but I'm taking you out tonight."

"No," Sandy replies.

"Yes. Be ready at 7:30 p.m. and wear something sexy. I have to meet a prospective client tonight, and I need you to have 'your girls' there to help me land him." I lie.

"What? When did you start using my body to land clients?"

"Tonight. I got the 411 that he likes big boobs, and you know I have little tits. So, tonight I need yours. Be ready at 7:30 or else."

"I hate you. If you were any kind of sister you would allow me to stay at home and wallow in self-pity. How much should I have out?"

"Unfortunately for you, I'm not any kind of sister. I am Cassandra Fiona Long-Pierce's sister, and I'm using you for my personal gain. Have everything out but your areolas."

"You're kidding, right?"

"Of course I am! I didn't tell you to have them exposed. I told you to have them there. I'm sure he can use his imagination to figure out the rest." I am not letting her go until she agrees to come.

"Okay," she says reluctantly. Now get off my phone and call Michael." The next sound I hear is the dial tone. Mean hussy.

Chapter 32

Two Can Play That Game
Sandy

My sister doesn't know a good deal when it's sitting in front of her. The man didn't ask her to marry him. He asked her to go to Jamaica. I'm glad I got the munchies and ordered some food from my favorite specialty grocery store, Sebastian's. Sebastian is a senior citizen, but his grandson, Armondo, is a sexy 21 year old who has been flirting with me since he was teenager, sacking my groceries. Back then I would completely ignore him, because he was a baby. He's all grown up now and property of the United States Army.

I called the store to see if I could get them to deliver my comfort foods, and Armondo happened to be there helping his grandfather out before he leaves for his first deployment in Iraq. He offered to deliver my groceries personally and here he is. I haven't seen him since he was home two years ago. The army definitely agrees with him. He's put on a few pounds and hit the gym. I don't know if it's the buzz cut or the long eyelashes, but I'm liking what I'm seeing.

I watch Armondo take my groceries out of their bags. The muscles in his arms look rock hard. The fitted shirt he has on accentuates the definition of his chest and the six pack that dwells beneath.

"Your total is $69.69, Mrs. Pierce," he says with a flirtatious smile. I see those braces he used to wear worked out nicely. I try to ignore his sexual innuendo and place

$70 in his hand. He hands me the receipt. The total really is $69.69.

"Is there anything else I can do for you, Mrs. Pierce?" Armando steps into my personal space with his body only inches from mine.

"Excuse my behavior, but you get more beautiful every time I see you. I know I shouldn't be so close to a married woman, but you've been the star of my fantasies since I was 15. Is Mr. Pierce still making you happy?"

I try to remain rigid. I can't succumb to this man. He's too young. I've got to act as if I'm not even the least bit phased by his advances.

"Mr. Pierce and I are separated at the moment."

"Really? How long have you two been split?"

"Not long. Almost 24 hours now."

"Twenty-four hours sounds like a fight, not a separation."

"After what he did, there is no way we are going to salvage this marriage. It's over," say.

"I'm sure it's lonely in this big house all by yourself. Why don't you let me keep you company? I know an unhappy woman when I see one, Mrs. Pierce. You can be my last delivery, and I can spend the rest of the day catering to you. Tell me what you need."

"I really don't know what I need. What I know is I'm tired. I'm tired of taking care of everybody else. I'm tired of being taken for granted. I'm tired of being the bigger woman. I wish someone would think about me sometimes. Being everybody's rock can be so draining. Even Tee. The love roller coaster she's on is wearing me out. I hope the Lord sends her a man soon so somebody else can listen to her problems. I need someone to tell me I'm beautiful and make me feel sexy and desirable. I need someone to not only say they love me, but show it, too. That's what I need," I say and then take a step back. He's too close. Armondo takes a step toward me closing the gap I created.

"I can do that and more," he whispers. "Allow me to help you forget about your troubles with an afternoon of passion and pleasure. And after your divorce is final I can give you a lifetime of love."

Armondo gently brings his lips to mine. His mouth tastes like cherry Jolly Ranchers, and I enjoy its sweetness as his tongue dances with mine. My body is hot and my sensitive areas are tingling with desire. At this moment my wedding vows mean nothing to me. Patrick, with his lying, cheating, conniving-self, means nothing to me. I want this Italian stud and I see no reason to deny myself.

"Show me what happens in your fantasies," I command.

"As you wish. I've been waiting for this opportunity for years."

Armando scoops me into his arms and takes me to my bedroom. I'm not a little woman by any means, but he maneuvers me with ease. I've always been what we in the south refer to as "thick." Growing up I was self-conscious about my large bottom, wide hips, and voluptuous breasts. I always felt fat next to skinny as a rail Tee. Yet, as we grew older, I figured I must not be too bad. I'm the one with the husband and kids while Ms. Not So Perfect can't keep a man. Now, I'm in the arms of a man who belongs in a Chippendale's calendar.

Before claiming me as his own, Armondo treats me to a sensual bubble bath, carefully cleaning and caressing every inch of me. I am surprised at the sounds I hear escaping from my throat as he explores my body. Each one is an audible confirmation of the pleasure he is evoking. Such an erotic experience only heightens my anticipation and my desire for him. Armondo dries me off and carries me to my bed. He entangles his body with mine for what feels like forever, drinking of my essence as if he were dehydrated. I see why so many older women go get a vibrant young thing. Cougarville doesn't seem like a bad place to reside. Maybe, after my divorce, I can move there permanently.

Chapter 33

Invitation for Two
Tee

I decided to wait a few hours before I called Michael. I can't make myself seem too eager. My fingers dance across the buttons as I dial his number and the butterflies in my stomach flutter when he utters his first syllable.

"Hello, pretty lady. I won't take no for an answer."

"That's good because my answer is yes. But I do have a question. How many rooms did you get?"

"I booked two, of course, but they are adjacent. If the monster under your bed should try to get you, scream and I'll come running," he teases.

"That's perfect. I will be packed and ready to board the plane first thing tomorrow morning."

"Great, I'm glad you accepted my invitation. I assure you that my intentions are innocent and honorable. I merely want to be able to go somewhere nice and take some time to get to know you. Overseas, people don't recognize me nearly as much as they do in the States."

"To be honest, I do have some reservations about going out of town with you so soon. I did just make your acquaintance this week. But, I decided to take a chance on you."

"Tee, I appreciate it. In return, I promise you the time of your life."

"I look forward to it, Michael. Oh, one more thing The I Will Live Foundation would like to reschedule the HIV/AIDS benefit. Do you have your schedule handy?"

"Yeah, I'm looking at it now."

"The date we're looking at is two months from now, Saturday, August 15th. Does that work for you?" I ask.

"Right now it's wide open. I'd be happy to come back to Memphis and speak then. I wouldn't mind going back to the children's hospital for another visit, too."

"Great! I'll let my client know you are available, and I'm sure I can arrange another hospital visit. I hate to rush off the phone but I need to get back to work. I have a new idea I'm working on, and I want to get it all out while my creative juices are still flowing."

"That's my little worker bee, Ms. Tee."

"Yep, that's me. I'll call you right before I pick up my sister for her surprise party so we can discuss the trip some more."

"Okay."

"Michael, thanks for inviting me. I really could use a getaway."

"We both could. I promise you that you will have my undivided attention in Jamaica. How did you manage to captivate me in 48 hours?" he asks.

"It's voodoo, baby! You better be good to me, or I'll give you a shrunken head," I tease.

"That's the last thing I need. Bye, beautiful. Call me later."

"I will handsome. Ciao."

I have several questions swirling around in my head, but I decide to wait until we are face to face to ask them. Those few moments on the roof left quite an impression on me. I truly do admire his newfound dedication to God and his commitment to enhancing the lives of others. I want him to know that I am proud of him for fighting his depression and using a life-altering situation as a testimony for the greatness of God.

An email alert pops up on my computer. Let me see what Patrick sent.

Chapter 34

Mommy Dearest
Michael

"Daddy, wake up! Daddy, wake up!" Michelle shouts while jumping up and down on my bed. She is forever introducing me to the exciting and not so exciting segments of parenthood. I am physically drained. I had another nightmare last night and I would really like to continue my afternoon nap, but I know Michelle needs some uncle/niece time. My parents brought her to my book signing yesterday, but I was so busy I barely got to speak to her.

I pretend like I'm still asleep and when I feel her crouch her little body next to mine to get a closer look, I tickle her until she can't take it anymore. For the next hour, I lay in bed with Michelle, answering all her questions about where I've been and what I've been doing. She really is a smart girl. I've got to see about getting her in preschool. I want to provide some balance and consistency in her life now that Becca is gone.

She keeps asking when her mother is coming home, but I have no answer. I know Becca's in town because she left a note for me at the check-out counter of the bookstore. This one read,

Hi. I like the book. Read it to Michelle. She'll love it.

At least she hasn't made any more attempts to cause me bodily harm. I'm getting a little tired of having to have armed guards everywhere I go. I decided not to tell Peter I'm going to Jamaica for the weekend. I'll suffer the consequences of one of his "this is for your own good" lectures when I get back. My mother calls Michelle and me downstairs to eat, interrupting our discussion about why she should eat her vegetables, even if she doesn't like them.

After our meal, my phone rings. It's Peter calling. He congratulates me on a successful book signing. The call is brief. As usual, he's busy working.

"Was that Mommy?"

"No, baby it wasn't. Would you like to talk to her?"

She nods her head yes.

"Let's try her cell phone and see if she answers." I have been calling randomly since she ran off, but Becca never answers. I called her cell phone carrier, and the customer service agent said that it hadn't been used in days. I figure it won't hurt to try her again. Maybe this time she'll pick up. The phone rings once.

"Hello, Michael. Have you come to your senses yet?" she answers.

"Mommy, I miss you so much. When are you coming back to get me?" Michelle is extremely excited to talk to her mom.

"Hello, Princess. I miss you too. I wish I could be there, but Mommy has a few things she needs to take care of. Are you having a good time with Grandma and Grandpa?"

"Yep. With Daddy, too. I love having a Daddy, Mommy. Why didn't you give me a Daddy, sooner? Hurry up and come get me so we can be Mommy and Daddy again."

"I'm trying to baby, but your Daddy won't cooperate. But I'm glad you are enjoying him. Is he there?"

"Yes ma'am."

"Let me talk to him. I love you."

"I love you too. Daddy, Mommy wants to talk to you." Michelle hands me the phone.

"That was low, Becca. Are you done trying to k-i-l-l me, yet?"

"I'll leave you alone for now Binky. And it's only because my baby loves having you around."

"Becca, come back to Akron and turn yourself in. We'll get you some help."

"All I want to do is give my child the two-parent home she deserves, and you think I'm crazy. Screw you, Michael. I'm not about to turn myself in for trying to be a good parent. I will give you some more time to think over my proposition."

Her breathing is hard. She doesn't sound like herself. I take the phone to my bedroom and shut the door.

"Will you listen to yourself? You actually think I'm going to marry you and you tried to run me over with a car. Didn't you hear your child say she needs both of us in her life? I'm committed to helping raise Michelle and that should be enough. Come back to Akron so we can sit down and talk about this!"

"No deals, Binky. I want the ring. I'll contact you soon to get an answer. I hope it won't be your FINAL answer. Take care of my baby." The phone goes click.

What am I going to do with that woman? What does she mean by she'll give me some more time to think it over. There's nothing to think about. At least she did say she would leave me alone for a little while. I hope she meant it, so I can go to Jamaica and not have to look over my shoulder. I hope she comes to her senses soon.

***

Becca

Yeah, I'll leave him alone--for now. I need to figure out a way to put an end to this game of cat and mouse. Michael makes finding him way too easy. His email and password are exactly the same as when we dated. All I have to do is go into his email and check the itinerary and flight reservations his booking agent sends. Then, I drive there and watch him. But I can't keep this up. All this driving is tiresome. The things we do for love. If that nappy headed girl in Memphis thinks she can have my man, she better think again. I will do whatever it takes to be with him. Michael Stokes is ALL mine.

Chapter 35

Surprise!
Tee

Sandy and I are in my car headed to what she believes is dinner with a prospective client. As we drive from her home to Mae Lillie's, I can't help but notice how happy she is. She is absolutely glowing. Instead of behaving like a woman who thinks she is headed for a divorce, she is acting like a woman in love. What's going on?

I promised Patrick I would try to smooth things over and get Sandy to this party, so I better get to the smoothing part.

"Have you talked to Patrick?"

"No. He called 15 times, but I would never answer. Eventually, I just turned off the ringers on all the phones. He left at least six voice mails, and he even sent roses to the house."

"I have something to tell you, but you're not going to like it. I talked to Patrick about what happened, and I believed him when he said he wasn't sleeping with Sheniqua."

"What are you doing talking to my husband about my marriage, Tee? Don't be so gullible. Why else would he pay all that woman's bills if he wasn't sleeping with her? It was probably hush money to keep her from telling me. What did he say?"

I giggle a little at my sister's curiosity. She hits me in the arm for doing so.

"Ouch! Patrick said he was paying her bills because she is an unemployed, struggling single mother, and he felt sorry for her. You and Patrick survived the affair, but her relationship didn't. She was living with her baby's daddy and their three kids when it took place. When he found out she had sex with Patrick, he left and he hasn't been by once to check on his kids. Sandy, that was almost a year ago. She couldn't find a job after Patrick fired her. She was getting unemployment and when that ran out she applied for public assistance, but it's not enough to support four people. You know how expensive kids can be. Patrick felt bad for her.

"Three months ago, she called him crying about the hard time she was having, and he promised to help her until he found her another job. She guilted him into it by arguing that he was partially responsible for her predicament, since the only reason he fired her was to save his marriage. She was actually good at her job. According to him, the stipulation of him helping her was that she would have no physical contact with him or his family. She wasn't even allowed to call. They only communicated through text messages."

"What else did he say?"

"He feels really dumb, because he realized it was all a ploy to get back in his life, even if it was at minimum capacity. Sheniqua didn't take the news well when Patrick texted her that he had found her a job at a new dental office and he would no longer be paying her bills. She had no reason to continue contacting him. That's why she called you. She wants to break you two up. That woman wants your husband, but I am thoroughly convinced your husband doesn't want her."

"Why do you believe him, Tee?"

"He forwarded me his cell phone records, complete with a transcript of their text conversations to prove it."

"Here, look at them," I say, handing her the document Patrick emailed to me this afternoon.

"He reiterated I don't know how many times that the situation was temporary and that you are the only woman for him. She was offering him sex, food, anything she could to get him to come over, but he wouldn't. If she called, he didn't answer."

"Tee, he took money out of our house to give to his mistress!"

"Former mistress. Don't you think I told him about himself? I let him know that his actions were unacceptable and he owes you an apology. Sandy, Patrick is a lot of things, but he's not heartless. That gold-digging woman saw an opportunity and she milked it for all it was worth. She knew Patrick was not going to let little children suffer."

Sandy looks distraught.

"What should I do? I'm so angry I could spit fire at him. He wasn't supposed to have any contact with her at all! That was our money, Tee! Money we work hard for every day!"

"I know you're upset, but I also know you still love your husband. Forgive him and move on. The only thing your husband is guilty of this time is showing compassion to a woman who doesn't deserve it. He is really sorry and he is sincere about making amends. He never wants you to feel the pain you felt when you found out about his affair again."

My sister begins to cry.

"Sandy, what's wrong? I thought you'd be happy to find out your husband isn't a low-down, lying adulterer."

"I am but, Tee. I did something vengeful today. If I had known this then, I wouldn't have done it," she sniffs.

I have to stop these water works before they ruin her make up. I can't have her walking into her party looking like a sad clown.

"Whatever it is, I'm sure it can be fixed. We can talk about how to do it later. I hate to sound cold and selfish, but stop crying because we are here. Get yourself together."

I drive onto the parking lot of the restaurant. Mae Lillie's is packed. I hope Sandy doesn't recognize the cars of any of our friends and family inside waiting for us.

"What are we doing here?"

"I told them to meet us here. If I'm going to wine and dine potential clients then, it's going to be at my family's restaurant. Mae Lillie's is just as good as any overpriced steak house."

"Thanks, sis, but I need to call my husband. This has all been a terrible mistake."

"I agree. Let me do the introductions. Then, excuse yourself. We're late. We need to get in there now."

Sandy looks at herself in the visor mirror and freshens up her make up. We exit my truck and walk to the glass double door entrance of the restaurant. I enter first and step to the left so as not to block Sandy's view when over one hundred people yell SURPRISE and HAPPY BIRTHDAY in our direction! Our mother, uncles, aunts, cousins, the girls, Edgar, and other close friends are all present, along with Sandy's in-laws, former co-workers, valued business associates, and restaurant staff. The room is decorated in our sorority colors, royal blue and white. Blue and white balloons are scattered around the restaurant and tall blue glass vases with white roses sit on each table. A large banner embroidered with the words Happy Birthday Cassandra hangs from the ceiling.

In front of the guests, stands an apologetic Patrick in a tailored black suit with a white shirt. He looks much better than he did yesterday. His hair and his goatee are neatly trimmed and lint free. Patrick smiles with pride at his one true love.

Sandy is wearing a black chiffon dress with spaghetti straps. Her ample cleavage is slightly peeping out at him from underneath. I give my brother in-law a thumbs-up to signal that everything is okay.

Sandy looks frightened at first, but after it mentally registers that I tricked her into coming to her own surprise party, she gives me a hug.

"I could kick your butt, Tina Long. Thank you! I've always wanted a surprise party!" she shrieks.

"You're welcome, but I don't deserve the credit for this grand event. This was all Patrick's idea. Although, I did help with the execution. Didn't you have something you wanted to say to your man? Why don't you go tell him now?" I gently push her forward.

Sandy trots over to her lawfully wedded husband and they engage in a passionate kiss. Several of the guests bellow out hoots and cheers. Patrick's lips emerge from against hers covered in red lipstick. My sister steps away from him to address the people who have come to help her celebrate her 36th birthday.

"Hello, everyone. This is a pleasant surprise. Thank you so much for coming. I understand that my husband, along with some help from my baby sister, is responsible for this birthday celebration. I love you both so much. But I especially love my husband. He is one of the most kind-hearted men I know, and I am so proud to be his wife! I am truly surprised, especially that all of you could keep a secret from me. Let's get this party started!"

She looks over at our cousin, Jeff, who is standing behind a table containing two turntables and a laptop. It is flanked by two large speakers on both sides.

"DJ Cousin Jeff, crank it up so I can boogey with my baby!"

He pushes a button and Michael Jackson's "Remember the Time" begins blaring through the speakers. Patrick mouths the words "I love you" and "I'm sorry" before leading his wife of 12 years to the dance floor. Ain't love grand!

This evening has turned out better than I expected. Well, almost. MacKenzie is here. Isn't he smart enough to know that after a breakup, all previously issued invitations are rescinded? He's talking to my mother, right now. She always did like him. Momma once said he reminds her of my father. Mac smiles at me. I frown at him. He sure does look good, but I'm still upset with him. I am not going to let the sight of him ruin my night. It's my sister's birthday, and I'm going to celebrate! Tomorrow, I will be lying on the beach with Michael Stokes and Mac will seem like a distant memory.

I pick up a glass of Chardonnay and down it in one gulp. Then, I take Edgar by the hand and head to the dance floor. I wonder what Sandy had to tell me. Whatever it was will have to wait until I get back from paradise. Judging from the smile on her face, I don't think it's that important now anyway.

Chapter 36

What A Tangled Web We Weave
Sandy

My husband and I lay snugly in each other's arms at the quiet bed and breakfast he whisked me to after the party. The bed is cozy and perfect for two lovers at play. The party was fantastic. Tee did an excellent job on the decorations, and it was nice seeing so many of the people I love in one setting. I don't remember the last time I danced or drank so much. Unfortunately, no amount of alcohol can make me forget my recent infidelity. I'm trying to block out anything that could prevent me from enjoying this magical moment of reconciliation. I feel terrible. I know I need to tell my husband what I did, but I'm so ashamed. It was wrong, and I was stupid. I'm scared if I tell him it will ruin everything.

"Baby," my husband's voice snaps me out of my thoughts.

"Yes, Patrick," I answer.

"Let's promise not to keep anymore secrets. None of this would have happened if I had told you that I wanted to help Sheniqua and gotten your feedback. That was our money, and I had no right to spend it on another woman and her kids without your permission. I'm sorry."

"I forgive you, Patrick. It's over. Let's move on. Your friend Dr. Green agreed to hire her, so she will be able to take care of herself and her children. From now on you are to have NO contact with her under any circumstances. Change your cell phone number and put her out of our lives forever. As far as I'm concerned it's over. This is my post-birthday party celebration, and I don't want to spend it discussing her."

"You're right. I love you." He reaches over and pushes my hair out of my face.

"I love you too, baby."

Patrick's eyes follow the length of my naked figure. He smiles and licks his lips. My husband is so fine. Good thing Armondo leaves for Iraq tomorrow. He's supposed to be gone for at least a year. Once he gets settled, I'll send him an email informing him of my decision to stay with my husband. Hopefully, by the time he returns home, he will have forgotten all about me and our sinful tryst. I don't think I'll tell anyone about my affair, not even Tee. It will be between me, Armondo, and the four walls. I can keep quiet but can my conscience?

Patrick begins slowly and softly kissing my body. I give my approval in the form of a low moan. My husband has always been an excellent lover—limber, passionate, and attentive. Our years together have made him quite knowledgeable of what I like and how I like it. Those sensual kisses ignite another love making session. He repeatedly takes me to the pinnacle of ecstasy. What was I thinking? Compared to him, Armondo is a rookie.

I understand why my sister no longer allows the men she dates to invade her body. She is holding out for what I have. What I experience with my man, my lover, my best friend, my provider, my protector, my HUSBAND could never be duplicated with a man who doesn't really know me and has to leave my side to return to his own home each day. What we have transcends mere sex. It's almost spiritual. Patrick and I share a home, a life, children and love. We have two beautiful children, and I couldn't imagine raising Donovin and Nicole without him. Having him there every day adds so much to their lives--our lives. Nothing compares to the immeasurable bliss I have when we're all together and having fun. Tee deserves to experience that.

I won't forget how blessed I am or do anything to compromise it again. Patrick gave me a birthday party, but on this night I give him complete forgiveness. I am finally able to relinquish the resentment I have because of his affair. He truly is a good man. We both made a mistake. Sheniqua and Armondo had our bodies, but they could never possess our hearts.

I really should confess but I can't. I'm afraid of how he would react. I'm not willing to take the chance of losing him or my wonderful life. What if he doesn't forgive me? *Forgive me, Father, for I have sinned.* I pray His forgiveness is enough.

Chapter 37

Jamaica, Me, and Tee
Michael

I'm walking along the beach in Montego Bay, Jamaica with one of the most beautiful women I have ever seen, listening to her relay the recent events of her life. As we stroll hand-in-hand on the private beach behind, Breezes, the resort I selected, I allow the warm sensation of the sand to penetrate my bare feet; the company of this woman penetrates my soul. If she were water, I would drink her in so she could continue to nourish me. Spending time with Tee does me so much good. I'm laughing hysterically as she tells me how she took off her belt and whooped a 19-year-old man.

"You can't be serious!" I yell.

"Yes, I am. I tore that tail up, too! You better not mess with me, playa', cause I'm a bad mamma jamma, especially when there's money involved!"

"So, how's he doing now?"

"Blak is doing fine. He moved back home with his parents, and they are working with his lawyer to try and negotiate with the record label to give him more creative control over his next album. So far, Lee's investigation has found that Blak made almost $2 million over the last year but only has about $400,000 left. They are scouring his records to see if his money was mismanaged. If they find anything, criminal charges could be filed."

"There's a lot of money to be made in the entertainment industry, but you've got to surround yourself with honest people. There are plenty of sharks out there, looking for a free meal," I say.

"I know. But how could you take advantage of a kid? It's like they have no shame." I find Tee's concern for others such a wonderful attribute.

"Some people don't. In their mind, it's survival of the fittest. That's why you have to be able to manage yourself and your money to a certain extent. A man who doesn't count his own money is a fool. Now, tell me more about your new business venture, Ms. Up and Coming Entrepreneur."

"I've created the 'I'm a Good Woman' brand and printed some t-shirts and mugs with the logo. Those are just a starting point, an attention getter, if you will. My goal is to create an entire line of motivational products for women. We all have a bad day, bad break up, and moments of low self-esteem. Whenever a woman anywhere feels that way, I want to have a product to lift her up and encourage her."

"I think that's a wonderful idea. Let me know if I can do anything to help."

"Michael, are you serious? Because I may be looking for an investor in the near future. I want to put on an annual conference, do a radio or television show, the whole nine."

"Put together a business proposal and I'll see what I can do. I've seen my fair share of women who have been beaten down by life and relationships that could use a little encouragement. I think you're on to something here."

Tee gives me a hug and peck on the cheek.

"You're so sweet. I could just eat you!" she says and playfully bites me in the spot she previously kissed.

"Oh, really? Be careful. This chocolate over here could give you a cavity after one bite. Speaking of eating, let's go back to the resort hotel and get ready for dinner. I hear there's a great restaurant on the premises. I could go for steak and lobster tails tonight."

"Sounds like a plan. I'll race you back to the hotel," Tee says and takes off running. Instead of running after her, I stand back and take in the view. This woman looks good coming and going.

It doesn't take long for me to get ready for dinner. I decide to wear my beige linen slacks and shirt with some brown sandals. I hope Tee is ready, too. I knock on her door, hoping she isn't one of those women who takes hours to get dressed. A vision of loveliness in a strapless tangerine dress with brown stilettos answers. Her hair is in twists and pulled up into some kind of hairstyle. I don't know what it's called, but I like the way it accentuates her long neck and excellent cheekbone structure. Her jewelry is simple: a gold necklace, gold bracelets, and a gold ring on her right ring finger. Her dress isn't tight but it follows the curves of her body nicely, leaving no doubt in my mind that God has been good to her. She looks like she is about to walk the red carpets of Hollywood. I try my best not to stare. I tell her she looks lovely and she gives me a compliment as well. I take her arm in mine and lead her down the hall. I am not the only one who notices how good Tee looks. A male hotel worker pushing a room service cart is staring at her so hard that he runs into another worker with a baggage cart. Yep, Ms. Tee is definitely a 10.

Over dinner, she and I talk about the Bible and how words written centuries ago are still applicable today. We talk about some of our personal struggles and how the word has helped us to overcome. I enjoy listening to her intellect and her Biblical knowledge. And she's funny. Tee never seems to run out of witty things to say. She tells me about her family, her friends, her job, and her many charitable endeavors. This woman is beautiful inside and out.

I consider telling her about Becca and Michelle now, but it doesn't seem like the right time. Something so serious doesn't belong in a first date. Besides, I have been focusing on them and work so much lately that it's nice to have some time for myself. I make a mental note to tell her before we leave. She deserves to know the entire truth before we take this thing any further.

Our waiter informs us that the resort also has a disco. After our abundant meal of lobster tails, steak, pork skewers, chicken, salad, vegetables, and chocolate cheese-cake, we head there to work it off with a little dancing. The DJ is playing a good mix of 70's, 80's, and 90's music. We dance to everything from The Jackson 5 to LL Cool J. Tee is an excellent dancer. And she must be in a really good mood because when the Percolator comes on, she does the dance all the way into a split. I'm impressed! After a couple of hours, the slight pain in my knee indicates that I'm about to overdo it. I suggest that we return to our rooms to get some rest. Tomorrow, we are taking a snorkeling cruise. I hope she lets me kiss her goodnight.

Chapter 38

Here We Go Again
Tee

    As we approach our respective doors, I invite Michael into my room. I'm not ready to end our evening. I've had such a wonderful time. I want to make the most of every moment in case our schedules prohibit us from seeing one another again soon. I tell him to have a seat on a white couch near the TV. Michael really did pick a nice resort. The rooms are spacious and decorated with contemporary furniture in an array of colors. I am looking forward to sleeping in the comfy king size bed. I turn on the TV and look for a movie. "Pretty Woman" with Julia Roberts and Richard Gere is on. I love that movie! Michael is such a gentleman. He is still standing, waiting for me to be seated first. I approach the coach, and he catches me completely off guard with a kiss. It begins soft and sweet but grows more passionate with each second. I know this type of kiss. It's the one that usually precedes disrobing. With my eyes closed and our lips still connected, I feel myself being lifted and carefully placed on the couch. Every part of my body is screaming yes, but my head is telling me NO WAY. THIS MAN IS NOT YOUR HUSBAND. Another voice works to quiet that one.

    Just let go and have fun for once. Remember MacKenzie? This is always the part where you lose your man. Don't lose this one. Guys like him don't come along every day. He's an NFL million- aire and he's yours for the taking. Aren't you tired of being a bride's maid and never a bride? Do you really expect a man like him to be with you if you don't have sex with him? This man can get it from any woman he wants.

Michael's mouth travels from my lips to my neck. I feel his large hands slide up my dress. I know I have to stop him before he begins to take my clothes off or I will have to repent in the morning. But it feels so good. I open my mouth to object, but no sound escapes my lips. Michael's mouth is working its way down to my cleavage and his hands are working their way up to my behind. He gently caresses the soft flesh. I open my mouth again to protest, but again no words escape, only a low moan. What is wrong with me? I'm usually extremely vocal about my celibacy and adamant about my dedication to stick to it. I have to put an end to this. I open my mouth to try again, but I realize that my attempts are futile. This man is my kryptonite and my super celibacy powers seem to have evaporated. My will of steel is now submissive goo. My body is about to give in to this man and I know it. *Father, give me strength.*

As if someone had entered the room and tapped him on the shoulder, Michael stops, removes his face and hands from my body, and turns around with his back toward me. I hear him murmur something quietly to himself before turning his face toward mine. There is remorse in his eyes. The expression on his face is one of a man who has done something dreadfully wrong.

"I'm sorry, Tee. I got carried away. I really am celibate, but this is all so new to me. I'm used to following a certain script and when I get to this point, I usually go in for the kill. Please forgive my behavior. I'm still in the process of rewriting my lines to reflect the way I live now. You are so beautiful," he says rising from the couch.

I reposition my dress to cover the areas that have been exposed.

"I understand. There is no need to apologize. I'm sorry. It's my fault. I shouldn't have invited you in so late. I wasn't thinking. But we were having such a good time. I didn't want the evening to end. I didn't mean to tempt you."

"Evidently, you have no idea how fine you are. You tempt a man by simply walking in the room. You're the first woman I've wanted to date since becoming celibate. This isn't going to be as easy as I thought."

"I understand. And no, it's not always easy to abstain from sex. The key is to pray for strength and to find someone who is on the same journey you are. I believe we've found that in each other. In the future we have to try to avoid situations like this one. And if it happens again, one of us has to continue to be strong enough to apply the brakes. I'm glad you were able to do so tonight."

"God will give you exactly what you ask for," whispers Michael, more to himself than to me.

"What do you mean?"

"I prayed for a beautiful, intelligent, kind, virtuous woman with a bangin' body, and that's what I got."

This man knows exactly what to say. I begin to blush.

"Thank you. You're pretty nice yourself, sir. Don't be so hard on yourself. I think you're doing everything right." He has to realize that this isn't all his fault.

"No, I'm not, but I'm trying. Don't worry. I'm not going anywhere, and I don't mind waiting. I know you're more than worth it. I should go to my room now. Sweet dreams, pretty lady."

Michael gives me a kiss on the cheek, and I watch him walk to the door that adjoins my room to his. As he opens it, the light coming from his room gives him an ethereal glow, illuminating the muscular edges of his finely toned body. His aura is beautiful—a reflection of the spirit that dwells within. Once again, he has left me in awe.

I briefly reflect on the evening's events before kneeling at the edge of the couch. I thank my Heavenly Father for allowing me to meet a godly man who loves him as much as I do and is able to be strong when I'm weak. I ask him to strengthen us both. I was really about to give in to temptation. This was the first time that I didn't have to be the one to say stop. I didn't even have to explain why we shouldn't have sex. Thank God for the wonderful man on the other side of that door who understands! That's the last time I give or accept an invitation to watch TV in a room with a bed. Temptation is a dangerous thing.

Chapter 39

The Truth Shall Set You Free
Michael

The next morning I awake to find Tee standing over me in jogging shorts and a tank top, telling me to get dressed, because we will be attending church services on the beach. I assume she's been working out or running, even with sweat on her forehead, she is radiant. We both dress and head to a secluded area of the beach where a white tent with portable air conditioners has been transformed into a sanctuary. The service is simple. There is one soloist singing hymns a cappella, and a Jamaican preacher is delivering the word. He is dressed in a white, short sleeved, button down shirt, black slacks, and shiny black shoes. His dark skin is the color of mahogany wood. His long dreadlocks are pulled into a ponytail.

There are about 50 or so people gathered under the tent for service. The preacher is standing with his back toward the beach with waves crashing and the tide rolling in and out as he speaks. Who needs an organist when you've got nature to back you up? His message is about Job and how he continuously trusted in God, even during his darkest hour.

"The enemy comes to kill, steal, and destroy. As long as you have breath in your body, you've still got joy and a reason to give praise to the Lord. Don't let the trials and tribulations of the world steal your joy. Do as Job did. Trust Him with all your heart, all your body, all your mind, and all your soul. God will never leave you nor forsake you. When the enemy attacks you, He is still with you. Allow Him to show you how awesome His power is. Submit to His will. Allow Him to use you. Be the man or woman God has called you to be, and watch Him move mountains on your behalf. He is mighty. He is sovereign. He is God. You are going to have some bad days. You may even lose some things or some people you hold dear. But continue to trust the one who allowed you to have them in the first place. He has the power to give it all back. But you must be patient. Your deliverance may not be immediate but it is coming."

The preacher has a thick Jamaican accent, but I understand every word perfectly. I know God is using him to reaffirm my commitment to Him. And like Job, everything I lost He's given back and added some awesome extras like Tee and Michelle.

After service, the congregants are invited to enjoy a continental breakfast in the back of the tent. It's mostly fruit, bagels, cereal, and yogurt. Healthy, yet satisfying. We meet the preacher and the soloist, who turns out to be his wife. Tee and I tell Reverend and Mrs. Gordon how much we enjoyed our first service on the beach. They thank us for coming and insist we come back again next time we are in Jamaica.

As we walk hand-in-hand back to the hotel, we pass by a young couple getting married. There are no bridesmaids or groomsmen. Just a preacher in a white robe, and the happy couple vowing to love, honor and cherish one another in front of about 15 guests. Tee has a dreamy, wistful look on her face.

"Do you ever think about getting married?" I ask.

"Yes. I know I will someday. I have to meet a man who is worthy of me first. Do you know anybody?"

"I just might."

She smiles and grips my hand a little tighter.

***

Tee is a little apprehensive about our snorkeling trip, because she can't swim. I assure her that everything will be fine. The concierge told me we will be in shallow waters and the ship's crew would issue the proper safety items. We arrive at our departure pier an hour early and sit down on a bench to wait. This is the perfect time to enlighten her on my current situation. I drape one arm around her small shoulders and let out all the stress I have been dealing with for the past few weeks.

At the conclusion, Tee kisses my face and says, "Michael, you're safe here with me. See these arms. Inside these arms lies the worry-free zone. I offer you escape from crazy ex-girlfriends, ungrateful brothers, and people who think your life is ruined because you can't run with an oblong ball anymore. God has a purpose for your life and He'll protect you. Don't worry, Michael. I won't let Psycho Barbie run me away. Also, I think it's honorable that you have committed yourself to raising a child who is not yours.

"Psalms 27:1 says 'The Lord is my light and my salvation; whom shall I fear? The Lord is the strength of my life; of whom shall I be afraid?'

"Nothing can harm you when God's got your back. I'll be right here."

"I'm glad you feel that way, Tee. I was afraid you would head in the other direction if I told you about Becca and Michelle. Thank you for your kinds words of encouragement.

It's amazing how this woman relaxes me. I wrap both of my arms around her and place a kiss on her neck.

Because Tee said it, I truly do believe everything is going
to end on a positive note.

Chapter 40

Revelation
Tee

I finally found out what's troubling the great Michael Stokes. It means a lot to me that he is willing to confide in me. I really don't think a crazy ex-girlfriend is anything I can't handle. I'm sure she'll move on once she realizes that he has a new woman in his life and he isn't coming back to her.

The sun feels good against my skin. Being encircled in Michael's embrace feels even better. I'm glad I came on this trip.

The Captain in charge of our snorkeling cruise soon calls for his passengers to board and we lazily make our way onto a small ship named Serenity with about 40 other guests. I am extremely excited and nervous. I've been near water this entire time, but haven't done more than get my feet wet walking along the shore. I love the sea.

I've been here once before, and it was here in Jamaica I fell in love with the beauty of water. Before Jamaica, I had only experienced open waters from the shorelines of Miami Beach. Jamaica's clean, sandy beaches and spar-kling, crystal blue waters always entice me to bathe in its cool refreshing liquidity, even though I can't swim. I usually stay as close to the shore as possible.

As we board, I notice that all of the guides on the boat are muscular men in swimming trunks. The Captain and the female bartender are the only ones fully clothed in white uniforms with gold buttons. This should be interesting. I can tell by the look on Michael's face he notices the all-male review guides too, but he doesn't comment. He has no reason to feel intimidated.

We have a seat at one of several plastic tables lined along the deck. The boat moves swiftly, smoothly, and quietly among the waves. There is a large, thick net stretched across the front of the ship that allows passengers to look down at the rushing water underneath. A few people are even lying across it to allow the gentle spray of salt water and wind to cool them. We are surrounded by water. I stand and watch as the pier gets smaller and smaller until it disappears from sight. In settings such as this, I can't help but admire the greatness of God. The beauty he fashioned is absolutely fascinating.

We arrive at our destination and our guides instruct us on how to properly use our life vests, goggles, and the long breathing tube we insert in our mouths. They have clearly been used before. I hope they sanitize them after every tour. They also provide optional fins. I've never used them, so I decide to take my chances with my bare feet. Michael selects a pair. We put on our equipment and climb down the ladder that runs along the side of the ship and into the sea. I squeal as the water envelopes me. My one piece bathing suit provides little protection from the chilly waters. Michael informed me that he is an excellent swimmer, so I hold on to him. I trust that between him and my orange life vest, I will stay afloat.

I am relieved that our sightseeing area is fairly shallow, but deep enough that my feet aren't touching the sea floor. We are told to simply stick our heads under water to get a glimpse of what the fishes see every day. I pull the goggles down from the top of my head, insert the breathing apparatus in my mouth, and place my head in face first. It's lovely down here under the sea. There's coral and other plant life dancing to and fro in the current, multi-colored fish, and small turtles. I even see a mama seahorse leading her babies. Absolutely gorgeous!

After about 30 minutes of shallow underwater exploration, our guides inform us that our snorkeling adventure is over and we have to re-board the ship. Once on board, I take off my life vest and have a seat.

During the return journey, our ship turns into a party. Gone is the peace and serenity we experienced while heading to our destination. Music pumps loudly through the speaker system and the bartender announces that she is now taking orders. The deck becomes the dance floor, and the shirtless guides make perfect partners for the bevy of unaccompanied women on the ship. A woman with braids in a bikini boldly asks Michael to dance. He politely declines. I know she saw he was with me, but I'm having way too good a time to get jealous. I can't blame her for trying. He is handsome.

It seems a school of dolphins heard the music and decided to join in the fun. About five of them appear on the left side of our ship. Their slim bodies glide effortlessly next to us, keeping in perfect pace with the ship. Each one reminds me of Flipper, the dolphin I used to watch on television as a child. They even put on a show for us, jumping into the air, turning somersaults, and emitting a sound that I know has to be laughter. The grey, shiny creatures are completely at ease in front of their human audience and appear to be enjoying the attention. Several of us clap and take pictures. Eventually, our new friends grow tired of performing and allow the ship to speed ahead. They swim backwards and flap their fins in what I assume are waves of good bye. I want to continue to look at them for as long as possible and run from the front of the ship to the back. One small dolphin continues to trail us. *That's right, little dolphin. Stay with me.* He's looking at me. I know he is. I lean slightly over the side to get a closer look as he glides through the water. I am mesmerized by the sheer beauty of this water mammal. He is magnificent. I lean a little further over the side to get a better view.

Suddenly, a hard push in my behind launches me over the side of the ship into the water. I am instantly overtaken in sheer panic. My heart is racing, the water is freezing, and I am a flailing mass of arms and legs! I have nothing and no one to help maintain my buoyancy. I scream for help, but I'm almost certain no one can hear me above the music. I scream again, but this time I call on the name of Jesus. "Jesus!" I can feel myself going under and take in a big gulp of precious oxygen. Where's Flipper? Isn't he supposed to save me? He is no where to be found.

I try to remember what I learned in my beginners swim class. I didn't learn to swim, but I did learn to float. I have to relax. The water will carry me. I stop struggling, tilt my head back, and I imagine myself weightless. In response to my releasing the panic, my legs travel to the surface of the water. All of me is floating and the current is tossing me gently from side to side. I lie on my back in the middle of this vast, blue body of water and look up at the clear blue sky. An unexplainable calmness comes over me. I know there is nothing to fear. God is with me. The ship circles back for me and before it reaches me, Michael launches himself into the water. *Thank you, Lord! Thank you!*

"Hold on, baby! I'm coming!" he shouts.

Those words are more melodious than any song lyrics I've ever heard. When he is close enough for me to touch, I grab his body and hold on for dear life. He takes off his life vest and places it on me.

"Are you okay, Tee? Baby, please say you're okay."

I smile and nod my head yes.

I'm freezing. The temperature of the water out here in the middle of the sea is significantly lower than what I experienced in the shallow waters near the coast. I wrap my arms tighter around my hero and wait for the ship to arrive. Once it reaches us, someone throws a white rope ladder down the side for us to climb.

We are greeted with applause and dry towels as we re-board the ship. The party has stopped and the other passengers are standing near the rails asking me if I am alright and what happened. Someone on board this vessel pushed me and I intend to find out whom.

"Who pushed me?" I shout angrily.

No one answers. Everyone is looking at me like I'm insane.

"Baby, what are you talking about? I thought you lost your balance and fell," Michael says.

"I did not. Someone came behind me and pushed me over board, and I want to know which one of you sick pranksters did it. Somebody just tried to kill me. I need to know who it is so I can punch you in the face!" My eyes travel around the ship looking for the guilty party.

"Baby, calm down. You're safe now. You're on board the ship and I got you. Nobody is going to harm you. I promise."

"How can you expect me to calm down?" I demand. "I could have drowned. Show yourself! Stop hiding!" I start pointing at people. "Was it you?" I say to a man in red swimming trunks. "Was it you?" I ask a woman in a big straw hat with a drink in her hand. I see the woman who asked Michael to dance earlier. "I bet it was you. Trying to get rid of me so you can have him to yourself? I'll snatch you by those braids and mop the bottom of this ship with them!"

Michael seems more embarrassed than concerned.

"Ma'am, I'm sorry" he says to the woman. "Tee, you've had a traumatic experience. Stop this. You're safe now. Everyone please excuse her. I'm sure you can understand why she's upset. Did anybody see someone push my lady friend?"

Several of the onlookers shake their heads or say no. I know someone had to see something.

"Are you sure, Tee? Maybe the boat shifted and the force pushed you over?"

"Someone tried to take me out and you're trying to convince me it was my imagination! Are you serious?"

Through clenched teeth and a cold, wet, shaking body, I say, "Didn't no force push me over, Michael Stokes. I felt a person push me over the side of this ship. I can't believe that you don't believe me?"

The Captain approaches us. "Ma'am I am sorry that this tragedy has befallen you, but please compose yourself and lower your voice. You're scaring the other passengers. Would you like to come below deck and calm yourself?"

"I think that's a good idea," Michael says.

"DJ, start back up the music. Margaritas for everyone!" announces The Captain. The invitation of more free liquor and dancing was all the other guests needed to resume their partying.

Michael and I follow the Captain to a flight of stairs that leads below deck and into a room with a faux suede furniture and pictures of dolphins arranged along the walls.

"I'm going to leave you two alone for a little while. I'll be back shortly to check on you. If you need anything, please let me know," he says and leaves the room.

The rug on the floor feels good beneath my cold feet. My body is still shaking, but warm tears are running down my cheeks. This is supposed to be a vacation. I am supposed to be having fun. Michael sits down in a large chair, places me in his lap and cradles me in his arms. There is a brown, fleece throw on the back of the couch. He gently wraps it around my shivering body, never disconnecting his eyes from mine and never saying a word.

"Baby, you believe me, don't you? Somebody pushed me," I whimper. "Michael, I'm so scared. Do you think Psycho Barbie is here?"

"Shhhhhh, rest." Michael kisses my lips to quiet me.

His actions speak louder than words ever could. The man who saved my life doesn't believe that someone tried to kill me. I bury my head in his chest in hopes of rapidly soaking up his body heat. I am hurt, but I don't dare push him away. At this moment I need him to comfort me and help keep me warm. I continue to nuzzle my frantic face in his chest.

He gently rocks me in his arms. A short time later, the boat gradually slows down and then comes to a complete stop. Michael suggests that we wait until the other passengers leave the ship before going upstairs. The Captain comes down to announce that the ship is clear and we can leave if we like. He is about to say something else, but Michael silences him with the wave of his hand.

"We'll be leaving now. Thank you for the snorkeling." He reaches into the small bag we brought with us and pulls out a $20 tip.

Michael escorts me to my room. I give him a hug and thank him for saving my life. I truly am grateful but it bothers me that he doesn't believe that I was pushed off the ship. I politely ask him to leave me alone, so I can get some rest. He doesn't object. He kisses me on my forehead and tells me he will return in a little while. I don't think he knows quite what to say or do right now. It's probably best if he does nothing. He's done more than enough at this point. I thank him again for his kindness and for saving my life.

I retreat to the room's balcony to let the rays of the sun warm me. The chill from the water went straight through to my bones, and I am still cold. A cup of hot tea would probably do me some good. I locate the phone to dial room service and notice that the message light is flashing. I hit the button and listen to a member of the staff informing me that there is a package for me at the front desk. Who would be sending me a package? Only my sister and my assistant know I'm here. I am tired, but my curiosity compels me to go downstairs. I slip on jeans and a t-shirt, exit my room and take the elevator down-stairs to the lobby.

Michael is already downstairs. He is talking to fans and signing autographs. I ignore him, walk over to the front desk, and inform the attendant that I have a pack-age there for me. I'm upstairs dealing with the scare of my life and Mr. Superstar is down here entertaining. I can't believe him! The attendant hands me a plain white envelope with my name on it. Inside is a handwritten note with no signature:

I came for Michael but got you instead. Did you enjoy your swim with the dolphins? He's taken. Walk away while you still can.

P.S. Tell Michael he helped me kick my fear of flying. I'll go anywhere for my man.

"Sir, do you know who left this," I ask the attendant.

"No, miss. It was already here when I started my shift. Is there a problem?"

"Yes, but I don't think it's one you can handle."

I walk over to Michael and push the note into his chest.

"You said we were safe here. If I'm in danger I think I deserve to know. Psycho Barbie is the one who pushed my overboard. How did she even know we were here?" I demand.

The fans awaiting their autographs take a few steps back. Michael looks totally bewildered. He removes the note from my hand and reads it. He then locks his arm in mine and leads me to a corner of the lobby away from his fans.

"Tee, I thought we would be safe here. I don't know how she found me. I didn't tell anyone I was coming and I made all the arrangements myself. And if she did find out, I didn't think she would come here because of her fear of flying. I am so sorry I put you in this predicament. I doubted you when you told me someone pushed you. I'm sorry for that, too."

His apology isn't enough right now. "Evidently she got over her fear. It's one thing when she is threatening your life, Mr. Stokes, but it's another thing when Psycho Barbie starts threatening mine!"

Once again all eyes are on us but I don't care and neither of us notices the hotel employee in a navy suit behind us. I am quite perturbed when he interrupts our conversation.

"Excuse, Mr. Stokes. This may be a bad time, but the hotel manager would like to see you," he says timidly.

"This is a bad time. We are having a very important conversation," Michael says in a less than cordial tone.

The worker shifts nervously. "I understand, sir, but the manager of this establishment would really like to speak to you. He says it's very important. Please follow me."

We table our discussion until later and do as the worker requests. He leads us through a door that reads "Employees Only" and down a winding corridor to the managerial suites. After passing three lavishly decorated offices, he ushers us into the fourth one. A large, dark-skinned man in a navy suit is seated behind a huge oak desk. He smiles widely and stands to greet us.

I read some information about Wellington Pompei online before I left home. According to the website, he is a native of Jamaica who takes great pride in running a resort that is frequented by the rich and famous. Breezes has developed a reputation for being private and virtually void of paparazzi. It is rumored that he pays them handsomely not to take pictures of his guests and in return celebrities and socialites pay handsomely to frolic along his private stretch of beach. After we exchange pleasantries, he asks us to have a seat. He also offers us a beverage. We both decline.

"Well then, I'll tell you why you're here. Mr. Stokes, I must apologize. We are usually quite good about protecting the privacy of our guests while they are on the resort grounds, but it seems that word of your being here has gotten back to the States and has circulated throughout the local media." He places before us the newest edition of the *Gossip Gazette*, and there on the front page is a picture of the two of us walking hand-in-hand on the bench. It reads,

"Michael Stokes Benched, Then Hitched?"

"Retired NFL great Michael Stokes is spotted walking along the beautiful Montego Bay beaches looking very cozy with Memphis event planner Tina Long. It seems he has found something other than football to occupy his newfound free time. Mr. Stokes is rarely seen in public with his love interests. We surmise this must be serious."

The picture must have been taken yesterday. Under different circumstances I might have been flattered. I look good in my white sundress. Having Michael Stokes standing next to me doesn't hurt either.

"I am perfectly willing to extend your stay an extra two days free of charge to make up for this mishap," Mr. Pompei says apologetically.

"Thank you, but no thank you. Ms. Long and I must leave now," announces Michael.

"Then, let me give you a voucher for two free nights at your convenience," Mr. Pompei adds.

"That will be fine. Tee, we need to leave now." Michael quickly rises from his seat.

"Why? I don't care about any tabloids. I care about a killer," I say.

"This is how the killer knew I was here. I've got to get you away from me and back home safely. As long as you are with me, you are in danger."

"Sir, is someone bothering you? We have excellent protection for our guests who are having problems with stalkers. I can arrange for an armed escort to take you to the airport if you wish."

"That would be wonderful. However, I'll need two: one who can stay with me and one who can stay with Ms. Long until we reach our separate destinations in the United States. Add the cost to my bill."

"Michael, I'm sure I'll be fine on the plane," I say.

"Baby, I can't take any chances. You read her note. You were right. It's one thing for her to threaten me. It's another for her to threaten you. You will have armed security escort you back to Memphis. Please don't argue with me."

I think about my unpleasant dip in the sea earlier and agree to go without further objection.

We thank Mr. Pompei for his concern and head to our rooms to pack. So much for my romantic Jamaican getaway. Michael promised me a weekend I wouldn't forget, and he definitely delivered.

Chapter 41

Parting Is Such Sweet Sorrow
Michael

I've had enough of this. I can't even go on vacation with a good woman without Becca ruining it. That woman is turning my life upside down.

Before we leave Mr. Pompei's office, he persuades us to alert the Jamaican authorities to the attempted murder on Tee's life. A couple of officers arrive to take our statements. They ask me to send them a picture of Becca as soon as possible. They also suggest that we alert the authorities once we return to the United States. Becca is making it harder and harder for me to keep her in Michelle's life. I really don't want Michelle to lose her mother to incarceration or a mental institution. I was hoping she could get over trying to be with me and focus on raising her daughter.

After giving our statements, we head to the airport accompanied by two armed security guards. We are both lucky enough to find flights that will be departing within the next couple of hours. After going through customs and security screening, we sit in one of the airport restaurants to talk.

"Tee, I have enjoyed my time with you, but until Becca is captured, I can't see you anymore. I couldn't forgive myself if something happened to you. No relationship, whether it be a friendship or more, can survive under these circumstances. I hope you can understand."

"Michael, I'm scared. Not for me, but for you. Don't I have a say in this?"

"No, baby, you don't. There's no other way. Give me a kiss." I attempt to guide her face to mine. She turns her head.

"No, my kisses are reserved for brave men who want to be with me. Not cowards who let crazy women drive them away. Leave me alone, Mr. Stokes. I'm sorry I ever met you!" she says.

Her words cut me like a knife. How was I being cowardly? Didn't she realize I was doing this for her own safety?

"Tee, you're being irrational," I say.

"Maybe I am, but I haven't felt this good about a man or with a man in a long time. You want me to put my feelings on pause. I don't think I can do that. Good luck catching your killer. I'm out! Let's go, whatever your name is," she says to one of the guards. "We have a plane to catch."

"So that's it, huh? When things don't go the way you want, you just leave. Is that how it works in Tee's world? I'm standing here telling you that I want to spend time with you, but not under these circumstances. I can't truly enjoy you if I'm surrounded by armed security, looking over my shoulder or trying to protect you the entire time. I've got to get Becca off my back. Stop being selfish! You forget that I have other people who depend on me, like my niece, my parents, and my siblings. I have to make sure I'm safe for their sakes, too. This isn't just about me." I had to make her understand.

"I get that, but at this moment I'm upset and I'm scared. I don't feel like being mature or rational. What if she kills you, Michael? I've had enough disappointments in my life. I don't think I can take anymore. The last thing I need to do is to fall in love and then lose you."

The sorrow in her voice wounds me more. "Tee, I'm sorry if this hurts you, but I'm more concerned about what Becca will do to you if I keep seeing you. She pushed you into the sea today." I let out an exasperated sigh. "You're right, you should go."

Tee nods. We both stand, and she gives me a slow kiss on the lips. Even with my mouth closed I can taste her peppermint lip gloss. She allows me to hold her tightly in my arms, and I hope it's not the last time I am able to do so.

I feel her body shake momentarily. She frees herself from me and says, "I have to go."

I stand there watching the woman of my dreams throw her brown Louis Vuitton bag over her shoulder, take her matching carry-on by the handle, and sashay through the terminal and out of my life. I promise myself it will be temporary. Becca is going to pay for this. I've been way too nice for way too long.

I pull out my cell phone and make a phone call to leave a simple message. "You got your wish, Becca. She's out of my life. Don't contact or touch her again or you'll be the one needing to be saved."

Chapter 42

Life Isn't Fair
Michael

It's been almost a month since I've seen or talked to Tee. I send her a text message every now and then. Sometimes she answers. Sometimes she doesn't. When she does, it's usually words of encouragement or Bible scriptures that are applicable to my situation. I decided that it's best if I don't call. But there isn't a day that I don't think about hopping on a plane and appearing on her doorstep to kiss her soft lips again. She deserves more than I can give her right now, and I'm not going to reenter her life until I can give her my best.

I have to go to Memphis next month for the Gala she rescheduled. She handled all the details through Peter. I told him the only way I would come is if she wasn't there. Peter relayed the news, caught more than an earful, and then finally persuaded her to do what I asked for the sake of her client. She didn't have much room to argue since the Foundation already paid me my money. Her assistant is going to handle this one without her. I have a feeling that Becca will be there, so I'm not going to give her another opportunity to try to take Tee out again.

Michelle asks regularly when her mother is coming back. I don't have an answer. She handles her absence pretty well until it's time to go to bed. Then, she is almost inconsolable, crying repeatedly, "I want my mommy."

Becca no longer answers her cell phone, but she has been sending packages to the house for me and Michelle.

Michelle gets toys, hand drawn pictures and she even sent a video of herself reading my book. Mine are gifts that you give to a lover: cake, candy, cards, poems, and flowers. I never eat any of the edible gifts in case they have been poisoned. Once, she sent naked pictures of herself. They made me want to vomit. There is nothing sexy about sagging breasts, a big stomach, and a flat behind.

I am still doing speaking engagements and book signings, but security is always in place. I really don't believe Becca would kill me, but I am certain that if I don't give her what she wants, she will cause me bodily harm. I've tried to meet with her several times but she refuses. She's smart enough to know that as soon as she shows her face, I'll have her arrested. I have been working with the police to try to construct an alternate plan to capture her. Maybe then I will stop having nightmares about her stabbing me.

I finally got Michelle to stop calling me Daddy, and Maxwell is warming up to the idea of being a father. He calls to talk to her every other day. She calls him Max Daddy. He says he likes it because it sounds like Mack Daddy. They are getting to know each other as best they can over the phone. When he comes home for fall break, they'll get to spend some one-on-one time together. He apologized for the way he acted when he was home but I'm thinking about spitting on him anyway.

Today is a typical Sunday. I wake up to Michelle jumping on my bed. We eat breakfast and get dressed for church. She really enjoys children's church. I figure it's because it's the only time she is around children her age. I want to put her in school, but I'm afraid to let her out of me or my parents' sight. On our way to church, I get a call from an unknown number on my cell phone. Whoever it is, I hope they have some good news. I could really use some.

Chapter 43

Silly of Me
Tee

Lillie Long is 62 years old, but doesn't look a day over 50. She prefers to be called by her middle name, Pearl, but to me and my sister she is Momma. If you ask me, her name should be sassy, because that's exactly what she is. She and I meet for Sunday Brunch at the Peabody Hotel once a month after church. Retirement seems to agree with her. Momma has been traveling a lot lately and is preparing to leave for Paris later this week with her best friend, Ms. Purdy. While we eat, I update her on my situation with Michael. She's not too pleased.

"Girl, what is wrong with you? This man's very presence in your life poses a threat to your ability to stay above water and you get mad at him when he says he can't see you until his mentally ill ex-girlfriend is captured? You should be ashamed of yourself, Tina. God brought you out of the lion's den and you're trying to run back in. You need to apologize to that boy but stay as far away from him as you can," she advises.

"Momma, I know you're right, but I have never met anyone like him. I know we would be good together."

"That may be true if his life were not in danger. How much can you enjoy him if either one of you is dead? Based on your description, he does seem like a very nice, respectable young man, but I don't know him. I know you. At least I thought I did. I raised you to think with your head as well as your heart. Baby, will you listen to yourself? You are not making sense. I'd rather you go back to MacKenzie than have to deal with this nonsense. This man has a lot of baggage."

"Momma, you would rather I go back to a man who tried to pressure me into having sex with him, insulted me, and then threw me out of his house? Would that really be better than being with a good Christian man who treats me like queen? You've been talking to him haven't you?"

"Yes. Mac still calls to check on me. I saw you two talking at Sandy's birthday party, and I thought you two might work things out. He says you won't return any of his calls. Why?"

"Because he's not the man for me and I see no need to waste his time or mine."

"Are you sure? He's really sorry."

Mac had even brainwashed my mother into thinking he was Mr. Right. I knew it was only a matter of time before she tried to convince me to give him another chance.

"I'm sure. I've let the idea of us being together go. You have to do the same."

"Ok. I'll mind my own business. I just want you to be happy. Now, back to this Michael. Let's say you get your wish. You two start dating again before this woman is caught and she kills him. Do you want to endure the pain of losing a loved one? Or worse, you get killed, too! Do you know what that would do to me? Are you trying to send me to the grave girl?"

Momma picks up her napkin and fans herself. She can be so dramatic, sometimes. But she does have some valid points.

"I'm sorry to upset you. I want to be happy, too. I want what you and Daddy had. He loved you and he would have done anything for you."

"And when the time is right, you will. You can't rush love, Tina. It has to blossom in its own time and it can't do that under stress and duress. If Michael is the one, God will bring him through this situation and back to you. You have to be patient." My mother takes her hand and places it on top of mine. "You always did want what you want when you wanted it. You and this man deserve to have the opportunity to love each other openly and honestly without worrying about someone else interfering. It's obvious he cares for you, and I'm glad he's smart enough to realize he needs to stay away from you until his situation improves. Listen to the man, baby. Stop being so silly and selfish. This separation is for your own good."

No one has ever been able to make me feel ashamed of my actions the way my mother can.

"I know. But it's hard feeling like the very thing you've been praying for is slipping through your fingers. I feel so helpless!" Now, I'm the one upset.

"Some things are out of our hands. Be patient Tina and wait on God. I love you and your sister so much. You both make me proud. I tell everybody that having you two was the best thing I ever did."

"Thank you, Momma. We love you too. Let's change the subject. You are so worked up you're starting to perspire. I would hate for you to mess up your new hat."

Momma is dressed in her Sunday best. She looks lovely in a classy silver suit with rhinestone buttons. She has it expertly complimented with a silver clutch and feathered hat. Sister Pearl, as they refer to her at church, loves her big hats.

"Changing the subject is a good idea. But do me a favor and consider calling Mac. It's not like you're seeing anybody else. How is I'm A Good Woman going? The women at the church conference last weekend ate it up."

I wish she would stop talking about Mac---permanently.

"They sure did. I sold 200 t-shirts and 100 mugs. I also collected the contact information for women who would be interested in attending an I'm A Good Woman conference. My working theme is "Progress Thru Pain". I'm hoping to land Dr. Juanita Bynum as the guest speaker."

She claps her hands together and exclaims, "Oooh baby, that sounds wonderful. You know how much I enjoy hearing Juanita!"

My mother and I continue to talk while we finish our meal. I know I need to call Michael and apologize for the way I behaved at the airport, but I can't. Part of the reason is pride. The other part is that I know the minute I hear his voice, I'm going to break down in tears and ask him to let me be close to him again. I can't believe he told me I couldn't come to my own event. I was looking forward to seeing him. Well, I've got news for him. I am going to see him. But he won't see me. I have to be there. It would be unprofessional for me not to be. It's my event, and I have to make sure everything runs smoothly.

I've been praying for Michael, Becca, and Michelle every day. I know God will keep him safe and deliver him from harm. I am trying to be patient, but it has never been one of my strengths. My phone rings. It's Michael. Something must be wrong, because he never calls.

"Hello," I say nervously.

"I know you're probably busy, but I couldn't wait to tell you, Tee, it's over."

"What?"

"It's over. Last night they caught Becca at a local pawn shop trying to sell my mother's jewelry. It's over. She's been arrested and taken to a secure mental facility for evaluation. She can't hurt you or me." There is undeniable happiness in his voice. It's as if he spooned honey into my ear. Those were the sweetest words I have ever heard.

"Tee, Baby, are you there?"

"How soon can you get here?" I blurt out.

"I can charter a plane as soon as we get off the phone, but I want to bring you to Akron. There are some very important people I want you to meet."

"I don't have a problem with that. Book it for tomorrow evening. I'll go anywhere you want me to Michael Stokes, as long as you're there waiting for me when that plane lands."

"Wild horses couldn't keep me from you now. I've missed you," he says.

"Same here," I try to hold in the squeal that's fighting to escape my throat. My prince is sending a chariot for me!

Chapter 44

Reunited
Michael

The plane I chartered lands on a private airstrip in Memphis. I didn't tell Tee that I was going to be on it. I wanted it to be a surprise. I can't wait to see her face. Rose petals are spread throughout the cabin, and I've arranged for her favorite candies along with sparkling grape juice to be served. A celebration is in order! Once we land, we are meeting my family for dinner. I know they are going to love her.

Tee boards the plan. Our eyes lock. She screams and runs into my arms. I pick her up and the kiss we share is indescribable. She is a sight to behold in a black silk top, skinny jeans and black stilettos. The old me would have begun taking off all her clothes right in front of the lone flight attendant assigned to the plane. Instead, I tell her how happy I am to see her and ask her if she would do me the honor of being my lady.

She smiles shyly and says, "I would like nothing better, Mr. Stokes."

I take the two flutes of juice the attendant has prepared for us and make a toast to new beginnings. Afterward, I ask Tee to join me in a prayer. We hold hands and thank God for bringing an end to my horrible situation and allowing us to see each other again. We ask him to bless our union and guide our relationship in the direction he would like it to go. At this moment, I believe I'm the happiest man in the world.

One month later..........

I've pretty much relocated to Memphis. Whenever I'm not working, I swing through Akron to spend time with my family and then head to the home of the blues and rock 'n roll to spend time with my girlfriend. Because of my travel schedule my parents and I decided the best place for Michelle is with them. She is enrolled in pre-school and seems to be adjusting to life without her mother pretty well.

As for me, I have turned in my playa's card and erased all the honeys' numbers from my phone. I'm focusing all my energy on laying the foundation for a great future with Ms. Tina Long. I'm even thinking about putting the bachelor pad in Miami up for sale since I'm hardly ever there. Tee says I should hold onto it for a getaway spot when the weather in Akron and Memphis gets too cold.

My family loves Tee. My mother told me that I've selected a fine Christian woman; my daddy already introduces her to people as his daughter-in law. Tomeka loves that fact that Tee is a fashionista, and the two have gone shopping together several times. What else could you expect from a teenager? She calls Tee the big sister she's always wanted. Max hasn't met her yet, but I'm sure he'll like her, too. Michelle and Tee get along wonderfully. I brought her to Memphis to visit and I enjoyed seeing Tee's maternal side. She's going to be an excellent mother. Whenever Michelle started crying for Becca or my parents, Tee found a way to dry up those tears. She's also careful to never say anything negative about Becca in front of Michelle. I appreciate that, because I don't want to ruin her memories of her mother, even if she is crazy.

Up until she abandoned her, Becca had been a pretty decent parent.

Becca is in an Akron mental institution awaiting her trial for theft and three counts of attempted murder. When questioned by police, she admitted to everything except stealing my mother's debit card. I have a feeling Maxwell took it in case I really did cut him off. We expect her to be confined to a mental institution for treatment for a very long time. I really do hope she gets herself together for Michelle's sake. Right now, Becca is allowed to have supervised calls with her twice a week.

Living in Memphis has taken some adjustment, but I like it. Like any city, Memphis has its challenges. But it's rich in culture and this southern hospitality is nice. I've never heard people call me "sir" so much in all my life. I've grown to love the music scene. Every day of the week you can find someone somewhere who can blow everything from R&B to blues to country to gospel. I'm taking it all in. I went to Graceland to see Elvis' mansion. We also visited the National Civil Rights Museum. I enjoyed learning the history of our people. I even stood in front of the balcony where Dr. Martin Luther King was killed and looked out of the window where the fatal shot was fired. It was a very solemn experience.

Things are going really well between me and Tee. I think she's even more beautiful, intelligent, and witty than I did when I first met her. This relationship is unlike any other I've had before. Not having sex with my girlfriend is different but in a good way. Tee and I spend hours talking and laughing. It's been fun getting to know her, and I can't seem to get enough of her! She is showing me how to express love in ways that don't include sex. I'm becoming a better person and a better Christian. It's not always easy but the bond we've made in one short month is stronger than any I've ever had with a woman. I'm truly blessed to have her in my life.

The day has finally arrived for me to make good on my promise to speak at the Give Life Gala. There are hundreds of people here at the Crystal Ballroom and Tee has outdone herself on the details.

"Dang! This is the third time Peter has called me in the last hour. I wonder what he wants. It must be important, because he never calls this many times in a row. I wish he would learn how to text, but he refuses to take the time to do so."

"Well, baby, it will have to wait. Nothing with this event has gone right: the menu was wrong; our entertainment got food poisoning and cancelled. Thank God Marquez, the pianist at my church, was available," says Tee. "It's almost time for me to introduce you. I've got to get you on stage on time," Tee says.

"Tee, relax. No one even noticed the menu was wrong. The food was delicious and the pianist is doing an excellent job. You can be so bossy when you're stressed."

"Who's stressed? I'm not stressed. Get ready to dazzle the audience with your dashing good looks and charm."

"I got this. Don't worry," I pat her hand for reassurance.

"Worry? Who's worried? Of course I'm worried. Pitt Chamberlain, one of the richest men in Memphis, is in the audience. I've been trying to land his annual charity ball for years. He wasn't happy with the way it was handled this year, and I hear he is in the market for a new firm to coordinate it. He allocates a massive budget for it.

Do you know what I could make off of an account like that? I have to get this thing perfect because ......"

"Will you listen to yourself? You're dating a millionaire and you're still worried about money. Why?" I ask.

"Michael, you act like we're married. You could leave me tomorrow and your money would go with you. As far as I'm concerned, until I have a ring on my finger, I still have to worry about money."

"Woman, what are you saying? Leave? What makes you think I would leave?"

"Nothing, but it's true. Say you die tomorrow. Because we're not married, I wouldn't get a dime. It would all go to your parents. As a single woman, I still have to think about my security and my mother's security. She's getting older and I have to make sure she will always be properly cared for."

"Tee, I didn't think we had been together long enough to talk about marriage. Is that what it will take to make you feel secure, a ring?"

"No. You're missing the point. I know it's too soon to be talking about marriage, but until you give me a reason not to, I still feel like I have to be somewhat independent."

"You talk like we don't have a future together. Do you think I come here because I don't have anything to do? I've basically relocated myself to be closer to you." Sometimes I just don't understand women.

"You are taking this the wrong way. Of course I think we have a future together. Michael, you are everything I want and need and more. You and your niece mean the world to me. It would be beautiful to have a home with both of you. But we're not there yet, and we both know it.

"Marquez is ending his song. I have to introduce you now. I know what I said may sound a little harsh, but advancement in my career is important to me. As your girlfriend, I'm not legally entitled to anything you have, but I am ever so grateful that you share it with me."

She blows me a kiss and straightens out her red evening gown before heading to the podium. My baby looks good. I'm a lucky man. But I don't think she realizes that everything I have is already hers—including my heart. I love that woman. I haven't told her yet, but I'm going to. Each time I try, the words won't come out. I try to show her by making sure she wants for nothing, but she won't let me. She still pays her own bills like she doesn't have a man. Why can't she see that as long as I'm around she doesn't have to worry about a thing? I feel my phone vibrate and check the caller I.D. It's Pops this time. I'll call him back after my speech.

Chapter 45

Growing Pains
Tee

That man can pick the most inopportune time to hold an intense discussion. I'm trying to catapult my career and he wants to talk about our future. I can't worry about that now. There's nothing to worry about. We're good together, and I am happy.

I walk on stage and scan the sea of people in the audience. Among them are some of Memphis' finest business men and women, philanthropists, and politicians. I shouldn't have worn this dress. It fits a little too snug on my behind and it keeps riding up. I hope no one notices. I glance back at our table and look at the man of my dreams. Beside him sits his therapist, Dr. Ida Foster. Michael insisted that she come when we found out she was in town this week. I reach the podium and adjust the attached microphone to my height. The stage lights are always so bright and hot. I need some water.

"Good evening, ladies and gentleman. On behalf of the I Will Live Foundation, I would like to thank you for attending the Give Life Gala. Over a decade ago, the world was introduced to a horrible virus that still has no cure. AIDS has claimed millions of lives over the years, but thanks to research and modern day medicine, women and men with HIV are living longer and healthier than they ever have before. It's not enough to develop medicines and other treatments to slow down the progression of the virus. We need to find a cure for it. That's why you're all here tonight. Proceeds from this wonderful event will go toward finding a cure for this disease. I urge each of you to get tested and protect yourself. We may not be able to cure the disease, yet, but we can prevent ourselves from contracting it. Get tested. Know your status and know your partner's status. If you have it, isn't it good to know that there are organizations like the I Will Live Foundation?

"I must say that I owe this Foundation more than my gratitude for allowing me coordinate this wonderful event. Because of it, I met an amazing man who stole my heart. He happens to be our speaker for tonight. He asked me not to focus on his football accomplishments during his introduction. However, I must announce that he recently received confirmation that he will be inducted into the NFL Hall of Fame. Although, he is very proud of his athletic accomplishments, he is more proud of the things he's been able to accomplish since retiring from the NFL. In less than six months, he has helped charitable organizations around the country raise more than a million dollars by speaking at events like this one and playing in celebrity golf tournaments. His first children's book, "Victory Is Mine," stayed on the New York Times Bestseller's list for six weeks straight, and he is currently working on a second one. He's a NFL great. He's a philanthropist, and a wonderful man. I'm proud to say he's my man. Please welcome the magnificent, Michael Stokes."

The crowd stands to their feet to welcome Michael. He strides confidently from our table toward the stairs. He mounts them effortlessly and crosses the stage to where I am standing. I am greeted with a quick peck on the lips, and he steps to the mic to begin his speech.

We are both startled by a loud crash in the back of the room. We look in the direction of the sound, and a woman in a server's uniform is running towards us screaming. Her blond hair is all over her head. She is thin—barely skin and bones. What is most vividly noticeable as she charges toward us is the hatred I see raging behind two emerald green eyes. This must be Becca.

"He's not your man he's mine! Michael, I told you I was gonna get you! You thought you could get rid of me! Well, I got something for you and your little nappy headed wench!" she screams in a voice that almost sounds demonic.

She jumps onstage landing on both feet. She pulls a large butcher knife from underneath her shirt and lunges at us. Luckily, she doesn't touch either of us.

"You bastard! If I can't have you no one can!" she screams. "Take this Michael!" She wields her knife at us again. This time, striking Michael in the right arm. She retrieves the blade from his flesh and blood flows from the wound.

"Noooo! Stop!" I scream.

She looks directly at me. The evil intensity in her eyes is petrifying. This woman is insane. "I got something for you too nappy head!"

I grab Michael's hand. We have to get away from her! I move quickly but I am not able to get out of her path fast enough. Michael steps between us and Becca stabs him in the right shoulder. I step from behind him. If I don't, she is going to stab him again in an attempt to get to me. I can't let that happen. I feel something sharp pierce me near the left side by my breast, followed by another sharp pain in the right side of my abdomen.

I hear Michael yell, "Becca, NO! What are you doing?"

She lets out a hideous laugh.

Everything seems to be moving in slow motion. Michael hits her in the face with his right fist. Blood continues to run down his arm. She stumbles to the floor. I look
down. My dress is covered in blood. It's my blood. I hear
people screaming. I begin to feel very weak. My knees
buckle beneath me. Michael catches me.

I hear three loud pops and a thud. Becca is lying on
the floor. A pool of blood forms around her body. Why is
Dr. Foster standing over her with a gun? Becca's green
eyes are wide open and they are staring directly at me and
Michael. She mouths the words, "I love you." Her eyes
roll back into her head.

My head is in Michael's lap. I can hear him calling my
name. I try to answer but the pain in my side and chest is
crippling. My vision blurs and then everything goes black.
I hope I'm not dying. I didn't have a chance to tell my
family and Michael that I love them. Lord, I can't die
now. My prince has finally come. We're supposed to live
happily ever after. The calmness I felt while in the sea
returns. Is it because I'm dying, or is it because everything
is going to be alright?

Chapter 46

The End?
Tee

I awake to the sounds of people whispering. I can't quite make out what they're saying, but I can tell they're talking about me. I open my eyes, but a white blinding light causes me to immediately shut them. I hear a familiar voice say, "Quiet everybody! I think she's waking up."

"How are you going to tell somebody to be quiet and you're the loudest thing up in here?" Is that my voice? It's so raspy. My throat is dry and my mouth tastes funny. I open my eyes again, this time they successfully adjust to the light. Momma, Sandy, Michael, and Edgar are all gathered around my bed, peering down at me. Michael's arm is in a sling.

"Hello to you, too. Next time you get stabbed and almost die, I'm going to kill you. Don't you dare scare me like that again," Sandy says.

"Who got stabbed?! Who almost died! You're kidding right? And who are you? Who are all of you?" I say.

"Oh, my. She's got amnesia," my mother says softly.

"I know who you are, Momma. I just wanted to get Sandy's blood pressure up."

"This is not the time to be playing, young lady. And you got my blood pressure up, not your sister's," she reprimands.

"Sorry. Would someone care to help me sit up and then tell me what happened? I feel awful."

"I think that's where I come in," Michael says and moves in closer. "Becca escaped from the mental institution where she was being held. That's why Peter kept calling me during the Gala. He was trying to warn me. She tried to kill both of us but you got the worst of it. Turns out my therapist isn't really a therapist at all. Dr. Foster is a retired cop who now does private security and investigation work. Peter hired her to provide extra security and to get me to give more information about Becca to help capture her. She happened to be in town working on a new case, and it's a good thing she accepted my invitation to the Gala. She shot and killed Becca before she could ..."

His voice trails off, but I knew what he meant.

"You lost a lot of blood," says Sandy. "We could have lost you. I don't think I've ever been so afraid. What would I do without you?" I reach for my sister's hand, but a sharp pain in my side halts my movements.

"Easy, baby. Those cuts are pretty deep. You required quite a few stitches. You need to take it easy," my mother advises.

"Sandy, I'm alive and I'm not going anywhere. Me and you are a team like Nettie and Celie from "The Color Purple." Me and you, we never part, la tee da da," I sing.

Sandy smiles.

I look at Edgar. "What's up, baby boy? You're mighty quiet over there."

"I've never been so happy to hear you call me baby boy in all my life. I love you, Tina Long. I want to tell you I'm sorry for every horrible, insensitive thing I ever said to you. I don't care if you ever have sex again. Become a nun for all I care. I'll support you 100%," he says.

"A nun? Not me. Whatever you said is in the past. Let's leave it there. I love you, too. As soon as I'm better, you and I are going to go shopping. I need you to help me pick out my fall and winter wardrobe."

"You got it, girlfriend! I will have you looking fierce!" says Edgar and snaps his fingers.

The door opens and the doctor enters. He is wearing a white lab coat and big oversized glasses. I bet he can do an x-ray without the machine in those.

"I see sleeping beauty is awake. I told you she would be around in a day or so. She still needs to rest, though. Hello, Ms. Long. I am Dr. Sabir." He pulls an instrument out of his pocket and tells me to open my eyes wide. He shines a light in each one and then puts it back in his pocket.

"Nice to meet you, Dr. Sabir. What's going on with me?" I know my family said I would be okay but I prefer to talk to a professional.

"You are a very lucky young lady. You were stabbed twice, but the knife missed your organs and nerves. However, you did lose a lot of blood and required a transfusion. You also required many stitches. You may feel weak for a few days. I would like to keep you here with us a couple more days for observation, and I want you to stay in bed. I am now going to have to ask your lovely family to leave so you can rest. I have never seen an unconscious woman have so many visitors. People have been coming here all times of the day and night to see you. We had to restrict your visitation to family. Once again, I apologize to your brother over there. Our staff did not believe you had a Hispanic brother until your sister vouched for him," he says looking at Sandy and Edgar.

I snicker. "Thank you, Dr. I truly appreciate you and your staff taking care of me."

"Yes, thank you, doctor, for everything you and the wonderful staff here have done for my baby. We will do as you say and leave Tina so she can get some rest," adds my mother.

"With all due respect, I'm not going anywhere," Michael says.

The Dr. Sabir looks Michael up and down from head to toe. "Okay, big man. You can stay, but the rest of you—out. Come back tomorrow."

After everyone leaves, Michael kisses me on my forehead and arranges the covers around me to keep me warm.

"I feel horrible about all of this. This should be me lying in this hospital bed, not you. Becca came into your life because of me. I'm your man, Tee. It's my job to protect you. I promise you nothing like this will ever happen again," he soothes.

"It's not your fault. Becca was mentally ill. I didn't want her to die, but I am relieved that she is no longer a part of our lives. I feel so sorry for Michelle. Is she okay?"

"Me, too. My parents said they would tell her the news but I don't think they've done it yet."

"Michael, I don't blame you. I need you in my life. I'm going to need you to get through this. I'm in pain right now, but having you here with me makes me feel better."

Michael smiles.

"I am so grateful that God spared my life. I'm tired. I'm going to sleep now. Do me a favor? Crawl in this bed with me and hold me."

"You got it, pretty lady." Michael climbs in my bed and snuggles up next to me. It's not long before I feel myself drifting to sleep. I hear Michael whisper the words, "I love you, Tina Long." They sound like the sweetest of honey being spooned in ear.

When I awoke I expected to feel Michael's strong arms still around me. Instead, Michael is nowhere to be seen but sitting beside me, holding my hand, is MacKenzie Elbert Patton, III. I rub my eyes and blink a few times to make sure I'm not dreaming.

"Mac, what are you doing here? Where's Michael?"

"I don't know. There's no one here but me and you. How are you feeling?"

"I'll live. Okay. You answered that question. What are you doing here? Shouldn't you be off having sex with whoever you replaced me with?"

"Even in a hospital bed, you're still feisty," he chuckles. "Be nice. I came to see how you are doing, and I have something I need to say."

"I'm listening."

"I've been by the hospital several times but because I wasn't family the nurses wouldn't let me in your room. I had to see you, so I snuck in here today. I was afraid I would never have the opportunity to tell you how I really feel. Tee, I was at the Gala, and I didn't realize how much I loved you until I saw that woman stab you. I'm sorry I hurt you. I was so stupid. I never met a woman who loved me they way you did or one who required so much work. Asking me to not make love to you was foreign to me. I didn't understand, or better yet I didn't want to understand. So, I pushed you away and it was the biggest mistake I ever made.

"I was used to hearing the words 'I love you' right before or after having sex with a woman. So, that was the way I believed someone who truly loved you behaved. I wasn't used to seeing love the way you displayed it. The constant encouragement, the massages, the chicken noodle soup when I was sick, the cute notes tucked into my briefcase, the prayers. You made me feel invincible and frustrated but I couldn't fully understand why, until now. I've dated four women since we broke up, and none of them compares to you. No matter how hard I try to see each one for who she is, I can't. All I can see is who she isn't. They're not you. I'm supposedly in a relation-ship now, but she's just a poor replacement for you. I need the prototype. I want you back, and I'm willing to do whatever it takes to prove it, if you'll let me. I miss you so much."

I am grinning from ear to ear, but my heart is un-touched. The man I once thought I wanted to spend the rest of my life with finally said all the things I wanted to hear. Even though I am enjoying this moment, I know it's too little, too late. My heart now belongs to someone else. Even though I am tired and medicated I have some things I needed to say to him, too.

"If you had said these words three months ago, I would have jumped out of this bed into your arms. I would have told you, 'Yes I still love you and I forgive you and we can start over'. I realized that you didn't understand the kind of love I had to give, because you had never experienced it before. I was patient with you in hopes that you would get it, but you didn't. Instead you kicked it back at me and hit me dead in the forehead with it. You really hurt me! But I'm over you. I've found someone who understands me and the decisions I've made regarding sex. It's not a chore for him to love me. It's easy. I'm not wondering after I turn down his advances if he will call me the next day, because he doesn't make advances. He says he realizes that some things are worth waiting for. Best of all he's a Christian. He's not perfect. He has his own issues, but he's not struggling to love me. That comes naturally. I like that.

"Toward the end of our relationship, I was always scared that you were going to leave me. I could see the unhappiness in your face. The night we broke up, you looked at me like you hated me. You thought that in order for us to have a healthy, loving relationship, we had to be pulling each other's clothes off every chance we got. Or maybe it was a blow to your ego that I wasn't trying to jump your bones like so many other women in Memphis. I wanted you to see that love was deeper than just the physical.

"To be honest with you, I don't think this change of heart came when you saw me attacked. I think it came when you saw me look at another man the same way I used to look at you—with admiration in my eyes and a smile that says, 'I'm the luckiest woman in the world.'

"Go home to your girlfriend, Mac. I know you didn't tell her you were coming here to profess your love to me," I end with, "I forgive you, but there's nothing here for you."

"I guess it's my turn to hurt. Tell Michael he's a lucky man." Mac lets go of my hand, kisses my cheek, and quietly leaves the room without looking back.

The bathroom toilet flushes and Michael slowly emerges from behind door.

"Michael, were you spying on me?" I ask smiling.

"I could lie, but I won't. I was using the bathroom when he came in. I heard you two talking so I listened. I needed to know how you felt about me. It's good to know your feelings for me are as strong as the ones I have for you," he says before rushing to my side and kissing my lips. Then, he lovingly caresses my face.

"I love you, Tee. I know I should have said it sooner, but for some reason I couldn't get the words out. I have no problem saving sex for marriage. If you keep looking at me the way you're looking at me now—like I'm the only thing that matters. That'll be enough until our wedding night. Will you marry me?"

"Yes, Michael. I'll marry you," I say with glee.

I finally heard the words I have been longing to hear. They are more beautiful than I ever imagined!

Michael leans in and kisses me like nothing else in the world matters but me.

Chapter 47

Happily Ever After
Tee

As I walk down the aisle, I see all my friends and family looking at me, smiling. There's my mother sitting in the front row. My sister is standing in the pulpit in her fuchsia, matron of honor, maternity dress. She and Patrick are expecting their third child. I couldn't pick one of the girls over the others, so I opted not to have a maid of honor. Tiffany, Lenora, Lenice, and Teresa all look beautiful in their matching shimmering grey bride's maids' dresses. Standing in front of them is Michael's niece, Michelle, and my niece, Nicole. They are both serving as flower girls. My nephew, Donovin, looks dashing in his black, ring bearer tux. Michael's father is his best man with Maxwell, Edgar, Peter and Patrick serving as groomsmen. Their pink and shimmering grey ties and handkerchiefs blend perfectly with the motif. I see my pastor, Pastor Jenkins, and next to him stands my husband-to-be, Michael Tyler Stokes, Jr. in a black suit with a fuchsia tie and that 1,000 watt smile I love so much.

I feel like a princess in my asymmetrical, one shoulder, white Vera Wang gown. She customized it for me with colorful accents of grey and fuchsia. I am holding a huge bouquet of lilies with Swarovski crystals winding throughout. My palms are sweating. The Memphis Symphony orchestra is playing the wedding song. The butterflies in my stomach won't stop fluttering, and my heart is beating like I'm running down this aisle instead of walking. It's nervous energy, but I don't mind. I've planned my greatest event and so far everything has gone perfectly in my fairytale wedding.

Everyone looks so happy, but no one could be happier than me. I appreciate their coming to share in our special moment. I focus my attention on the man who loves me like no other. He's a former NFL player, a man of God, my provider, my protector, my hero, the future father of my children, and the man of my dreams. As I make my way down the aisle, that song my sister and I used to play as children resonates in my head, "Someday My Prince Will Come." Someday has finally arrived.

God truly has answered my prayers. Psalms 37:4–5 says,

"Delight yourself in the Lord, and He shall give you the desires of your heart. Commit your way to the Lord, trust also in Him, and He shall bring it to pass."

Thank you, Father, for being true to your word.

I's about to get married and I's about to get me some, too! I hope Michael got plenty of rest, because playing in the Super Bowl won't compare to the workout he's going to get tonight.

THE END

Someday, Too

Coming Summer 2011

Chapter 1

Marital Bliss

Today is the last day of Mr. and Mrs. Michael Stokes' honeymoon. For the past week the newlyweds have been living in marital bliss on the beautiful island of Anguilla. Although, neither Michael nor Tee could tell you much about the island itself. The two had been celibate for a combination of four years and waited until their wedding night to fully explore one another. They spent most of the week repeatedly consummating their marriage.

Michael loves waking up each morning to the love of his life. He had always been of the mindset that you saw the true essence of a woman in the morning. How a woman started her day said a lot about her. He didn't believe in subjecting himself to the essence of any woman. You had to be special and this woman is more special than any other. She is his wife.

It's the dawn of a new day for both of them. While Tee quietly slumbered, he pulled back the covers to admire her beauty. She stirred a little in response to his act. The morning light that streamed through the blinds of their cottage cast a soft glow on her naked body. Michael delighted in every inch of her--from her shoulder-length braids to her French manicured toes. As he visually feasted on his bride, his eyes drifted to the scars that served as physical reminders of the multiple stitches that were once on left side of her right breast and the right side of her abdomen. Sadness briefly interrupted his joy as he remembered the day that his mentally-ill ex-girlfriend, Becca, attacked the two of them with a knife during a charity event, where he was serving as the guest speaker. The scars from the cuts he received on his right arm during the altercation seemed miniscule next to Tee's deep puncture wounds. That was almost two month ago, and he still blamed himself for her misfortune but thanked God every day that it had not been any worse. He didn't know what he would have done if he had lost her. It was the attack that made him realize that he didn't want to live without her. Michael was determined to make sure that all of Tee's days from that day forth were good ones.

October had been a busy month for both of them. After his hospital bedside proposal, Michael and Tee decided that they wanted to get married as soon as possible and get all of the ugliness out of the way before the ceremony. Tee harbored no ill will toward Becca or her daughter, Michelle. The gratitude and newfound zeal for life she had dwarfed any anger she might have once had. She went out of her way to make Becca's death as painless as possible for her soon-to-be niece.

After she recovered, Tee, an event planner by trade, took it upon herself to plan Becca's memorial service and it was Tee who insisted that Michael hire the woman who had killed her, private investigator Ida Foster, to try and locate Becca's family and invite them to mourn, too. Unfortunately, none were found because Rebecca DeFoy was not her birth name and whoever she used to be had been very well hidden and long-forgotten.

So, they proceeded with the service, but the only attendees were members of the Stokes family: Michael; his parents, Michael, Sr. and Vanessa; his brother and Michelle's father, Maxwell; his sister, Tomeka; Michelle;

and his fiancée, Tee. Tee's family could not bring themselves to attend the funeral of the woman who had almost robbed them of her. It was a brief but beautiful graveside service that was solely dedicated to giving a four-year-old girl the opportunity to say good bye to the only family she had known, until five months ago when her mother revealed to Michael her existence. They buried Becca in Michael's hometown of Akron, Ohio so that Michelle could visit her whenever she desired.

Two weeks later, Michael and Tee became man and wife during a breathtaking ceremony held at Tee's church. It was orchestrated by Tee as well. Michael, a retired NFL player turned motivational speaker and author, had a lucrative bank account and spared no expense on his bride. After everything Tee had been through, she deserved to have her dream wedding. Her diamond and platinum wedding ring was so huge, he nicknamed it Godzilla.

But Tee's greatest desire was not a grand wedding but to begin their lives together. God had finally answered her prayers and she did not see any reason for delay.

Michael enjoyed having her all to himself the past seven days. He used his index finger to gently trace her scars, and then, softly kissed each one. He was startled when Tee let out a hearty laugh and said, "Good morning, Mr. Stokes. I guess you are to blame for the cold air that has invaded my space. You do know I'm naked, right?"

"I'm sorry, pretty lady. I didn't mean to wake you. I was just admiring one of God's greatest creations. You look so adorable when you are asleep."

"Oh really? Is that all you're going to do is admire?"

"I was but if you have something else in mind I may be able to accommodate you?" said Michael.

"I most certainly do. Come here and I'll show you," Tee said seductively.

Chapter 2

Guess Who?

While Tee took a shower, Michael ordered room service so they could eat out on the patio one last time. Their cottage held a magnificent view of the Caribbean and the coolness of the morning was the perfect time to enjoy it.

He ordered assorted fruits, bagels with cream cheese and bacon. He was setting the trays on their small patio table when he heard the familiar chime of his cell phone. He had been avoiding phone calls all week, and he usually let them roll over to voice mail but since his honeymoon was almost over he figured he might as well take the call. What could it hurt? Tee was busy at the moment. He didn't recognize the number but decided to answer it anyway. He immediately wished he hadn't.

"Hello Binky. Are you enjoying your honeymoon?"

That voice sent a chilling panic through his entire body. This had to be a mistake. The madness in his life was over, and he had just begun a wonderful life with the woman he loved.

"Becca?"

"What's wrong? You don't sound happy to hear from me. You sound as if you heard a ghost."

"But y-y-you're dead. I buried you," Michael stammered.

"Are you sure? If I'm dead how am I on the phone talking to you?"

"Whoever this is, this is not funny. I'm going to find out who you are, and I'm going to beat you until you can no longer utter a single word."

"Michael calm down. There's no need for violence. I'm only calling to congratulate you on your wedding. I have no intentions of bothering you or your bride for the time being. I want the two of you to be happy and take really good care of Michelle for me. But be aware that I am watching and when the time is right you'll see me again. Whether it's in this life or the next."

"Look, whoever you are, don't call this number or try to contact me again!" Michael shouted.

"Oh, you'll be hearing from me again. You can bet your life on that. But no worries, I plan to give you plenty of time to enjoy your family. So keep doing your speaking engagements, write another book, and make some babies, Then, I'm going to come take it all away because the life you share with that woman is supposed to be mine."

The phone clicked, indicating that the caller had hung up.

What Tee saw when she emerged from the shower sent the beat of her heart into overdrive, her new husband was lying motionless on the floor.

Stay Connected

Website
www.imagoodwoman.com

Facebook Fan Page
http://www.facebook.com/pages/Im-A-Good-
Woman/119858378087901

Twitter
www.twitter.com/imagoodwoman

Email
Imagoodwoman2@yahoo.com

LaVergne, TN USA
17 March 2011
220497LV00001B/1/P